SUMMER PEOPLE

SUMMER PEOPLE

SARA HOSEY

CamCat Books

CamCat Publishing, LLC
Brentwood, Tennessee 37027
camcatpublishing.com

Hardcover ISBN 9780744302509
Paperback ISBN 9780744302516
Large-Print Paperback ISBN 9780744302530
eBook ISBN 9780744302547
Audiobook ISBN 9780744302561

Library of Congress Control Number: 2022952382

Book and cover design by Maryann Appel

5   3   1   2   4

FOR JESS, JOHN, AND JULES

THE DAY CHRISTMAS MILLER AND LEXI REYES found a body floating facedown in the lake hadn't started off weird and terrifying. In fact, it had been a happy enough day.

Christmas had been anxious, but she'd also been hopeful and excited. Her best friend, Lexi, a "summer person" from Pennsylvania, was finally arriving in Sweet Lake, New York, that afternoon. Graduation, just ten days earlier, already felt like the distant past.

To kill time as she waited, Christmas raked algae from the lake. Only June and it was worse than she'd ever seen it, the algae a scum on the top of the water in the shallow areas and growing in puffy, slimy clouds in the deeper water. The absolute center of the lake was the only place you could escape it.

She frowned, imagining Lexi's reaction, and worked harder, pulling out the blue-green substance in clumps, the algae clinging to the tines of the rake like mermaid's hair or long wisps of alien matter—or like a toxic mucous, the green snot indicating the Earth's fever. She dragged the algae toward the shore and then heaved it up and dumped it on land, where it would bake dry in the sun, turning into hard, matte-colored mounds that dotted the Millers' shoreline for the rest of the summer. At this rate, the lake might be unswim-mable by August. Or, if you did go in, you'd come out with burning eyes or a rash, as Christmas's father did one year.

When they were kids, Lexi and Christmas had spent all day in the lake, reading aloud to each other from waterlogged paperbacks as they floated in tubes, diving in to cool down ("here, hold the book for a minute"). Hours swimming and playing, treading water while they talked about everything, as though being in the water together dissolved the barrier between their minds, making them permeable to each other.

But last summer, Lexi had refused to swim in the lake at all. She was disgusted by the algae and would only go in from her grand-father's boat, in the middle of the lake, and then only to water ski. If she could have skied without getting wet at all, she would have. She told Christmas that she wanted to have children some day and that she didn't want them to have fins. "I hear they're expensive to remove," she'd deadpanned.

Christmas raked harder. It was almost as if she took its pres-ence personally, or as if Lexi's disgust somehow extended to the en-tire community and even to Christmas herself. Lexi had teased her in the past about being too attached to the town, but back then it had been okay because Lexi had seemed to share Christmas's love of Sweet Lake. In the past few years, Lexi's stays had started get-ting shorter—and one year she spent only two weeks total at Sweet Lake. But this year she was staying for two whole months. Christ-mas had set up jobs for them at a community day camp, working Mondays through Thursdays in the basement of the new town hall complex—the same complex at which a meeting was to take place that evening, a meeting to discuss the algae blooms.

Christmas channeled her fear and frustration into the physi-cal labor. The movement-with-a-purpose allowed her brain to dis-engage a bit, to quiet, to be in the moment and not skittering over today, yesterday, tomorrow. And it helped to keep her from checking her phone every two minutes to see if Lexi had arrived yet.

She was so involved in her raking and thinking that the roaring vehicle was almost upon her by the time she saw it. Of course, it was Cash Ford on his fluorescent yellow Jet Ski whose zipping around she'd pretended to ignore earlier. But now she looked up to see him careening into the shallow water, coming to a dramatic, splashy stop about twenty feet away. He called out, "What the hell are you doing?"

Christmas stood in the churning water, the waves from Cash's Jet Ski lapping her ankles. "Hi, Cash," she said. Cash, naturally, was not wearing a life jacket; his tan chest and arms bulged with muscles. She suspected he was flexing, showing off, and she involuntarily rolled her eyes. "Trying to get rid of some of this algae," she said, her voice a bit squeaky, she thought.

Cash hooted. "That's the dumbest thing I ever heard. You think that's gonna make a difference?"

"Well," Christmas spluttered, finding herself, as she often did, at a loss when faced with her former classmate's combination of swagger, rudeness, and, sometimes, surprising insight. "Maybe if everyone did this at their lakefront . . . maybe it would help a little." Even as she said it, she knew it wasn't true.

Cash smirked. "Stop wasting your time and come for a ride with me."

Christmas shook her head. "No thanks."

"Aw, come on, Chrissy," he said. "You know you want to."

Christmas's phone, which she'd left on the dock, vibrated. She waded over quickly to retrieve it. Her eyes on her phone, she said to Cash, "I have plans."

Just got in, Lexi had texted Christmas.

Christmas texted back: *Yay! I am waiting on the dock!*

When Christmas looked up again, Cash had unceremoniously zoomed off. She bit her lip. She hadn't meant to be inconsiderate;

she'd simply been distracted by Lexi's text. Although even if Lexi wasn't heading over, there was no way Christmas would have gone Jet Skiing with Cash Ford.

She'd known Cash since they were kids and had a clear memory of first encountering him at a summer library program, when he'd refused to read aloud, refused the ice-cream sandwich he was offered as a treat, and told the librarian that she had a fat ass and shouldn't have one either. The librarian had scowled and told Cash to put his head down, that she'd have his mother come pick him up if he was going to be so miserable, but Cash didn't even do that; he stalked out across the parking lot and sat defiantly on top of a big rock.

Christmas remembered her relief when he left. She'd felt bad for the librarian, who Christmas could see was fighting back tears. And, more generally, having Cash around made Christmas nervous, made any situation suddenly unpredictable. Later, when Christmas's family relocated to Sweet Lake full time (at ten, she became summer people no more), she and Cash were put in the Resource Room together, and Christmas learned that he, too, had a learning disability. As a result, and to Christmas's chagrin, she and Cash were placed in the same class every year, and often had "extra help" together. That they had this difference in common might have inclined Christmas to be a bit more generous toward Cash, but it didn't. Instead, it only made her want to further distance herself from him.

Cash probably felt the same way, Christmas reasoned. She assumed that Cash thought she was a kiss-ass, a nerd, a prude. She had to admit, though, that he was usually pretty nice to her, always inviting her to his bonfires (there were many alcohol-fueled parties in a nearby field his dad owned), and once giving her a lift home when he saw her out jogging in a dangerous thunderstorm. And there'd been kind of a thing between them, recently, after the prom.

But still. They were like oil and water, Christmas thought, at that moment noticing a rainbow-colored slick on the surface of the lake. Probably left behind by Cash's stupid Jet Ski.

Christmas looked out at the reflection of the cloudless sky in the water. With the exception of Cash at the far end, the lake was serene, with only one fishing boat floating in the center and an orange kayak over by a small inlet that she recognized as belonging to her friends Curly, so-called because he was totally bald, and his husband, Lemuel "Lemy" Kang-LaSalle.

Climbing up onto the shore, Christmas grabbed the plump pink duffel—packed earlier with a change of clothes and her ADHD meds—that waited for her on the sloping, clover-filled lawn. She'd been wearing her swimsuit all day and she was ready to go.

Christmas's earliness, her inability to concentrate on anything else when she knew she had something coming up, this, she had learned, was one of her "ADHD things," and discovering that it was—if not a symptom, a related condition—was somewhat comforting. Because she had ADHD, she had trouble gauging time and how long things would take. And because she was a people pleaser, because she had anxiety and hated disappointing anyone, she had developed a compulsion for earliness as an overcompensation for what would probably have otherwise been chronic lateness.

Medication helped. A bit.

Christmas stowed her phone in the bag and waited.

And then she'd heard the sputtering of a speedboat come to life, the sound distorted by the flat water as the vehicle backed up from the dock, a buzz as Lexi's grandfather put the boat in gear and pointed it west, toward Christmas's house. She skipped down to the end of the dock and waved, her arms wide and joyful, as though they didn't know exactly where she was, as though the boat was an airplane landing in the fog, as though Lexi was a long-lost traveler at last returned home.

CHRISTMAS BOARDED THE BOAT AND THE GIRLS embraced and squealed and embraced again. Christmas said, "Hi, Mr. Hansen," and Lexi's grandfather nodded solemnly in return.

The girls complimented each other—"You look amazing" and "You're the one who looks amazing!"—and it was true: they'd both grown out of their earlier teenage awkwardness. For Lexi, this meant she'd come to appreciate her curly hair, which she used to try to straighten and tame. Now, a longish, wild, yet stylish bob framed her angular face. And Christmas, who was once too skinny, all knees and elbows, had put on a little weight and become more muscular, and she seemed to have finally won her battle with acne, though faint scars remained on her cheeks.

The friends beamed at each other, the purring of the motor an echo of their vibrating contentment. They'd been texting all morning in anticipation of their first ski of the summer, and they continued talking as Lexi put on her ski belt and the boat moved into the deeper water.

"Mom's already on the road back to Philly," Lexi said. "It's like she's allergic to this place."

She cast an apologetic glance at her grandfather.

Christmas fed the towline into the water. The boat idling, Lexi gave her friend another hug and said, "This is going to be a great summer." She crossed her eyes and stuck out her tongue and leaned over the side of the boat so that she fell sideways, plunging into the water. Her head appeared and she gasped.

"Oh my God, it's cold!"

Christmas handed a ski over the side of the boat.

Lexi paddled herself into position and then gave the thumbs-up. Christmas turned to Mr. Hansen. "She's ready!"

The engine roared and the boat pitched forward. There was a moment of Lexi teetering before she was up, smiling, tossing her head with delight and then careening back and forth, weaving over the wake, showboating, waving and mugging, making Christmas laugh. In the hum of the motor, in the cool June afternoon, time stopped, and Christmas felt a sensation akin to, but more pleasant than, boredom. Lexi was happy.

The lake was gorgeous. Life felt stunning and eternal, and Christmas was overwhelmed with gratitude as she watched her friend water ski, and she tried to tell herself to mark it and appreciate it, this, the first of many more summer days on Sweet Lake.

After two big laps, Lexi released the tow bar dramatically and put one hand on the back of her head and one hand on her hip, like an old-fashioned pinup. Her body continued forward on the ski until finally, as though on a delay, she began to sink, still holding the pose. Christmas rapped Mr. Hansen on the shoulder. "She's down!" The old man slowed the engine and turned the big steering wheel.

"That was amazing," Lexi declared as the boat bobbed near enough for Christmas to lower the ladder.

Lexi climbed up, shimmering and dripping, panting and smiling.

Christmas dove in. Like Lexi, Christmas burst up from the sharply cold water gasping for breath. Her light brown hair, black from the water, covered her face, and she slicked it back and looked up at Lexi. "I want two skis," she said.

Lexi rolled her eyes at Christmas's cautiousness. Two skis were the stuff of novices; they'd moved away from that years ago. "You're gonna drop one, I hope," Lexi said, retrieving the second ski from where it was stowed along the side of the boat.

"I'll see how I feel," Christmas answered.

"Live dangerously," Lexi said, laughing, pushing the ski so it would glide to where Christmas was treading water.

Christmas paddled herself to the rope, which slid like a snake just slightly submerged. When she got to the bar, she held on and was dragged a bit by the idling boat and, with her legs bent and her skis pointed up, she enjoyed the familiar tension forecasting the push that would soon send her upright to stand on the water.

"I'm ready," Christmas called, excited, but also trembling a bit, her stomach fluttering. She'd been skiing since she was eleven, but still, she was fearful in the moment before the boat took off, the moment before she was lifted.

And lifted she was: pulled to standing, blue-black water, so smooth, passing between her skis. Immediately, her body remembered what to do, and she slid across the wake, catching air, racing up alongside the boat only to lose speed, start to sink and be again yanked forward, pitching back across the wake. Lexi waved, gave her a thumbs-up. She held up her phone, taking photos and videos they'd never watch.

Who invented waterskiing? What kind of person thought it would be a good idea to pull a person at high speeds across the water? Christmas marveled at human inventiveness, lunacy.

She dropped a ski in front of the Hansens' house, wavered, found her balance again. And again across the wake. And again and again. In these moments, flying across the water, Christmas was her most competent, her most confident. She was good at this. So good at this.

But then Lexi was frowning. She was talking to her grandfather, who craned his neck to look behind him as he scowled. He waved an arm as though to say, *get lost,* and Christmas turned to see that she was being trailed by Cash on his obnoxious Jet Ski. This was not the first time he had annoyed Mr. Hansen by driving too close to a skier. Like dolphins, some Jet Skiers liked to play in the speedboats' wakes; unlike dolphins, the Jet Skiers were reckless teenage boys operating hundreds of pounds of equipment.

Mr. Hansen was endlessly outraged by what he called "those morons," who wouldn't stop until someone had gotten really hurt. Lexi and Christmas always assured Mr. Hansen that they never fell anyway—at least not accidentally. But with Cash behind her now, Christmas was self-conscious.

It wasn't her own ability she worried about. Instead, it was Cash's overconfidence that scared her. He was way too close; she could sense him right behind her, believed she could feel the breeze as the Jet Ski cut across her wake.

And, unused to the specific exertion of waterskiing, she'd gotten incredibly, alarmingly tired. Her arms and back ached, and her legs shook. She wanted to simply drop the rope and stop skiing, but she was afraid that if she did, Cash, incautious or distracted, would run her over. She imagined the accident, imagined the dull thump of her head against the front of the machine, her ski flying straight up like a straw thrown into a fan, her body sinking to the bottom of the lake.

Meanwhile, Mr. Hansen twisted in his seat, obviously furious, his mouth open, his curses and recriminations unintelligible under the sound of the motor. She knew it was irrational, but Christmas felt guilty, as though she were somehow responsible, as though she had summoned Cash by turning him down earlier.

Cash accelerated until he was right next to Christmas. Their eyes met and she waved him away—the hand that held the bar was quivering—and he smirked and dropped back before appearing again on her other side. She pulled up, tried to ski closer to the boat and away from Cash so she could drop the rope, but there he was, right beside her again, no longer simply an annoyance but a true threat.

"Go away!" Christmas shouted. Her breath was shallow, and she was afraid she might cry.

Her arms and legs shook ever more violently from the strain. Her fingers, clutching the bar, felt frozen and locked. What was he trying to do? What was wrong with him?

The rope began to slacken and Christmas realized that Mr. Hansen was gradually slowing the boat. Although she didn't sink immediately, it became more and more difficult to stay upright on the ski. Mr. Hansen was counting on Cash losing interest once there was no more wake to jump over.

But Cash didn't go away. He continued to slice closely—too closely—at high speeds, his Jet Ski making a thunderous noise as it leaped over its own waves.

"What is your problem?" Christmas tried to scream over the din as she sank. Her ski slid off and she clutched it to her chest, feeling ridiculous and vulnerable: just a head, bobbing in the water.

"Goddammit!" Mr. Hansen hollered from the boat.

Cash whooped, gunned his engine, and—finally—took off, zooming across the waves.

Christmas flushed with relief. The heat in her body made the water feel warm and though her muscles continued to spasm and shiver, she was suddenly sublimely comfortable. She dunked her head under the water and wiped the tears from her face. Emerging, she took deep breaths before she paddled to the boat, where Lexi and Mr. Hansen continued to rage.

"Could have killed you—"

"Are you okay? You looked really scared—"

"—call his father if I thought it would do any good."

Christmas climbed up the ladder and Lexi put a towel around her shoulders.

"But you sure looked good out there, girl," Lexi said, grinning.

"Son of a bitch," Mr. Hansen said.

3

"**H**E'S OBVIOUSLY A SOCIOPATH," Lexi said as they reclined on deck chairs on the small slate patio, drying off.

The sun, which had just a moment before felt so heavenly on Christmas's face, disappeared, and the air noticeably cooled. She shivered and squinted up at the obstructing cloud.

"Do you think he's gonna pull that nonsense every time we ski this summer?" Lexi asked, blinking behind her sunglasses, pushing a black curl out of her face. "I'm afraid my grandfather might murder him. Like, for real. He's probably gonna arm me with a crossbow and tell me to shoot at Cash while I'm skiing." Lexi mimed lifting the weapon and gazing through the sight.

Christmas made a face and sat up too. "Cash Ford would probably think it was sexy or something."

"Eww," Lexi said. "More like Trash Ford."

Christmas swallowed an impulse to defend Cash. Though Lexi's estimation was not completely inaccurate, Christmas also knew that Cash wasn't always terrible. And he hadn't had the easiest life either. His family was well-known in Sweet Lake (his grandfather had operated an auto shop that was positioned somewhat ostentatiously on an acre of lakefront) and his dad, who had inherited the shop, was roundly adored. Mr. Ford was handsome—even for an old guy—in a sort of Matt Damon way, with a wide, easy smile and the same tousled blond hair as Cash, though his was graying at the temples. He was rich and showy about it, but he was also friendly and generous. All the local sports teams, PTAs, and fun runs knew he was good for a donation or sponsorship; he'd recently funded a new steeple on the local church. He wasn't the mayor, but maybe that was because he didn't need to be.

Cash's mom had been a beauty queen, also locally famous. She'd died of cancer when Cash was nine, and he had always seemed a bit feral after that. He had his dad to look after him, of course, but Mr. Ford never really seemed all that concerned about what Cash got up to, what trouble he was in, which classes he was failing. When Cash was acting extra obnoxious, Christmas tried to remember that he'd lost his mom, but it was hard because Cash lacked his parents' charisma.

Christmas opened her mouth, about to confess something she'd been meaning to tell Lexi, when Lexi's phone vibrated. They both looked at it, Christmas snapping her mouth shut. Lexi, her hair back in her face, unselfconsciously smiled at the phone before texting back. "Sorry," she said, catching Christmas's eye. "That's Martha. You're gonna love her. I'm trying to convince her to take a few days off work—she works all the time—and come up. She's just . . ." Lexi trailed off and her eyes rolled up to the sky and she shook her head as she searched for the words. "She's the best."

"Cool," Christmas agreed weakly, though her mind snagged on those words: *the best.*

It wasn't that Christmas didn't want Lexi to have other friends. Or maybe it was. Though Christmas herself didn't really have other close friends, she was self-aware enough to know that this was not a normal way of being, that most people liked to have several dear friends. So she would never actually give voice to her concern that Lexi was going to replace her, that Lexi, like Christmas, only had enough room in her heart for one best friend.

Maybe if Christmas had lived somewhere else—somewhere bigger—it would have been easier. It wasn't as though she was bullied or persecuted. She said hi to everyone, had a group that she'd sat with at lunch for the four long years of high school. She had one classmate, Madison, whom she saw outside of school, but that was mostly because Madison insisted on it.

But if she were being honest, Christmas might admit that she hadn't truly pursued friendships with her classmates. Though she pretended to be offended that after seven years most still considered her summer people, she was also to blame for her isolation. She was shy, of course, but more than that, her parents had not discouraged an attitude of apartness, perhaps even superiority. And Christmas knew that, even though her family had their own small-town scandal, folks in Sweet Lake still regarded her parents, both former teachers, with a little bit of awe, considering them a certain brand of eccentric intellectual.

Ultimately, it didn't matter. Christmas had graduated and was starting college in the fall. She would meet new people there.

But mostly it didn't matter because she had always had Lexi and always would.

Christmas knew what true friendship was. She knew what it was to meet someone and love them right away. Friends at first sight.

The Hansens' house was about a half mile down the road from the Millers' and Christmas's parents had known Lexi's grandparents well enough to say hello. When Christmas was seven, Mrs. Hansen (who was, sort of embarrassingly, around the same age as Christmas's mother, Allie), told Allie that her granddaughter, who was also seven, was staying for the summer. Would Christmas like to come over and play?

Christmas, who didn't go to a lot of people's houses even back in Queens, was agitated, fretful about the playdate. But when she walked into the Hansens' house, Lexi had taken her hand and led Christmas upstairs where there was a dollhouse, a box of Hot Wheels, and several ancient Barbies.

Lexi was not put off by Christmas's shyness or her nervous thumb-sucking, and also shared Christmas's interest in intense imaginative play. The two spent that first afternoon spinning out an elaborate drama involving the Barbies, and Christmas recalled how wonderful it felt for a committed daydreamer to find her collaborator.

And, perhaps even more exciting, was that when it was time to leave, they made plans to do it again the next day.

Lexi's phone buzzed. Christmas watched—flexing her fingers, which were stiff, the skin raw and ready to callous after only one ski—and wondered if Lexi was texting that person Martha yet again.

"Sorry, sorry," Lexi said again, the smile from the text exchange still playing on her lips. "Hey, do you want to go to that mini-golf place after dinner? I was just telling Martha about it—how it's, like, authentically vintage but not because it's trying to be cool but just because they have literally not updated it in a million years. I told her I'd send pictures."

Christmas grimaced apologetically. "We—I—have that meeting tonight. The meeting about the algae?"

"Oh, that's right," Lexi said, nodding. "My grandparents want to go to that meeting too. Do I have to go?"

"It's at the new town hall complex—you'll get a preview of where we'll be working tomorrow if you come," Christmas said. "The camp is in the lower-level classrooms."

"Imagine passing up such an enticing opportunity," Lexi said. "But yeah, if it's important to my Chrissy, I'll come. We can do mini-golf tomorrow night. Are your parents going to this meeting?"

"Civic engagement isn't really their vibe." Christmas wrinkled her nose.

"I mean, can you blame them?"

"That's a loaded question," Christmas returned.

"Will we be the only non-gray-hairs there?"

"Probably."

"Girls," Mrs. Hansen called from an upstairs window. "Come in and eat."

"Coming," Lexi called back. She looked at Christmas. "She made lasagna."

"Yum. I love your grandma's lasagna."

"How dare you," Lexi joked. "Talking about my grammie like that."

"I mean, everyone around here loves Kathy's lasagna. It's famous."

"I had no idea my grandmother was so promiscuous. Culinarily speaking, that is."

"Let's just say she knows her way around a meat layer."

"Too far," Lexi laughed, rising.

Dinner was happy with the Hansens. Not generally effusive people, Lexi's grandparents beamed at their granddaughter as she sat down to eat, and their warmth extended to and included Christmas. The lasagna was, as predicted, delicious.

Cleaning up, Christmas reminded everyone that they'd have to leave soon if they wanted to make it to the meeting on time. Lexi jumped in the shower and Christmas, eager to get moving, waited in the kitchen with Mr. Hansen.

The Hansens' place was basically identical to the Millers': a squat wood-frame house that appeared, from the front, to be only one story, but which was perched on an incline and had a low-ceilinged third story with two bedrooms and a bath, and a lower-level family room with sliding glass doors leading to the lake. The houses had been built as vacation homes in the 1950s, back when "upstate" was still a destination, and though in recent years more and more Brooklynites were gravitating to the area, Sweet Lake had obviously seen better days. One snarky blogger, observing the close-set, peeling-paint homes, with sinking porches and unattractive satellite dishes positioned prominently on front roofs, dismissed the whole area as *Catskill Crappy.*

But Christmas liked their houses. They were comfortable and always infused with the smells from outdoors: cut grass in the summer, snow in the winter, wet leaves and mud in the spring and fall, and the dank, deep, lovely smell of the lake all year-round.

Christmas and Mr. Hansen stood in near silence, Mr. Hansen intermittently jiggling his keys and Christmas checking her phone. Her friend Lemy had texted to see if she needed a ride to the meeting that night; her friend Madison had texted, too, to ask if she wanted to hang out afterward. Christmas politely declined both offers.

Perhaps noticing Christmas's neck rolling and nervous habit of shifting from foot to foot, Mr. Hansen assured her, "We'll get out the door eventually." He paused and cleared his throat. "Though I don't generally put much stock in having meetings about things."

"My parents think it's a waste of time too," Christmas told him. "But I'm happy that people are talking about doing something."

"'Talking about doing something,'" Mr. Hansen repeated skeptically. He shrugged. "With Bill Ford running the show, who knows. I have heard that most everyone will be there. Worried about their property value. That's one thing people care about: money."

"Okay, let's go," Lexi called, rushing into the kitchen, her grandmother right behind her. "Who's ready to go solve some problems?"

W HEN THEY FINALLY ARRIVED AT TOWN HALL, the main meeting room, which smelled of fresh paint and practically squeaked with newness, was already packed. Dan and Gina Lopez immediately rose, offering their seats to Lexi's grandparents, but there didn't seem to be any other vacant spots.

Lemy caught Christmas's eye and mouthed, "Sorry," gesturing to the occupied space beside him.

Christmas's friend Madison, however, began waving and pointing to a chair that she'd saved with her enormous purse. When Madison noticed Lexi beside Christmas, she immediately popped up and sat on the lap of the guy beside her—her fiancé, Owen—and waved even more vigorously. Christmas pulled Lexi's hand and the two of them moved awkwardly down the row to the empty seats.

"Thanks," Christmas whispered to Madison.

"Of course!" Madison chirped, leaning forward. "Hi, Lexi! Did you just get to town?"

"Yeah," Lexi said, smiling and pushing her hair out of her eyes. "Hey."

Owen nodded a greeting over Madison's shoulder.

Christmas didn't know Owen well. He was older than them, in his twenties, and Christmas had the sense that he only tolerated her because of Madison. And why Madison—sweet, adorable, cheerleader Madison—tolerated Christmas was itself a bit of a mystery.

Assigned to be lab partners in nineth grade bio, Madison assumed an immediate intimacy with Christmas, acting as if they'd always been—and always would be—friends, and then attentively maintaining their relationship, inviting Christmas to parties and clubs, tryouts and events. Christmas said yes around every third invitation. She enjoyed Madison and appreciated that Madison seemed to accept that she wasn't the kind of friend who needed to hang out every day.

Madison and Owen's Fourth of July party was coming up that weekend, and Christmas had tried to beg off, but Madison wouldn't hear of it, even going so far as to insist that Owen would pick Christmas up and bring her to the party if she needed a ride. "I know your summer person will be here," Madison had said, rolling her eyes. "She can be your plus-one."

Though Christmas turned her attention to the meeting, which had already moved past the preliminary greeting and introductions, Madison began to feverishly whisper about the party. "Owen got some serious fireworks," she said, her breath hot on Christmas's ear. "There's no furniture in the house—he sleeps on a mattress on the floor—but help me, Jesus, has he got the fixings for this party. Lanterns, lots of meat, two kegs. I'm going to decorate." Madison continued talking, but Christmas tuned her out and tried to hear what Mr. Ford, who stood behind a podium in the front of the room, was saying.

Meanwhile, out of the corner of her eye, Christmas could see that Lexi was, as usual, texting. "What, are you live-tweeting the meeting?" Christmas whispered.

Lexi blew out her lips. "Yeah. It's a real nail-biter."

Christmas tried to listen. Mr. Ford called for nominations for the board of the association. The board, which Mr. Ford would presumably lead, would collect dues, hire a firm to do research, and then recommend a course of action for addressing the algae.

Two local guys Christmas didn't know well volunteered and then, to her surprise, Owen nominated himself. Christmas leaned forward to give him an approving nod. Then, Mr. Ford gestured to the far side of the room. "Yes? Did you want to nominate yourself?"

As Christmas craned her neck to see who he was talking to, a curly-haired woman stood up. Christmas didn't recognize her. A dark-haired and handsome guy was sitting with the woman, watching her, his face set and serious.

No one else had seemed to feel the need to stand up to speak.

"I don't want to nominate myself, but I do have a comment," the woman said.

Christmas looked harder, trying to place the woman. Probably just summer people.

"All nominees for the board are male," the woman continued. "White male, it appears to me. Does anyone else find that problematic?" Some people tittered with nervous laughter.

"Oh, for Pete's sake," a man sitting near Christmas groaned. "Go back to Brooklyn," he muttered.

Christmas, fizzing with anxiety at the prospect of public conflict, kept her eyes locked on Mr. Ford, whose smile was indulgent but suggested his patience was wearing thin.

"I'm not sure we've met, ma'am," Mr. Ford said. "Do you own land in Sweet Lake? You know you have to be a property owner in the community to—"

"I'm Naomi Gold," the woman interrupted. "And I am a property owner. I have to admit we have not been here as much as we would have liked in recent summers—honestly, I was in the middle of a divorce last year—but I own the blue house across from the church." Christmas knew the house. Once or twice a summer, some-one mowed the tall grass; otherwise, the place mostly sat, looking overgrown and abandoned.

"Divorced. You don't say," Mr. Ford said, still smiling. There was scattered laughter.

"Excuse me," Naomi countered, looking out from under sculpt-ed eyebrows, one hand on her hip.

Mr. Ford raised his palm in apology. "Aww, just teasing," he said. "But, now, are you volunteering to run for that board position or not, Miss Gold?"

"It's Dr. Gold," Naomi called back, archly.

"You're a medical doctor?" Mr. Ford asked, clearly ready to con-tinue teasing. "It's always good to have a doctor in the house."

"I'm an EdD," Naomi Gold responded.

Mr. Ford tilted his head and asked, "Now wasn't that what af-flicted Bob Dole?"

Several people laughed loudly.

Christmas didn't get it and turned to Lexi. "Erectile dysfunction joke," Lexi grumbled, barely looking up from her phone. "Eww."

She still didn't understand the joke completely, but that didn't matter; the whole exchange struck Christmas as wildly unfair. Mr. Ford, well-known, beloved, respected, already had everyone on his side. She wished this Dr. Gold would just sit back down and let it go.

Christmas turned to look and was relieved to see Dr. Gold smil-ing, as though to prove she was a good sport. "I believe Bob Dole had several problems, but a doctorate in education was not one of them." She cleared her throat as though she wanted to say some more, but then shook her head, her curls bouncing. "But to my point. I thought the lack of diversity was worth mentioning. And while I'm not run-ning—I don't think I'd get many votes anyway—I hope that any women, people of color, or others from underrepresented groups who might be interested would consider it. You'd have my support."

When Christmas glanced at Lexi, her friend shrugged, as though to suggest the woman wasn't wrong, before returning to her phone. Christmas thought that the handful of non-white people in town (including Curly, who was Chinese American, Dan and Gina Lopez, and Lexi herself, who was half Dominican) probably did not appreciate Naomi Gold's call for people of color to step forward. If they volunteered now, it would seem like they were doing it just because some summer person said they should.

Mr. Ford paused and nodded. "All right then, Dr. Gold. Thank you for your contribution." He turned his face toward the general crowd. "Are there any females or," he cleared his voice, "better yet females who are *people of color* here to answer Dr. Gold's call? I see Lemy has a hand raised. Now, Lemy, we all appreciate Curly's ethnicity as well as your personal proclivities, but I'm pretty sure you still won't qualify."

"Ha, ha," Lemy said, not laughing. Lemy—tall, red-haired, and handsome—looked severe—and more serious than Christmas had ever seen him. "I'll be on your board. And I want to nominate Chrissy. Christmas Miller."

Lemy and Curly shifted in their seats and gazed expectantly at Christmas. It seemed as though the whole room, with the creaking noise of a slowly turning ship, was adjusting itself in order to locate her.

Taken by surprise, Christmas shook her head, no. Sure, she and Lemy and Curly had talked about the algae, but she didn't want to be in a leadership position. She certainly didn't want to have to speak in public.

She could feel the blood rushing to her face, and she looked at the floor. "I don't," she stuttered, feeling countless eyes burning into her. "I can't. I'm not . . ."

"She can," Curly called out, half to Christmas and half to Mr. Ford, as Madison squirmed with delight and then poked her encouragingly in the ribs. "She knows more about this stuff than most people," he added.

"Chrissy," Mr. Ford said, a human lighthouse, beaming at her as though this was his own brilliant idea. "You'll accept the nomination and bring a feminine touch to our board?"

Christmas rolled her neck. She was aware that she was blinking too much, but she couldn't stop it. "I don't think I . . ." she began.

"Just do it, Christmas," Madison whispered. "You'll be great. Plus, this meeting's gone on too long already."

"We're counting on you, Christmas," Curly called.

Christmas turned to Lexi, who dragged her eyes away from her phone and offered a small nod, as though to say, "Why not?"

"All right," Christmas said at last, looking up and meeting Curly's smiling eyes. "Thanks?"

Lemy wasn't finished though, and he stood, gesturing for Christmas to do the same. "Tell them about Cornell," he urged.

"Oh," Christmas said, her mind suddenly blank. "Yeah. Well. They do . . . there's a lab, I guess."

"They'll test the lake for free," Lemy interjected, trying to help her out. "Christmas has already been in touch with them. We can find out exactly what's in the water. And who," he said angrily, casting his eyes over the audience, "exactly, is responsible."

From the back of the room, someone bellowed: "The goddammed lake is poisoned and the sooner you people face that, the better."

A number of people shouted out protests. Christmas turned to see Mr. Cunningham, a big man with blotchy cheeks and an ugly scowl, leaning against the back wall. Mr. Cunningham continued. "It's poisoned. Get over it. There isn't anything we can do about it."

Lemy cut in. "Well, that's what we're here to work on, Carl. Finding some solutions to the algae."

Mr. Cunningham made a dismissive gesture, throwing his hands out as if to say Lemy could shove it.

"Now, Carl raises an interesting issue," Mr. Ford said. "Instead of wasting our energy on finding out what the problem is, maybe we should just figure out how to live with it. Or maybe prohibit lake use altogether." Someone booed. "Maybe we could fill it in?" Ford continued shrugging.

"I've seen you and your son out there fishing and swimming," Curly called out.

"I have never swum in that swamp, and I never will," Mr. Ford retorted, laughing. As usual, the room laughed with him. "I barely know how to swim! And if my sweet son wants to eat the fish, well. Can't possibly give him more brain damage than he already has." Though, again, the tone was supposedly one of good-natured ribbing, Christmas's stomach sank as she realized what a terrible thing it was for a father to say about his son, what a terrible thing to have the whole town laugh at you. She scanned the room quickly. She'd noticed Cash lurking in the back of the room when they'd come in but didn't see him now. She hoped he'd slipped out to smoke and hadn't heard what his father had said, even as a joke.

"You don't really care about cleaning up the lake because it's your shop that's polluting it," Lemy shouted at Mr. Ford. Christmas noticed that Lemy's face was flushed and that he was furious, his anger, it seemed to her, almost out of control. His eyes darted from Mr. Ford to Curly and then back to Mr. Ford. "You're dumping. Everyone knows you're dumping."

"Aww, now, that's not true at all," Mr. Ford said, grimacing dramatically.

"It's your shop and Cunningham's cows," Lemy added. "You're using our lake as your own runoff lagoons. There should be no businesses on the waterfront. Our Lake Board should demand that the town rezone—"

Lemy was cut off by Mr. Cunningham bellowing for him to shut his mouth.

"*You* shut your mouth!" Lemy shouted back.

"Listen, you tree-hugging fag—" Mr. Cunningham said, pointing his finger at Lemy and stepping forward.

There were audible gasps, and the rest of Mr. Cunningham's tirade was drowned out by shouts of protest and the sound of chairs scraping as people began to rise, moving toward the ensuing fight or hustling toward the exit.

"What the?" Lexi said, standing and looking at Christmas, openmouthed.

Christmas shook her head. Her pulse beat in her forehead; the already-overwhelming situation had suddenly turned dangerous.

There was more shouting as some of the men—including Owen—pressed toward where Mr. Cunningham stood, still hollering and cursing, ostensibly to quell whatever fight was about to break out. "Owen!" Madison called, following after him.

Lexi grabbed Christmas's arm. "Let's get out of here," she said.

They made their way with the rest of those who wanted nothing to do with the melee, Lexi's hand clasped tightly around Christmas's wrist, releasing her only when they stumbled out to the parking lot where stunned groups stood under the lights, hugging themselves against the chilly mountain air and trying to make sense of what had just happened. Christmas and Lexi found Lexi's grandparents, and the four of them shook their heads with disbelief and disapproval.

"Really! What was that all about?" Mrs. Hansen said, holding a hand out to Lexi, who allowed herself to be pulled in under her grandmother's arm.

"I'll tell you what it was about, Grammie," Lexi said, her eyes wide and angry. "Homophobia. I can't believe that people up here talk like that."

"Well," Christmas began, making a face and shuffling her feet. Her heart continued to beat in her temples; she hoped Lemy and Curly were all right, and she let out a small, weird, nervous giggle.

"Are you laughing?" Lexi asked, looking at Christmas incredulously.

"No," Christmas said, shaking her head. "I wasn't laughing. It's just . . . that was just . . ." She wanted to say more—of course she wasn't laughing; she was in a state of shock. She was so shocked, in fact, that words failed her.

"Nice, Christmas," Lexi said curtly. Her mouth turned down in a disgusted frown. "I mean, really." In that moment, Lexi sounded just like her grammie, but Christmas knew better than to share this out loud.

Before Christmas could object or explain, Mr. Hansen stuck an arm out, as though to corral them toward the truck. "All right. Let's not stand around in the parking lot all night." To Christmas, he said, "Are you coming home with us?"

"If that's okay," Christmas said haltingly. She always stayed at the Hansens' house when Lexi was in town, but she suddenly felt unsure.

"Of course," Lexi said, blinking impatiently and then walking away toward the truck, leaving Christmas to follow.

Sitting in the collapsible jump seats in the back of the old Nissan King Cab, Lexi stared at her phone, and Christmas looked into the darkness. Their knees glanced together with each bump in the road until Christmas pulled her legs in closer, trying to make herself as small as possible.

THE MEETING HAD THROWN EVERYTHING OFF.

Christmas wished she'd gone alone, that she hadn't forced Lexi to come with her. And she wanted to explain that she hadn't been laughing at what Mr. Cunningham had said. Of course she thought it was disgusting. And Lemy was one of her few actual friends in Sweet Lake! Christmas didn't understand why Lexi was so angry with her; she should know that Christmas sometimes had inappropriate nervous reactions.

But Christmas couldn't find a way to reprise the conversation and, if she were being honest, perhaps didn't really want to, as she was acutely afraid of what Lexi might say. A few different ideas skittered around the corners of Christmas's mind, ideas that seemed to slip away into darkness as soon as she turned her attention to them.

One thing was clear: Lexi was unhappy. And for the rest of the evening, Christmas's attempts at small talk or jokes based on their shared past fell flat. She floundered, unable to find that familiar, joyful connection she usually had with Lexi, her best friend, the person Christmas waited for all year long.

Down in the first-floor den, the girls grabbed fleece blankets and settled onto the couch to watch *Okja,* a movie Lemy and Curly had recommended to Christmas. She had already seen it—and wept throughout—and wanted to share this with Lexi. Lexi, however, almost immediately fell asleep.

And, for her part, instead of watching, Christmas ruminated and stewed. Although Christmas knew she would sound like a boomer, she couldn't help but feel offended that Lexi never put her phone down long enough to finish a conversation. Christmas would be in the middle of a story, or about to tell a joke, and she'd glance over to see Lexi totally focused on another text, giving Christmas only a distracted "uh-huh," or a forced laugh.

All these intrusions had to be from Martha—that girl with the old-fashioned name. Christmas couldn't help but be hurt that Lexi seemed to prefer the company of this other, absent person to her own supposed best friend, who was right beside her.

As if on cue, Lexi's phone lit up and vibrated, waking her.

"Oh," Lexi said, opening one eye and then the other. She looked at her phone.

"Your girlfriend?" Christmas tried to tease.

In the dim light of the television, Lexi peered at Christmas from her end of the sofa, her mouth in a snarl. "What?"

"Is that Margaret or Marsha or whatever?" Christmas said, weakly, surprised by Lexi's response. "She just texts you a lot."

"Martha," Lexi said, her tone clipped. She sat up and texted furiously with her thumbs before laying the phone facedown again. Christmas pretended to be watching the movie.

Lexi sat up abruptly and said, "I have some pot. Want to go out on the dock?"

"Okay," Christmas said. She paused the movie.

Christmas wasn't really into weed. She had learned the hard way that if she had too much, she'd get super anxious. But she'd vape to put Lexi at ease because if she didn't, Lexi would complain that Christmas was making her feel like a drug addict. And Christmas already felt as though she'd screwed up too much.

Christmas located her flip-flops while Lexi went upstairs to grab her vape pen. Then, without speaking, they each wrapped blankets around their shoulders and went out the sliding glass door to the lake.

The cold air was sharp and felt good in Christmas's lungs. They walked down the short lawn and then out to the end of Lexi's grandparents' dock, where the pier widened, and sat in the lake-facing Adirondack chairs.

Christmas longed for something casual to say—an observation about the beauty of the lake at night, or the swampy-sweet smell of the air, or sounds of the lapping waves and noisy bullfrogs—but she was afraid she'd come off as trying too hard. Instead, she waited to be passed the pen and murmured, "Thanks," before taking a shallow drag.

"Look at all the stars," Lexi said, and Christmas was momentarily, and perhaps pathetically, heartened.

"Remember that meteor shower a few years ago?" Christmas asked. "The shooting stars were practically nonstop." Christmas and Lexi kept their voices low; Lexi's grandparents were already asleep, and the girls knew, all too well, how voices carried across the lake.

"I do love it up here, despite all the terrible people," Lexi said softly, still looking at the sky.

"They're not all terrible," Christmas protested. She handed the pen to Lexi. "I'm not terrible."

"No," Lexi said. "You're not. Which is why I don't understand how you survived. Or why you didn't hit the road the minute you got your diploma. Like my mom." She sighed. "At least your parents finally got Wi-Fi. Are you amazed that you lived without it for so long?"

"I am," Christmas conceded, relieved to be able to pretend to ignore Lexi's astounding and vaguely offensive suggestion that Christmas should leave Sweet Lake. "It was pretty ridiculous."

Although they'd had cable and cell phones, Christmas's parents had resisted getting high-speed Internet long past the time when this position was in any way defensible. And though Christmas experienced an almost physical relief when she was able to get online easily from home (no longer having to go to school or the library), she did also suspect that her parents had been right, that something ineffable had been lost. Back then, she'd believed that the three of them were still on the same team, and that team didn't mind being different, or old-fashioned, or a little isolated. She wondered when she had stopped feeling that way.

"I would have run away if I were you," Lexi said. "Honestly. To be stuck here, with these people, and not even been able to escape into Netflix for a few hours."

"What are you talking about, 'these people'?" Christmas said. She remained distantly incredulous, as though she knew that Lexi didn't really mean what she said. Plus, she might think she was too good for Sweet Lake, but Lexi was technically more Sweet Lake than anyone: like the Fords and the Cunninghams and the La-Salles, the Hansens had lived in the area for several generations, and that meant something to the people of Sweet Lake. And though her mother had fled at eighteen, she'd actually grown up in the very house behind them.

"You know," Lexi said. "People here look at me as though I'm exotic, or they're afraid I'm part of the advance crew of brown people that's going to descend on them. It's, like, totally toxic to spend more than a few days here."

Christmas stifled a gasp. Was Lexi saying she regretted planning to stay for the whole summer? Would she return to Pennsylvania early? Was she already unhappy?

"Oh, please," Christmas managed. "It's not that bad."

"Uh, yeah, it is," Lexi said snappishly. "That display at the meeting? Even you can't pretend that one away."

"I don't pretend things away."

"You're so . . . willfully naïve."

Christmas had the sense that this was something Lexi had already thought about, had already articulated for herself. Was this how Lexi talked about her when she told Martha about Sweet Lake? That Christmas was naïve?

Lexi continued, "You must know how much it sucks here. But you refuse to admit it to me or even to yourself."

Christmas realized she was on the cusp of true anger; it was like seeing a lightning flash in the distance. It was still possible that the storm might shift suddenly, might never hit, but not if Lexi kept going in this direction.

Lexi continued. "You're unwilling to push back. Your parents only got the Internet because the school made them do it. You don't ever stand up to them. Or anyone. I really worry about you staying here. Stagnating here."

"Oh my God," Christmas said, trying to smile as though she was shocked, to conceal the anger she felt bubbling up inside her. "Where is this coming from?"

"You make too many excuses for people. When they do things you don't like, you avert your eyes. You're in denial. I don't know why you tolerate—"

"I'm nonconfrontational, fine," Christmas interrupted. "But at least I'm . . . steady. At least I'm not so uncomfortable being who I am that I have to change my whole identity every fifteen minutes."

"What? Change my whole identity?" Lexi said, laughing, but clearly offended. "I don't even know what you're talking about."

"Remember the year you tried to get me to start smoking cigarettes?" Christmas asked. "'Cause that was sooo wild and rebellious.

But by the end of the summer you were all into wellness and 'self-care' and begging me to go to yoga with you every day? Although that might have been more about that summer people yoga guy you thought was totally cool. What was his name? River or Leif or Sky or something?"

"Stop," Lexi said, annoyed. "I was fourteen."

"Fifteen," Christmas corrected.

"Jesus Christ," Lexi said. "What, are you taking notes? Why are you acting like this? I'm sorry that it's a problem for you that I've, I don't know," she shook her head, "continued to develop as a person and am not okay with homophobia. It's not my fault that the people here are just as gross as this disgusting lake."

"Fine," Christmas said. "I mean, I get it. You've made it perfectly clear how much you hate it here." Christmas felt her throat tightening. She knew she would cry if she kept talking and she was grateful for the darkness of the night. She considered rising, leaving, simply going home.

"What?" Lexi asked. "Christmas," she moaned. "God, you're so sensitive. So now if I disagree with you, your feelings are going to be hurt?"

Lexi made this last remark as though to have hurtable feelings was the most contemptible, irritating thing in the world.

Christmas almost couldn't speak. "I'm not—" Christmas began but had to stop. She cleared her throat. Willing herself not to cry was, naturally, having the opposite effect. She managed to squeak out: "I just feel . . . yeah, that meeting was messed up, but even before that, you decided you're too cool to be here and you'd rather be on your phone and when you're not on your phone all you want to do is tell me much you hate it here."

"Maybe I am too cool to be here," Lexi snapped. "And yeah, maybe I would rather be on my phone," she added. At that moment, the phone, resting on the arm of Lexi's chair, lit up again. She continued, her tone nasty and clipped, "Believe it or not, not everything is about you and your beloved lake. There's something I've been wanting to tell you."

Christmas waited, but Lexi didn't speak right away.

And then the quiet was disturbed by a groaning noise and a loud, sloppy splash. It was hard to tell exactly where the noise came from, but both girls instinctively turned their heads to the right, as though they'd be able to see through the darkness.

"What kind of nut goes swimming in the middle of the night?" Lexi asked, her voice still full of contempt. She sucked on the vape pen and exhaled a puff of smoke.

"That doesn't sound like swimming," Christmas said.

They sat, listening. The little hairs on Christmas's arms stood up.

"Probably a drunk fell in the lake," Lexi said.

Christmas shook her head, no. "I think we should go see."

Lexi made a small noise of impatience but gestured to the canoe tied up next to the speedboat. "After you," she whispered. She rose and stuck the vape pen in her pocket.

Christmas rose, too, relieved to have a distraction from their argument, but at the same time she was suddenly terrified of going out on the dark lake in the middle of the night. She didn't know what it was, if it was the tiny amount of pot she'd consumed or the fight with Lexi or even the gentle lapping of the waves that seemed almost aggressively quiet, but something was definitely off.

"Let's go," she whispered.

THE NOISE COULD HAVE BEEN AN OVERSIZED WATERBIRD diving for a fish or maybe a loose branch finally breaking free and splashing down into the water. But there had been a strange, strangled, human sound too. And even if the sound had been amplified by the quiet of the lake in the dark night, Christmas—and maybe Lexi—knew it was something big and maybe terrible.

Wordlessly, Lexi untied the canoe and Christmas stepped in, then held on to the dock as Lexi boarded. Christmas sat in the front, a cold trickle of sweat running down her spine.

"I think the noise came from over by Cunningham's Woods," Christmas said softly.

"I'll steer us that way," Lexi said.

Cunningham's Woods was a large lot of untouched trees adjacent to Cunningham's Farm, itself several acres of lakefront property, some of which was used as a cow pasture. Although most of the shoreline was gently lit by the houses along the perimeter of the lake, the woods, empty of people, were extra dark.

Christmas and Lexi moved forward in thick blackness, Christmas squinting ahead.

She could just make out some of the trees along the shore.

"Did you bring your phone?" Christmas asked. "Can you turn on your flashlight?"

She heard Lexi laying down her paddle and, a moment later, the area directly in front of Christmas was illuminated. The dark water rippled before her, and Christmas moved the boat closer to the shore.

She was just about to tell Lexi that they should turn around, that it was too dark to see anything anyway, when Lexi, the light bouncing and then returning to a certain spot, whispered, "There's something floating up ahead."

And in the moonlight, Christmas could see it too. A large lump near the shore, half submerged, lapped by gentle waves.

Christmas saw flannel. Then, the rest of a body registered, like one of those old Polaroid pictures, the image emerging gradually. It was a person, and he was floating facedown.

"Oh my god," Lexi gasped. "I think—are they alive? Should we help?"

Christmas didn't answer. Though there was a steep drop-off in the water in front of Cunningham's Woods—Christmas knew this because she knew the lake bottom, had spent countless days of every summer boating and swimming and fishing this lake—the person was floating in such a way to suggest shallow water, that their knees and hands were resting on the lake floor. She pulled the canoe a little closer. "Hey! Are you okay?" she called, as though the person would simply roll over, pop up, and say hello.

Until that moment, Christmas had felt as though she were trying to move through glue, that the canoe was so slow and heavy. But something switched, suddenly, and she saw what it was that she would need to do. Unlike the bouncing beam in Lexi's shaking hand, Christmas's mind narrowed and focused and steadied. She'd read before that an ADHD brain could come in handy in a crisis. It certainly seemed to be the case in this situation. She brought the canoe in closer and, when she was certain it was shallow enough, she lay down her oar, pushed off her flip-flops, and scrambled out of the boat, careful not to tip Lexi over.

"What are you doing!" Lexi cried, her voice high and panicky. "We need to get help. We need to go back."

Christmas had been correct about the depth; a glacial lake, Sweet Lake stayed shallow for twenty, thirty, sometimes forty feet from the shore. Here, they were only ten feet from land. As she stepped in, the water rose up to her thighs, but the lake sloped up dramatically as she waded toward the body. The rocks were sharp and slippery, and she moved as fast as she could without falling.

Lexi gasped behind her. "Ohmygodohmygodohmygod."

Christmas paused a few feet from the body—it was a man. She was afraid to touch him. In that split second, she couldn't decide if it would be worse if he were alive or dead. Dead, she concluded quickly. That would be worse.

She pushed. He rolled easily onto his back. Christmas gasped and recoiled. The man's face was swollen and shiny and covered in green slime, but she recognized him.

"It's Lemy!"

The green substance was algae from the lake, and Christmas wiped at it, trying to move it away from his eyes and mouth, but his skin looked so tender and painful, his eyes swollen shut, pursed together, that she didn't want to touch him, to hurt him further.

Then she realized: Lemy wasn't breathing.

"Help me!" Christmas cried to Lexi. "We need to get him out of the water."

When Lexi didn't move, Christmas clasped Lemy's ankles and began dragging him to the shore, slipping every few steps on the rocky lake bottom. "Stop shining that light in my eyes and get over here!" Christmas shouted.

In the shallower water, Lemy got caught on the rocks. "Lexi, come on," Christmas growled, but her friend remained immobilized in the canoe.

Christmas began to swing Lemy's body, positioning him so that his head was mostly on land. She put a hand over Lemy's mouth but didn't feel any breath.

She heard Lexi's quavering voice. "I'm trying to call 911."

"There's no signal on the lake!" Christmas bellowed over her shoulder.

She positioned Lemy on his side and pounded on his back. Then, she turned him faceup again and, putting one hand on top of the other on his chest, began pushing down. She remembered from the mandatory CPR class she'd taken at school that she was supposed to do thirty compressions, but she kept losing her count. Behind her, she heard Lexi finally splashing toward land.

Christmas tilted Lemy's head back and held his nose closed. She blew into his mouth and, with one hand on his chest, felt her own breath inflating his lungs. She thought how strange, and marveled at how in some ways, bodies are such simple machines: a tube connected to bellows.

Lemy suddenly gasped and began to vomit. Alarmed, Christmas fell backward onto the heels of her hands, sliding on the slippery rocks and splashing down into the lake before sitting forward again, pulling him on to his side so that the water could drain out of his body.

Lexi whimpered and backed away.

7

WHEN CHRISTMAS REMEMBERED IT LATER, time seemed distorted, at once both fast and slow. The paddle over to Cunningham's Woods seemed to take years, but dragging Lemy to shore, pounding his chest, breathing into his mouth—that was all mere moments. Lexi ran, crashing into the woods, closer to the road, and was able to get a signal; she called the police and then her grandparents and then, fast and slow as they waited for help, Lexi alternately screaming for help and pacing, cursing, looking at her phone. Her grandparents came quickly in the motorboat, and the police did, too, their blue-and-red flashing lights illuminating the woods as they made their way toward the flare Mr. Hansen had set off to let them know where they were.

Wrapped in a scratchy blanket, Christmas talked to Officer Ben Pappas, a guy only a few years older than her and who had a younger sister in Christmas's graduating class. Then time sped up again and suddenly he and another officer were driving her home, just down the road. Her parents had been called, but she'd told them not to come, assured them that she was on her way. Back at her house, Ben walked her in and told her parents she was a "real hero."

She gave them a succinct version of events and took a shower so hot her skin seared. She'd never before felt so repulsed by the lake and itchy and desperate to get it off her. But it wasn't just the lake—it was the damp wet heaviness of Lemy's clothes, his cold lips, his disfigured face.

After her shower, she was unsure of what to do with herself. Should she try to sleep? She was way too wired. Should she call Lexi? No, she wouldn't want to risk waking her. She could pull up a show on her phone, but that felt too callous.

She forced herself to get in bed, where she lay with her eyes open, roiling.

Lexi's arrival that afternoon seemed like it had happened eons earlier, in a happier, better time. And yet, even those more placid hours had been marked by worry and fear. Despite the drama of the last few hours, she couldn't help but wonder and fret, tossing and turning, about whatever it was that Lexi wanted to tell her. Maybe Martha really was her girlfriend; maybe that was why she'd gotten so annoyed when Christmas had teased her.

Christmas felt a deep, aching, shame and regret, a longing for a do-over, an anger that life afforded no such opportunities to simply take things back.

Lexi had certainly had more "experience" than Christmas, and this was something that had come up—come between them—before. Christmas had kissed—and only kissed—a total of two boys, while Lexi had apparently kissed so many people that she'd lost count, and had done other things as well, things she had begun to tell Christmas about, but which made Christmas blush and mumble, "I don't need the details."

"You're such an innocent," Lexi had sighed. "You don't know what you're missing."

"I'm such an innocent," Christmas returned, "that I don't even want to know what I'm missing."

Now, Christmas considered, maybe it shouldn't have mattered that Christmas didn't want to know. If Lexi had wanted to tell her, to share it with her, she should have listened. Even if it had made her uncomfortable. She probably should have listened.

W OKEN BY THE ALARM ON HER PHONE—the sound of chirping birds—
her mind snapped right into worry mode.

She moved quickly: dressing, swallowing her medicine, lacing
her sneakers, then stashing her phone and pepper spray in her fanny pack—double-checking but stopping herself from checking a
third time.

Running would help her sort out the events of the day before.
The morning was chilly and foggy, the lake shrouded in a pretty,
gray mist. It was, mercifully, too early and cool for the bugs and just
the right time to catch the riotous morning songs of the birds, many
of whom congregated in the Miller front yard, which was dotted
with an absurd assortment of her father's homemade birdhouses
and feeders.

After the initial pain of getting started, Christmas began to
tune out, letting the run and the rhythm take over her body, while
her mind, following its own pattern, continued to review the recent
events: Lemy unconscious, his flannel shirt floating in the water,
Lexi complaining about "these people," the sound of the splash
cutting through the dark night, Lexi angrily accusing Christmas of

laughing at the "f-word." The run did its next trick—or maybe the medicine kicked in—because Christmas was able to turn it off, or at least turn it down. Then she was just moving and not thinking at all.

After a while, though, her mind wandered, again, back to Lemy. Who could have done that to him? Was it about the fight at the meeting?

Lemy—one of the kindest, funniest, smartest people Christmas knew—was the opposite of the "ignorant" rednecks that Lexi seemed to think populated Sweet Lake. Christmas wished she had said that last night, wished she had pointed to Lemy and Curly as examples of the cool locals.

Lemy and Curly lived in Lemy's family's Victorian farmhouse, the porch adorned with a rainbow flag and the front lawn featuring BLM and antifracking signs. These men cared about the lake as much as Christmas did, which Christmas had discovered after she'd started an environmental club at the high school as her senior service project.

One of its goals was to investigate the algae blooms. Although the club never got past writing up their mission statement, their endeavors were reported in the local paper. One day, when Christmas was sitting on her dock, Lemy and Curly paddled up in their kayaks. They told her they were proud of her, thought she was doing great work, and invited to come to their house that afternoon for tea or coffee. ("Or a soda. I don't know what the kids drink these days," Lemy had said.)

Despite their age difference and Christmas's initial shyness, Lemy and Curly put her at ease almost immediately. She'd gone over to their house and drunk peppermint tea and the three of them had a wide-ranging conversation about the lake and the community, the stubbornness of some of the old families, the recent return of the beloved heron to the lake, composting, and what Curly called "radical recycling."

In Lemy and Curly's house, Christmas found examples of a certain kind of adult, an idea of the sort she might like to be: unaffected, appreciative of nature and the lake, worldly, knowledgeable, and casually sophisticated. They drove a car that ran on the leftover oil from the restaurant where Curly worked as a chef, the same restaurant from which he often brought home copious leftovers that he and Christmas and Lemy shared, sitting together at the big dining table made of reclaimed wood from a local barn.

After that first visit, a precedent was set: though they would devote a portion of Christmas's visit to discussing environmental issues, they would also turn to conversations about social justice, art, and politics. Lemy and Curly seemed to delight in introducing Christmas to authors, shows, and ideas; she was a happy, enthusiastic student. They loaned her books by bell hooks and Peter Singer, texted her links to articles in *The Sun* and to movies by Bong Joon-ho (like *Okja*). Curly sometimes tried to teach her how to cook, but she was both uninterested and not good at reading recipes, which put cooking squarely on the list of activities Christmas (not unhappily) eschewed.

"I'd rather just eat," she'd once told Curly, not trying to be funny, but making Lemy crow with laughter nevertheless.

9

CHRISTMAS RAN FOUR MILES THE DAY after she found Lemy in the lake, returning home just as the sun had really settled itself in the sky, the lake's mist now burned off completely. The Millers always left the front door unlocked—a good thing, because Christmas had never met a key she couldn't lose. Entering, she stepped out of her muddy sneakers in the hall, hoping to grab something to eat and avoid further discussion of the previous night's events before she headed to work. Her parents, however, were lying in wait.

"That you, Chris?" her father called.

"Yeah." She padded down the hall to where her mother and father sat, drinking coffee in the kitchen.

Her parents, like Christmas, were small, lean people, and they fit comfortably around the round kitchen table at which they ate all their meals. Once, Christmas's Aunt Inez had joked that the Millers were the picture of the three bears, and they'd all laughed, because it was true. Christmas thought of this again as she regarded them in their mismatched wooden chairs around the table, her dad, in his old Dickies jeans, and her mom, still in her robe and pajama pants. They looked back at her with expectant eyes.

"Good morning," her mother said. Her face was drawn and pale, her eyes sort of vacant, not yet truly awake. She smiled weakly, as though it was an effort to pull up the corners of her lips. "How's our hero feeling today?"

Christmas waved her mother's comment away and went to the fridge for water. "Any updates on Lemy?"

"Ben Pappas called while you were out," her father answered, nodding. "Lemy's in a coma, unfortunately."

"A coma," Christmas repeated. She slumped against the counter. "Oh, God."

Her father continued. "Ben said they had some follow-up questions for you. I told him you'd be at work today, and he said he'd track you down later."

"Okay," Christmas said. She took a long drink of the water.

"There's oatmeal on the stove if you'd like it," her father said.

Christmas finished her water before turning to the stove to dish out some of the hot cereal—leave it to her parents to eat oatmeal in late June. She could feel them watching her as she stirred in brown sugar.

"Sounds like you saved Lemy's life," her father said when she sat down with her bowl.

Christmas made an affirmative noise and took a big spoonful of oatmeal, unsure of how to respond.

"What do you think happened?" her mother asked slowly, looking at Christmas over her coffee. "Do you think he just got drunk and fell in the lake?"

Drunken mishaps were not without precedent. Some might even say they were a bit of a Sweet Lake tradition, even in the Millers' own household.

And while drinking was always a popular local pastime, most of the tragic deaths lately were the consequence of drugs: meth, heroin, or pills.

Though the folks who died that way didn't usually drown. Instead, they died inside, in their own or other's houses, or once, in the bathroom of the local bar, the Velvet Cup.

"No," Christmas said, looking at her oatmeal. "Someone had beaten him up."

Her mother frowned and shook her head. "He was probably bloated from being in the water."

"He definitely wasn't waterlogged," Christmas protested, Lemy's face looming in front of her eyes. She scooped up some warm mush and then dropped the spoon back in the bowl. Her appetite had vanished. "Lexi and I heard him fall in—that's why we went to investigate. He'd only been in the water for a few minutes—for however long it took us to get in the canoe and paddle over there and . . ." Christmas stopped, remembering, again, the flannel shirt, his eyes swollen shut. "I think he was dumped."

"But you didn't actually see anything, did you?" her mother asked. "Let's not jump to conclusions. The last thing we need is for you to stir up trouble."

Christmas opened her mouth to protest, but her father cut her off.

"Eat your breakfast," he said, without meeting her gaze. "Your mother's right that you have no way of knowing how Lemy wound up in that condition. And with this whole town on edge over the algae, the last thing anyone should be doing is suggesting that this was some sort of foul play."

Christmas looked at each of her parents in turn, incredulous. "Why does it feel like I'm in trouble?"

"Don't be ridiculous," her mother said. She let her eyes close for a long moment, as though Christmas were trying her patience. She spoke extra slowly. "We're just pointing out that you don't really know what happened, and we don't want you to be responsible for giving people the wrong idea."

"That's right," Christmas's father said. "The less we speculate about what happened, the better. Now eat your oatmeal. You need to eat, Christmas."

"Who's speculating?" Christmas said, heated now. It was in moments like these that she felt acutely the injustice of being an only child, of not having a sibling ally there to verify that she wasn't crazy, that her parents were the ones acting up. "I know exactly what I heard and what I saw."

"I think everybody needs to calm down," her father said.

"I don't need to calm down!" Christmas shot back, pushing out her chair and standing. "I found my friend almost drowned—almost dead—last night. And for some reason you guys are twisting it, like somehow I'm trying to be dramatic about it."

"No one is twisting it," her mother said, shaking her head. "I was only saying that the last thing we need is a crowd of angry villagers looking for someone to blame, especially not after that flare-up at the meeting—"

"Were you at that meeting?" Christmas asked, frowning. She hadn't seen her parents there.

Her mother paused and said, "I heard about it."

The room was silent, Christmas's question—*from who?*—left unsaid.

"The point is," her father said wearily, "I think we can all agree that we are a low-profile family. And while we are glad that you had the presence of mind and ability to save a life, the incident has been stressful for all of us."

"Oh my God, Dad," Christmas said, grimacing. "Has the fact that someone almost died been stressful for you and Mom? I suppose I should have just turned the boat around and left him there to die. I wouldn't want to stress you two out."

"Don't use that tone," Christmas's mother said, her eyebrows drawn together. She took a shallow breath before adding, "It's not about us. And it's not about you either. You've had your time in the spotlight."

"My 'time in the spotlight'?" Christmas repeated, stung. "I didn't rescue Lemy to get attention."

"Well, then, it won't be hard for you to move on."

"I can't believe this," Christmas started, her voice louder and a bit shriller than she'd intended.

Her mouth open to continue, she was interrupted by her father banging his palms on the table so hard that the cups and bowls bounced and clattered. Christmas's mother's shoulders jumped. "That's enough," Christmas's father said. "Christmas, we know you're tired and . . . overwrought. But we're not the enemy here."

Christmas faced her father, though her knees were weak and her voice whinier than she would have liked. "I'm not the enemy either," she said.

"Let's just have our breakfast in peace," her father said. "We don't need to talk about this anymore. You haven't touched your food."

Christmas shoved a huge spoonful of the oatmeal in her mouth and carried the bowl over to the garbage. She dumped the rest and, with a final glare at her father, stormed from the room.

10

C HRISTMAS FUMED AS SHE POUNDED UP THE STAIRS to the shower. Her father was always protecting her mother, always covering for her. It was the only time Christmas every really saw him angry: when someone dared suggest that his precious wife wasn't quite as perfect as he believed.

But her mom was far, far from perfect.

Her father's devotion, of course, had been a cherished part of the family narrative for so long that Christmas, even in her private moments, approached any criticism of their relationship obliquely, as though considering it head-on would demonstrate a dangerous lack of gratitude and respect. And Christmas did love her parents. She appreciated the steadfastness of their commitment to each other and to her. As a child, she took comfort in their Team Miller mentality, the safety of their family unit, or what some might even call insularity.

They were all painfully shy. That her parents had even ever found each other was itself a miracle: Allie and Tom (almost-forty and forty-five when they met), had both accepted that they'd never partner up. But then, a mutual friend, a woman who was not a blood relation but whom Christmas called Aunt Inez, insisted that they both come to her dinner party. Though each initially said yes to the invitation, they'd also each tried to beg off at the last minute, a move that Aunt Inez had anticipated, knowing her friends better than they knew themselves. In order to prevent them from canceling, she had assigned them crucial tasks: Tom was to bring the fish from the good market by his house and Allie was to bring her wonderful chocolate cake. Inez would brook no excuses and she told them that she needed their contributions, thanks very much, she'd see them at seven.

When Christmas was young, Inez would tell this story, laughing and smiling at her friends. She would say that she deliberately seated them together, but that the bookish introverts—both New York City public school teachers—had studiously ignored each other, eating their food as though they were at a silent retreat.

Then, after dinner, she'd sent the two of them off to wash and dry the dishes. She'd thought the whole thing was a bust until, straining to listen at the door, she heard a few mumbled words and even a chuckle. Something magical was happening in that galley kitchen.

Christmas's parents were inseparable after that night and eloped at city hall six months later. And fast on the heels of the wedding, when Christmas's mother was forty-one and her father forty-seven, Christmas was born, and their family was complete.

Christmas had loved that story, had loved the way her mother would smile and look down at the carpet when Inez told it, how her father might lean over and pat her mother's hand happily. But Inez didn't tell the story anymore because they didn't see Inez anymore. She and Christmas's mother had had a "falling out." Her parents wouldn't say what had happened, and Christmas had been well trained by her parents not to pry. But she had her suspicions. And what she knew for sure was that once the Millers lost a person, they weren't soon replaced. This was especially true after they moved upstate.

Christmas's father had inherited the Sweet Lake house from his parents around the time Christmas was born. It was their country place, a second home, and the new little family spent every summer, all summer, at the lake.

Before the move, the Millers were happy with their two-bedroom apartment in Queens and the summers at the lake house.

Then at some point, Christmas found she simply couldn't seem to keep up with her classmates in school. She'd always been a bit scattered, disorganized, sloppy even, but what was adorable and forgivable when she was five seemed to become obnoxious and somehow offensive when she was seven, and then eight. "The state of your desk is . . . unacceptable," her second-grade teacher had informed her, and Christmas couldn't disagree: it was jammed full of worksheets and crumpled papers, broken pencils, moldy water bottles, ancient, half-eaten bags of chips, an apple core, a shoelace, several pennies, seven capless Chapsticks, and gum wrappers. In third grade, her teacher repeatedly intoned, "Eyes over here, Chrissy," catching Christmas gazing out the window, lost in her own thoughts. "Let's try to stay with the class."

Frustrated and bored, Christmas particularly liked to daydream during math lessons. She simply couldn't remember the concepts or formulas, even just a few minutes after the teacher reviewed them. She couldn't get purchase on the numbers; they never stayed put or did what they were supposed to do. And while letters didn't swim away when she read them, she couldn't get a hold of them either when it was time to write; weekly spelling tests were exercises in torture. She regularly cried at her desk, the exam before her looking like a crime scene, with scrawled words erased over and over again until the paper ripped through, stained and damp from her tears and sweaty hands.

Homework was its own unique hell. Her otherwise gentle, funny, understanding parents—trained educators, professionally patient—became frustrated and accusatory. Though they never said it out loud, Christmas could sense that her academic struggles were shameful to them, that her failures as a student, they seemed to think, evidenced their failures as parents and teachers. "Why can't you just memorize it?" her mother might hiss. "We just went over this," her father would groan, not bothering to disguise his disappointment. They'd complain that she wasn't concentrating, that she was being lazy, deliberately obtuse. They'd throw up their hands. "I don't know what to do."

Things went from bad to worse when Christmas's class moved on to telling time.

An analog clock was a confounding puzzle.

"I can't do it," she tried once to explain to her father, as they sat at the kitchen table on a Sunday afternoon.

Together, they looked at a piece of paper covered in little circles with numbers and arrows.

"If the big hand is on the three," her father had said. "And the little hand is on the seven, then it's . . ." He gestured for her to finish the sentence.

Christmas couldn't contain the tears. "Dad," she'd said. "I can't see it the way you see it. I can't do it. I'm just stupid."

Her father gathered his breath, about to scold her, tell her she was wrong, that she wasn't stupid, that she needed to try harder, but then he put his hands over his eyes and exhaled.

"Allie," he'd called to Christmas's mother, who was a few steps away in the little kitchen. "Allie, will you come over here a minute?"

Her mother padded into the room, carrying a dish towel and a glass of wine. Christmas thought her mother had been summoned to relieve her fed-up dad, but when she sat down, he gently put his hand over Christmas's.

"Your mother and I have been talking about this, Chrissy. I think we've made a mistake. I'm sorry I yelled at you all those times before. I know you're trying."

Christmas, nervous, was afraid that next, her parents would tell her she was simply too dumb to continue with school. Would they be shipping her off somewhere terrible, a home for stupid, sloppy girls?

"I'll try harder," she spluttered.

"No, honey, no," her mother put in. "It's our fault. We're going to have you tested for some learning disabilities. We should have done this sooner—we should have recognized the signs sooner. But when it's your own kid . . ." Her mother trailed off and took a sip of wine.

Christmas's father looked at her, his big gray eyes filled with concern. "We're gonna figure this out together," he said.

After that night, Christmas was put through a battery of tests and evaluations, which ultimately indicated that she had an undetermined processing disorder/learning disability that was related to or exacerbated by Attention Deficit Hyperactivity Disorder (ADHD).

"It sometimes goes unrecognized in girls," the doctor had explained to them. "We think of ADHD kids as the stereotype of the boy bouncing off the walls, so when it manifests a bit differently—in your daughter's case, the retention problems, but also the sloppiness, the forgetfulness, the distractibility when doing nonpreferred activities—we don't always catch it right away. And because she's sweet and doesn't get into trouble and because she's smart, she's been flying under the radar. And it seems to me that she's developed some fairly complicated, if effective, work-arounds. But it can get pretty exhausting, can't it, Chrissy?" the doctor asked.

Christmas nodded, though she wasn't completely sure she understood. What he said next, however, made perfect sense, so much so that Christmas would think of it, often, over and over again.

"Some people with ADHD," the doctor said, "are like ducks swimming on a smooth lake. They look completely graceful and effortless. But under the water, they are paddling so hard. A lot harder than other folks. Maybe even a lot harder than they have to."

It was as a result of her diagnosis that they'd moved upstate full time. The school Christmas attended in Queens provided minimal support, while, according to their research, Sweet Lake Public School had plenty of resources for Christmas. They discussed it as a family and concluded that they would give up the apartment and be summer people no more.

Christmas's mother found a job at a private school less than an hour away. Despite her shyness, she was a natural teacher. She loved her students, her new school, her colleagues. Once, Christmas's dad took Christmas over to the school for a holiday concert, and they'd arrived early and been allowed to surprise Christmas's mom in her classroom. Before they entered, Christmas and her father peered through the little window in the door and had seen her mother transformed: striding around the room, laughing, gesturing joyfully. She looked to Christmas like the beloved and respected teachers on television shows, lit from within, her students charmed and captivated. She was so different, teaching, than she was one-on-one with anyone who wasn't Christmas or her dad. Around other people, her mother's expression became guarded, her face seemingly always tilted toward the ground, on a spot just past her shoes.

The Millers were happy in those days, when Christmas's mother was teaching at the Prep. Her father had retired when they'd moved, and he seemed to settle comfortably into his new role as a stay-at-home parent, which allowed him to build his birdhouses but also to keep track of Christmas's IEPs, treatments, and appointments. He took her to and from school, helped with her homework, researched and implemented family menus designed to support the management of her ADHD, and generally administered their lives.

Their days were unhurried and quiet, but also full. They skied in the winters and, when the lake froze, Christmas's dad would shovel out a skating rink. They raised quail, though a clever predator laid waste to their small covey, and the three of them were too heart-broken to try again. Christmas and her father fished and went to the movies together, and in the warmer months, she and her mother hiked and visited barn sales and thrift stores. And the summers, of course, were slow and lovely, full of Lexi and waterskiing, bike rides, and long afternoons spent floating on the lake.

Things changed when Christmas started high school and her mother had a car accident.

Christmas's mother had been driving home from a party at her school when she'd hit a deer.

Christmas's mother had been extremely drunk.

CHRISTMAS'S MOTHER'S DRINKING WAS LIKE another person in the family—a troubled second cousin or disturbed step-uncle—an entity that they all knew about, pretended not to mind, but really wished would mercifully disappear, stop showing up for holidays. Her mother had a problem that no one called a problem because Christmas and her father didn't want her to feel like they were judging her, because they didn't want to upset her and make her feel so bad that she'd have to have a drink. So, they said nothing.

Up until the accident, Christmas had assumed everyone's parents drank as much as hers did—which was pretty much all the time. Her parents drank to celebrate special occasions, but they also drank to unwind from work. They enjoyed having iced drinks outside on a sunny day, and they also liked to warm up with toddies or a couple of glasses of scotch on a brisk evening. They might order beers when they went out for lunch or share a six-pack at home. They drank as they prepared dinner, with dinner, and after dinner.

They didn't seem to get drunk. It wasn't always a problem. But, sometimes, it was. Sometimes, they had screaming arguments that escalated inevitably as her mother had another glass and then another, and only ended with her collapsing on the floor and crying until she passed out. There was the time Christmas's mom fell down the stairs and broke her wrist. And the time when, her feelings hurt about something innocuous Christmas's father had said, she'd stumbled out into a snowstorm, barefoot, and Christmas's father had to follow her in the car, begging her to get inside. One time, she'd caught Christmas rolling her eyes and become uncontrollably irate, taken a family photograph from the wall, and thrown it at Christmas, screaming that she was an ingrate and a snotty little bitch.

She'd apologized the next day, sulky and morose. But it was the same each time, with her promises to "cut way down," "back off," "really watch it." And she did. Sometimes for a few weeks or even a month or two.

When Christmas was in middle school, her father quietly stopped drinking. Christmas only noticed because her mother pointed it out. "Can I get you a beer?" she might ask as they settled in front of Sunday afternoon football, and when he demurred, she'd purse her lips and pretend to tease, "You're a teetotaler now?"

"Just don't want one," he might answer, eyes still on the television. Though he never addressed this with Christmas, it seemed he was hoping her mother might take the hint and follow suit. But Christmas didn't know if her parents ever actually talked about it. Because Christmas and her mother certainly hadn't. Though she had never been overtly instructed, Christmas knew it was out of bounds to name her mother's alcoholism. And if her comments ever veered too close, she could see a visible change in both of her parents. They became like houses boarded up for a storm.

Even after the accident.

Christmas's mother had been in the hospital for two days and then rehab for another week. When she'd come home, she'd sworn off alcohol, had promised seven ways to tomorrow that she would never drink again.

Her school let her pretend that she was retiring. At first, Christmas's mother put on a happy face. She said she'd finally have time to read, paint again, organize the basement. But she was clearly depressed. She slept all day or stared vacantly at the TV, wishing, Christmas thought, she could be starting the countdown to her first drink.

Christmas watched her. When she'd come in for a hug, she put her nose into her mother's neck, sniffing, looking for evidence. A few times, Christmas had noticed the unmistakable sour stink, but to Christmas's relief, these small lapses never seemed to lead to full-blown collapses.

Lately, however, Christmas's mother had been going to the Velvet Cup again, the local dive. Though Christmas knew her father was loath to confront her mother, Christmas was nevertheless shocked he allowed this, that he went along with her mother's bizarre claim that she was only going to the bar to see people, to socialize. (And when did her parents ever socialize?) This excuse reminded Christmas of the old joke her parents used to tell: a guy who said he bought *Playboy* magazine for the articles.

The Cup—was that where her mother had "heard" about the Lake Association meeting?

Christmas kept replaying the conversation from breakfast in her mind as she got ready for work. She'd wondered if perhaps camp would be canceled because of the accident, but the camp director, Shelley, hadn't called; Christmas supposed that the world wasn't going to suddenly stop spinning just because her friend was in the hospital. After her shower, Christmas was incapable of focusing her mind on anything but leaving. She paced and forced herself to wait on checking in with Lexi.

With only twenty minutes to go before they had to be at the town hall, she texted to say she was leaving and asked if Lexi wanted-ed to bike over together.

Lexi didn't respond right away, and Christmas wondered if she had overslept. Christmas was not only increasingly worried about being late, but she had a desperate need simply to talk to Lexi about the night before: about finding Lemy, as well as about her parents' weirdness, and of course their own, difficult, fraught conversation from the previous day. There was so much she wanted to process with her—Christmas knew they wouldn't have enough time at camp—but still she hoped. Maybe afterward, they could go out in the rowboat or take a bike ride to the old bridge, and just unpack it all.

When Lexi finally replied, it was too late to bike. Lexi wrote that she'd just woken up and that her grandfather would drive them. Christmas went out to wait at the top of the driveway, pretending to be immersed in her phone until Mr. Hansen pulled in.

As Christmas climbed into the cab, she noted that Lexi had dark circles under her eyes. She and Lexi both squeezed in the front, and Lexi stared blankly at the road ahead.

"How are you feeling today?" Mr. Hansen asked.

"I'm fine," Christmas said softly. *Unlike everyone else, apparently,* she might have added. Instead, she sat in silence with them for the rest of the mercifully brief ride.

Deposited in front of the town hall, Christmas hung back at the entry for a moment. She touched her friend's arm. "Are you okay?" she asked.

Lexi looked at her, seemingly startled. She feigned a smile. "Yeah," she said, unconvincingly. She yanked open the front door. "Just tired."

Lexi barreled through the door, not even bothering to hold it for her friend. Christmas was left behind, wondering just how and when things had gotten so bad.

C HRISTMAS WANTED TO TALK TO LEXI. But once inside, they were immediately swept up in preparations for the week's camp. First, to Christmas's chagrin, was paperwork.

"I need you two to fill these out," the camp director, Shelley, said, waving paper-clipped forms.

Christmas immediately shot a look at Lexi, who pretended not to notice.

Forms were one of the true banes of Christmas's existence. The tiny boxes always confounded her, and she'd put her last name where her first name should be, her phone number where her social security number was supposed to go. She'd scribble out her mistakes until the whole thing was unintelligible, and then she'd have to ask for another. Mercifully, more and more "paperwork" was online these days and thus easier for Christmas to understand and to correct. But the stack that Shelley held out was the old-fashioned kind. The worst kind.

Again, Christmas looked desperately at her friend. Christmas was a little afraid of Shelley, someone she knew to be sort of abrasive. Plus, Christmas didn't want to look stupid for not being able to complete a straightforward task. Would Shelley fire her if she thought she was too big of an idiot to be a camp counselor?

Lexi knew Christmas struggled with this stuff. Was she in such a bad mood that she wouldn't help her? Apparently. Lexi was already sitting at one of the small desks, frowning at the boxes in front of her. Christmas then looked helplessly at Shelley, who was pouring blue paint from a large plastic jug into a smaller plastic cup.

"Can I do the paperwork at home?" Christmas asked. "I just . . . I promise to bring it tomorrow."

Shelley looked up skeptically. "I suppose that's fine," she said. "Come and fill up these paint jars for me. I need to set up the easels."

Christmas, slightly relieved, put the forms with her stuff in the kitchen and got to work. Each camp session was a different theme— nature, sports, theater; the first week was arts and crafts.

Even before all the paints were ready at their easels, Lexi had finished her paperwork with a flourish, brought it to Shelley's office, and then announced that a little boy—five minutes early—was waiting in the hall.

"Come on in," Shelley called from the back of the room where she was reorganizing colorful plastic bins. "That'll be Eli. His parents always drop him off early."

"Hey," Christmas said, she hoped brightly, as the boy edged into the room. "I'm Christmas and this is Lexi. You're Eli?"

He nodded. "Your name is Christmas? Like the holiday?"

"It sure is," Christmas answered. "Easy to remember, huh?"

"Arbor Day, will you get Eli set up at an easel?" Shelley said, winking at the child.

After Eli, the children began to arrive in a steady trickle and the quiet, clean room was filled with noise and activity. Christmas and Lexi didn't have a moment to themselves for the rest of the day.

It probably wouldn't have mattered anyway, Christmas thought. She and Lexi could be stranded on a desert island, and Lexi still wouldn't talk to her. She seemed normal to anyone who didn't know better, but Christmas wasn't fooled: she saw how short Lexi was with the kids, how unwilling to joke around or laugh, how, when she thought no one was looking, her face fell into a deep frown. And worse: how she wouldn't meet Christmas's eye.

As the terrible day wore on, Christmas became more and more aware of what she needed to do. She had to be direct. She would use their time on the walk home to express her regret about laughing at the meeting and her embarrassment about being jealous that Lexi had a new close friend. She'd ask to learn more about Martha. In fact, they could talk or not talk about whatever Lexi wanted: Martha or finding Lemy or anything else that might be on Lexi's mind.

Though it would be hard for Christmas, who hated any sort of confrontation, she knew she had to do it. She was optimistic. She believed Lexi would understand. And once they'd smoothed things over, maybe they could try to figure out what had really happened to Lemy. Christmas would propose that they talk to Curly and maybe even visit the shoreline to look for clues, evidence, anything unusual or out of place.

As they climbed the stairs at the end of the day, Christmas began, "So I wanted to tell you—" But Lexi interrupted her.

"My grandpa's picking us up." Again, Lexi wouldn't look at her. "We can drop you home. Like I said, I'm pretty tired from last night. I think I just need to chill with my grandparents today."

Christmas was dumbfounded. Never in their history of summers together had they spent free time apart.

And when they exited the building, there was Mr. Hansen, waiting in his truck.

All of Christmas's energy had to be channeled into not crying. As they drove home, she looked out the window and tried to think about her next run. If she could just make it home, get her sneakers on, and get out of the house again, she'd be okay. And so again she sat silently in the cab, but this time, Lexi talked, though not to her: she told her grandfather about the kids, crafts, and Shelley. When they finally got to her house, Christmas grabbed her backpack and darted from the truck, feeling rude, but knowing she could not manage a "thank you" without betraying the sob she was holding in her throat.

13

CHRISTMAS RARELY RAN TWICE IN ONE DAY, but it happened some-times: days when the anxiety or the energy or the noise just got to be too much. On those days, the only thing she could do was to run. Her parents didn't question it; she knew they probably figured that she was still working out what had happened with Lemy the night before.

She ran a different route from the one she had taken in the morning and rather than push, she allowed herself a slow jog down the quiet country roads. Despite her turmoil, and the biting flies that pursued her on a particularly leafy stretch, she began to appreciate the beauty around her: the bright green of the trees arching over her head, the chuckle of a small stream that ran along the shoulder of the road. And after about a mile, it started to happen: some of the pain started to fall away. She thought of the old *Iron Man* movies, the way he would walk and his armor would assemble or disassemble it-self around him. That was how she felt when she ran, the iron falling from her body, the trouble gradually detaching itself. She imagined leaving it on the ground behind her, although, of course, it some-times snapped back on when she stopped running.

But for a few miles, at least, she was lighter.

Running, she let herself cry a little bit, her face scrunched up and her breath uneven. She reviewed each of Lexi's words and looks, how she'd sighed impatiently when Christmas asked for help distributing lunches, how she'd barely smiled when Christmas asked if Lexi's grammie was making anything particularly perverse for dinner. How cold she'd been all day. How unlike her usual self.

Christmas cringed, thinking again of how she'd stuck her foot in her mouth when she'd teased Lexi about Martha, and then again about the times when Lexi had tried to talk to her about dating and "hooking up" and, one time in particular, when Lexi had said she'd kissed two different people at the same party. Christmas had said "Eww," and Lexi had called her a prude.

It was true, of course. Christmas knew she was uptight about dating, relationships, and sex. It all remained sort of scary and mysterious to her, and it had never been something she felt at ease talking about. Both of her parents, too, were incredibly awkward about the subject and couldn't bring themselves to discuss anything beyond the basics of reproduction with her, instead leaving a stack of helpful books on her desk.

But of course, Christmas knew it wasn't her parents' fault that Lexi was upset with her.

She also knew that "rejection sensitivity" was an ADHD symptom, that being disliked or criticized could be extra painful for people like her. There was no denying that her academic success was largely a result of her profound fear of disappointing her teachers. But feeling like she'd let her best friend down—this was a new level of awful.

The run allowed her to develop a plan. First, she would fix things with Lexi. Then she would check in with Curly. And finally, she would settle something else that was bothering her: she'd talk to her dad, make sure her mother wasn't drinking again.

She chugged along, sweating, and unhappy with the high temperature. Christmas liked it colder, freezing even, but running outside in the winter could be difficult or impossible once the snow hit the ground and there was no shoulder to run to on. Though she found it torturous, Christmas ran on the treadmill in the den during those frozen weeks. But upstate summers were glorious for running, especially early in the morning, when the ground was still wet and the air crisp.

She didn't usually see many people out on her runs. A car or truck would pass now and then—usually it was someone Christmas knew—and they'd give her a honk or a wave. Christmas preferred the solitude, although once, the summer before, she'd been jogging on a relatively quiet side road when she'd run into Gary George, a kind of scary locally known drug-user. Gary had been walking toward her and she'd seen him from a half a mile out, although at first she didn't know who it was. As she neared, his stagger suggested that the individual was either old or somehow impaired. Closer, Christmas recognized Gary's generally disheveled appearance, his dirty hair, his paranoid scowl. Though she was afraid of Gary, she was too polite to turn around and jog in the opposite direction. She knew this was absurd and ridiculous and yet she kept jogging, shrinking the space between them.

When they were ten feet from each other, he stopped walking and, swaying in place, stared at her.

"I need to borrow that," he said, his words slurry and aggressive. He pointed at Christmas's armband, where her phone was strapped.

Christmas slowed, took out one earbud. "I don't get a signal out here," she squeaked, immediately cursing herself. He'd know now, of course, that she couldn't call the police.

Then, he'd lunged at her. She jumped and sprinted away as he yelled a stream of vulgarities and threats. She ran, hard and fast down the road. Obviously, she could outrun Gary George, but still her heart was pounding in her head, and her arms and legs tingled with fear. She saw a truck cresting the hill in front of her and, as it approached, she waved at it, more frightened than she wanted to admit.

It was Mr. Ford. He pulled over, his window already down. "You all right?" he asked, worried. "You look like you've seen a ghost."

"I'm so sorry to bother you," Christmas said. "I just saw Gary George. Down there. And he kinda tried to grab me."

Mr. Ford nodded good-humoredly. "That tracks. Jump in and let me drive you home."

Christmas climbed in the trunk. Her heart was still pounding, but she felt so relieved to be in Mr. Ford's calming presence. "I know I'm being stupid," Christmas said.

"Not at all," Mr. Ford said. He drove forward and, a moment later, they were upon Gary.

Mr. Ford pulled up alongside him. Christmas shifted uncomfortably in the seat, wishing Mr. Ford had just kept going.

Gary—greasy, with wild eyes and scarred, spotted skin—looked angrily at the car before leaning down and putting his hands on Mr. Ford's windowsill.

"Gary," Mr. Ford barked, "you ever bother this girl again you'll have me to answer to."

Unsteady on his feet, Gary looked at Christmas and then back at Mr. Ford. "That girl? Never seen that girl before in my life." His teeth —several of which were missing—were dark and jagged-looking.

"Goddammit, Gary," Mr. Ford said, then he moved quickly, his hands darting out and clutching Gary's collar. He pulled Gary's face close, through the open window. Though he remained completely calm, Mr. Ford revealed in that moment that he, too, could be scary; Christmas had never seen him like this before. "Chrissy Miller is a friend of mine, and if you ever even look at her again, you'll be sorry."

"Yeah, yeah," Gary said, his wild eyes rolling.

Mr. Ford released Gary and he stumbled backward. "All right then," Mr. Ford said. He put the car in drive again and they continued along the dusty road. "He's mostly harmless," Mr. Ford said after a moment. "But you should carry some bear spray with you if you're gonna run out here all by yourself. We do have some unsavory characters in Sweet Lake."

"I will," Christmas said, grateful to Mr. Ford.

The next day, there was a small black cylinder of Mace waiting for her in the mailbox.

Christmas thought of that rescue again as she noted a guy cycling toward her from the opposite direction.

14

S HE DIDN'T RECOGNIZE HIM, though that wasn't so strange; she was on a road a bit farther from her house than usual. And it was late June. There would be lots of summer people around in the coming weeks, biking and walking and generally clogging up the area until Labor Day.

But not long after he passed her, he turned and cycled up behind her. When she nervously moved to the side, he pulled over and stopped. Christmas realized she hadn't brought her Mace. She'd assiduously carried it since that day with Gary, but she'd left it behind that afternoon in her hurry to get out of the house.

The guy, who looked to be about her age, must have realized that he was scaring her, so he sort of waved a greeting, as though to indicate he was harmless. Christmas stopped a few yards away, uncertain. Panting, she waited with her hands on her hips, trying to look confident.

His curly black hair sprang out from underneath a blue bike helmet. He wore a faded Radiohead T-shirt, blue jeans, and Converse sneakers. The T-shirt alone would have recommended him, but he was also really cute. He looked familiar, but she couldn't quite place him. He wasn't from school. Maybe he was from Quartz or Honeysuckle?

"Hey. Sorry," the guy said. "I'm lost. I'm trying to get back to Sweet Lake, but I really have no idea if I'm going in the right direction, and I can't get a signal on my phone."

Christmas smiled. This was no Gary George situation.

"You were going the right way before," she said. "You want to go back down this road," she walked a little closer so that she didn't have to raise her voice and used her thumb to indicate behind her. "And up the hill and then take a right over by . . . you know where the old restaurant used to be?" Christmas realized that the usual landmarks wouldn't help with this summer person. It was, in fact, a rather twisted path home. "Where exactly are you trying to get to?"

"I supposed it's . . . the northern part maybe?"

"Whose house?"

"It's ours . . . it's a blue cottage. My mom is Naomi Gold."

Christmas thought of Dr. Gold at the lake meeting, and she suddenly realized where she knew the guy from. He'd been there too. He'd seemed older, but maybe that was just because he looked so serious—and handsome—sitting there, listening to Naomi.

"Sure, I know the house," Christmas said. She pursed her lips, thinking for a minute. "You know what? I need to turn around and head back anyway. I lost track of time, and I ran farther than I meant to. If you don't mind going slow, I'll jog and you can ride next to me."

"Really?" The guy smiled widely and slumped a little with relief. "That would be so nice. I could ride you on the handlebars if you want."

"I'd rather run," Christmas said, laughing a little bit. The guy remounted and pedaled up next to her as she began a slow trot.

"Let me know if I'm going too fast," he said.

"I will," Christmas said, speeding up to a pace that would allow him to pedal along beside her without losing his balance and falling over. "This good?"

"Great," he said. "But I can't believe you lost track of time running. I hate running so much, I'm totally aware of every second passing by. I'd much rather bike. I'm Rory, by the way."

"Like on *Gilmore Girls*?"

"Well, it's a boy's name too," Rory said, with a weariness that suggested he had heard this remark before. "And you're Chrissy, right? I remember you from that lake meeting."

"Christmas, actually," Christmas said, cringing inwardly. Though there were several people in town who knew her by her nickname, she'd long ago abandoned it. "My name is Christmas."

"That's a pretty unusual name too."

"It is," Christmas agreed. Rory waited for her to continue. "I was born on December 25. My mom didn't think she would ever have kids, and so then when I came along, she said I was the best Christmas present she ever got." Christmas smiled, thinking of her mother telling the story. Her mother had also said that she felt about Christmas the person the way that other people felt about the holiday: that she was a cause for joy and celebration, and a bit magical. Christmas felt a twinge of sadness and regret. Her mother mostly drove her crazy, but she also missed her somehow, missed the way they used to be.

"That's really nice," Rory said. "So, do you live in Sweet Lake?"

"Yeah, we're almost directly across the lake from you. Our house is white—or it was once. We have about two million bird houses in front?"

"Sure, I know that house," Rory said. "Do you ever sell any?" He was referencing, she knew, the hand-painted sign her father had hung, advertising "Bird homes, condos, bungalows, and ranches— bat homes too!—$25 each!"

"That's my dad. He sells a few each summer. But he makes at least twenty each year, so we have a surplus." She laughed. "Have you guys been coming up a while now?"

"My parents bought the house four years ago, but I never wanted to come. I was pretty bratty about it."

"What do you mean?"

"I gave them a hard time. I wanted to be at home—we're from Brooklyn—playing baseball and hanging out with my friends. So, whenever my folks would come up, I'd make a big fuss until they'd let me stay with friends for the weekend. And if they forced me to come up, well, I made them even more miserable. I'd stay indoors the whole time, looking at my phone." Rory was silent for a moment. Then, he added, "I like it now though."

Christmas smiled and cut a glance at Rory. She was surprised by how comfortable she was with him. Maybe it was the run that relaxed her, or that she could talk to him mostly without looking at him.

"What changed?" she asked.

"I don't know. I guess I'm starting to get it—the appeal of an 'escape.' I really, really needed to get out of Brooklyn this year." They continued in a silence for a moment and then he added, "Maybe I'm just turning into a senior citizen. But I like waking up and hearing birds instead of car alarms. I enjoy the peace and quiet and all that stuff. Do you live here year-round?"

"Yeah," Christmas answered. "We lived in Queens, but we moved up full time when I was ten."

They'd encountered a long, steep incline and so they both fell silent, panting as they crested the hill.

When they reached the top and began the descent, Rory rode his bike in a zigzag behind Christmas, back and forth across the road as she dashed, allowing the downward slope to let her build momentum, almost as though she were flying. Near the bottom, he pulled up alongside her and they started to talk again.

"So, do you like living here?" Rory asked.

"I love it."

"That must have been hard, though, when you moved," Rory said. "Leaving your friends and all that."

Christmas shrugged. She didn't tell him that she hadn't had that many close friends down in the city.

Instead, she said, "It was definitely an adjustment. But I always felt more at home here, in our house at the lake. Plus, we moved for the school."

"Are the schools up here good?"

"I don't know if they're objectively good, but the elementary school here was better than the school I was in downstate. Resources and support, that sort of thing. I have some learning disabilities and they weren't really able to deal with them at my old school."

"Oh, makes sense," Rory said, nodding. Christmas couldn't tell if it made him uncomfortable that she'd brought up her learning disabilities.

"I have dysgraphia," she said. "Or some kind of written-expression disorder. The jury's still out. It's basically like I have dyslexia but with writing." Christmas paused. Was this boring? She couldn't tell. He seemed interested. She thought about her doctor downstate, who explained that her challenges were "idiosyncratic." He had also floated the idea that Christmas might be on the spectrum, suggesting that some of her ADHD things overlapped with autism-things. She did not mention this to Rory, however, instead saying, "I also have ADHD. Sometimes that makes it hard for me to concentrate, but it also makes me extra motivated." She saw Rory nodding in her peripheral vision. "It's like I have a responsibility to do well. To prove that I'm smart or whatever." She surprised herself; she hadn't realized that she'd ever really felt that way until she'd said it out loud. "I was pretty far behind when we moved here," she added. "But I just graduated with a 3.8 GPA."

"That's awesome," Rory said. A moment later, he added, "A couple of people at my school had ADHD and they were at the top of our class too."

Christmas looked at Rory and this time, he looked back. "ADHD can be good and bad, I think," she said. "Like, I can get super focused. Which, again, can sometimes create problems if I'm too focused on the wrong thing. But if I have a problem to solve, I can be sort of like a pit bull about it. I can't stop worrying about it until it's resolved. And I'm never late. Again, I can be obsessive about it, but I also secretly believe it's important to be on time for things and I judge people who aren't." She cut a wry glance at Rory.

"Mental note," Rory said. "She doesn't like lateness."

Christmas laughed. Was he flirting with her? Yes. He was flirting with her.

"Am I pedaling too fast?" Rory asked.

"A little," Christmas conceded, suddenly aware that she was breathing hard. Rory put on the brakes, coasting smoothly now, on a somewhat-level road. At a fork, Christmas gestured to the right and they continued along at an easier pace.

"You must run track," Rory said.

Christmas shook her head. "No. I guess I should have. But I suppose I'm more of a lone wolf."

"You woulda been a track star," Rory said. "You still could? In college?"

"Maybe," Christmas said. "Are you . . . What year are you in school?"

"I just graduated too," Rory said. "I'm going to Cornell in the fall."

"Wow," Christmas said. "Cornell. You must be excited."

Rory shrugged. "I'm working on getting excited. I'm mostly just nervous. My sister went there—she just graduated—and she really loved it. But what about you? Where are you going?"

"I'm going to CCC," Christmas said, glad that the flush she had from running would hide whatever color was spreading across her face and neck, embarrassed to have proudly mentioned her GPA. "The community college. Just for the first two years. You know."

"That's cool," Rory said, trying perhaps a bit too hard to sound upbeat.

"Yeah," Christmas said. She hadn't felt ambivalent about her plans before; not only were plenty of the kids from her graduating class going to community college (if they were going to college at all), but her parents were big proponents of public educations and "democracy's colleges" and, since they were also basically not rich, had suggested the community college route was somehow more virtuous than her other options.

But now it felt unimpressive, embarrassing, knowing that Rory was going to Cornell.

They passed town hall, which was set on a hill overlooking the lake. Christmas was happy to change the subject and, nodding ahead to where the lake was visible through some trees, asked, "Do you know where we are now?"

"Oh yeah, I see it," Rory said. "But I never would have found my way back. I probably would've pedaled forever, an ancient mariner on a bicycle. You basically saved my life."

Christmas smiled appreciatively, but his last remark reminded her of Lemy, and she also remembered, with a sudden sinking feeling, all the things she had been running to forget: Lemy in the lake, the weirdness with her parents, the fight with Lexi. She wished they weren't back already; she wished she could keep running beside Rory so that she could stay with him in that place out of time, moving together.

He was easy to talk to and she found herself wanting to tell him more: about Lemy, about Lexi.

"Do you really know which house is mine?" Rory asked.

"Sure," Christmas answered. "I know the houses around the lake pretty well. Plus, at the Lake Association meeting, your mother said you had the place across from the church."

"Good memory," Rory said. "Weren't you, like, elected to the board?"

"We technically never had the elections," Christmas said, frowning.

"Yeah. That whole meeting was out of control," Rory said, raising his eyebrows.

When Christmas didn't comment, Rory continued. "What do you think is causing the algae?"

Christmas shrugged. "I don't know. Maybe the cows. Maybe the auto shop. Maybe it's global warming."

"We humans are the worst. We treat the entire world like it's one big toilet bowl."

After a pause, Christmas agreed. "I guess we do."

They were approaching another fork in the road: to the right was Christmas's house, to the left, Rory's. Christmas slowed and Rory did too, riding in a loop around her before coming to a stop and putting one foot on the ground. Christmas stood, panting a little, hands on her hips again. She glanced down and was startled to realize she was wearing a sweat-drenched bright orange Mets T-shirt, pink shorts, and teal sneakers.

She inwardly cringed. She wanted to assure him that she did not normally dress like this. Instead, she muttered, "Um, I guess this is where we say goodbye."

"Thanks so much for bringing me back," Rory said. "That was super nice. And it was really cool talking to you."

"Yeah," Christmas agreed. She looked up and smiled, unable to stop thinking about how sweaty she was. It was so much easier when they had their eyes on the road ahead of them! But she liked looking at Rory, who really was amazingly cute: sharp-featured with high cheekbones and bright brown eyes, he was tall and thin, with ropy muscles.

"We should do it again sometime," Rory said.

Christmas felt herself flushing and was then grateful for the fact that she was probably already pretty red in the face. "I run every day. But mostly in the morning. And besides, don't I go too slow for you?"

Rory shrugged. "You ever bike?"

"I do, actually."

"We could go for a bike ride sometime, if you want. You could show me, you know, some cool spots." He seemed suddenly embarrassed. "Or whatever."

"Yeah. That'd be fun," Christmas said. She wanted to add, "My friend Lexi and I love to bike around." She didn't, of course, but the thought of Lexi provoked another thought: in a flash she saw herself, abandoned again, the next afternoon stretching out in front of her, alone without Lexi. She said, quickly, "How about tomorrow? I work until around three thirty. I can swing by your house after. Like, four thirty?"

"That'd be awesome," Rory said. His eyes crinkled as he smiled. "I'll see you tomorrow, track star."

"Sounds good," Christmas said. She stood awkwardly for another moment before giving what she felt was a super dorky little wave and taking off again, jogging away.

"I'll be ready on time," Rory called after her.

Christmas looked back and smiled to let him know she got the joke, before she started to sprint, and then to really run hard, propelled forward with a lightness, as though she were filled with bubbles lifting her a few inches above the road.

CHRISTMAS SAT ON THE COUCH, scrolling on her phone. Her father watched the Mets game from his recliner while her mother snoozed in hers. Christmas texted Curly to ask about Lemy, but he didn't respond. She stopped herself from texting Lexi. Thinking about Rory, reviewing the details of their conversation, gave her mind something else to settle on, but still, the thing with Lexi was always there, like a pot simmering on a back burner.

In her hand, the phone vibrated. It was Lexi.

sry about today, just tired. I think im coming down with something and gonna actually stay home from work tmw. dont worry, ill call and let Shelley know.

Christmas's heart pounded in her chest. A part of her wanted to cling to the lie that Lexi really was coming down with something. But a larger part of her knew better—knew her friend better—and knew that even sick, Lexi was never mean or distant. She'd never pushed Christmas away before.

Christmas had no idea how to respond and was sitting, staring at the screen, trying to slow her breathing, when the doorbell rang. Christmas looked up to see her parents, wide-eyed. They both stared back at Christmas expectantly. They weren't used to unannounced visitors.

Or announced ones either, really.

"Oh my god, you guys," Christmas said, exasperated. She heaved herself off the couch. "Fine. I'll get it."

She padded down the hall and pulled open the front door. Ben Pappas, blond and baby-faced, stood beside another uniformed officer. Officer Schaefer was also youngish, but where Ben tended toward the cherubic, Officer Schaefer was thin-faced and severe-looking with a pointy chin and sharp nose.

They stepped awkwardly inside and explained they had a few more questions for Christmas.

Christmas sensed her parents behind her in the hallway, buzzing and nervous. Immediately claustrophobic in the narrow hall, she took a step back.

"Yeah, sure. Come in." She moved toward the kitchen and bumped into her parents, who murmured greetings to the cops before following her.

They filed into the kitchen, the cops' boots and belts creaking. Christmas's father grabbed a spare chair from the pantry, where it served as a stepstool, and they assembled themselves at the little table while Christmas's mother bustled around near the sink, preparing coffee that everyone had already politely declined. Once settled, Officer Schaefer said, "We really appreciate what you did last night, Christmas."

"You handled yourself like a real pro," Ben added.

"Is there any news on Lemy?" Christmas asked.

Ben shook his head. "He's still in a coma, unfortunately."

"Are you any closer to knowing what happened?" Christmas looked from one cop to the other.

Though Ben frowned instead of answering, Officer Schaefer said, "That's why we're here. Now, tell us again what happened, with as much detail as you can. Sometimes the things people think aren't important turn out to be really helpful in the investigation."

Christmas sighed. "I really don't think I left anything out last night."

"Did you hear any vehicles or notice anyone on the road around the lake? Or other boats?"

"I didn't hear any other boats," Christmas said. "But it wouldn't be unusual for a car to be on the road, so it's not something I would have noticed. Besides, we were talking and looking at the stars." Christmas thought vaguely about the vape pen and the fact that they were still only seventeen and bit her lip.

"Okay," Officer Schaefer said. "Now, how well do you know Lemy LaSalle?"

Christmas squirmed a little. "He's a friend of mine."

"Isn't he quite a bit older than you?" Officer Schaefer asked.

"I guess," Christmas said, shrugging.

"Doesn't seem to me like you all would have a lot in common," Ben said.

Christmas made a face. "That's not true. Lemy and Curly have always been really nice to me. We care about a lot of the same stuff."

"What kind of stuff is that?" Ben asked.

Christmas shrugged again, a bit sheepish, feeling that specific kind of shame associated, in some families, with "showing off." She didn't want Ben and Officer Schaefer to think she thought she was smart and sophisticated. But they'd asked what she and Lemy and Curly had talked about and so she told them: "Environmentalism. Climate change. Things like that. We talk about the algae, about the lake. We love the lake."

When neither officer responded, Christmas added, awkwardly, "It's not weird."

She looked at her father for confirmation. He nodded, to suggest that what she had said was fine.

"Just . . . two adult men who hang around with a teenage girl," Ben began, spreading his hands out as though asking someone to complete the thought.

Christmas was so surprised by the direction the conversation was taking that she was momentarily at a loss for words. Her mother furrowed her brow as she put a mug of coffee in front of each of the officers, who offered curt smiles to thank her.

"You can't be serious," Christmas said at last. "Even if it was weird, which it totally isn't, Ben—"

"Officer Pappas," her father interrupted. Ben waved a hand to suggest Christmas's lack of formality was fine.

"My friendship with Lemy and Curly has nothing to do with Lemy getting beaten up."

"So you do believe that someone intentionally . . ." Officer Schaefer seemed to search for a word. "Deposited Lemy in the lake?" She put her hands around the coffee mug as though to warm them.

"Of course," Christmas said, heatedly.

"Mrs. Miller," Officer Schaefer said, swiveling her head, as though she'd just remembered that Christmas's mother was in the room. "You were at the Velvet Cup last night, weren't you?"

"Me?" Christmas's mother said, as though she, too, was surprised by her own presence.

"Did you see Lemy?" Officer Schaefer asked.

Christmas twisted in her seat to look up at her mother, who opened her mouth and then shut it again before saying, "Sure. There was a crowd of people after the meeting."

"And did you observe anything out of the ordinary? Did you speak to Mr. LaSalle?"

"Who, Lemy?" Christmas's mother said, absurdly. "No, no I didn't talk to him."

"What were you doing at the Velvet Cup, Mrs. Miller?"

"What was I doing? I was unwinding." Christmas's mother's eyes darted around the room. "I had a seltzer. It's not a crime. It's not a crime to . . . want to get out of the house."

"No one said it was, ma'am," Ben said.

"Don't 'ma'am' me," Christmas's mother snapped. "I don't even understand what this . . . interrogation is about. A guy got drunk and fell in the lake."

"Was he visibly impaired when you observed him at the Velvet Cup, Mrs. Miller?" Officer Schaefer asked.

"I didn't observe him or anything else at the Cup," Christmas's mother said.

"But maybe you noticed the general feeling last night," Officer Schaefer pressed. "Were people wound up? Upset about what happened at the meeting?"

Christmas's mother shook her head as she took Christmas's father's empty mug and brought it to the sink. "The whole thing . . . sounds like a lot of showboating was going on at the meeting."

"Mr. Cunningham called Lemy the f-word," Christmas said facing forward, the officer's attention directed back at her. They waited and she added, cringing, "You know. Fag."

"We had heard that," Officer Schaefer said.

Everyone sat silently for a moment. Christmas wondered if this was a cop trick, that they thought if they stayed quiet, someone would dive into the breach to relieve the tension. Well, they didn't know the Millers.

They were masters of allowing awkward silences to stretch on long past what others considered reasonable. Christmas's father stared at the tabletop and her mother scrubbed the mug more vigorously than necessary. Christmas, too, just waited, although she started to roll her neck and wiggle her jaw to release some of the tension that rested there.

Finally, mercifully, Ben tapped the table.

"We'll let you folks get back to your evening," he said. To Christmas, he said kindly, "I'm sorry about your friend and I hope he comes out of this okay. You probably saved his life, Chrissy."

Christmas, overwhelmed, couldn't make sense of the conversation that had just happened. She nodded absently and stayed seated, forcing her father to rise to the occasion and see them to the door.

Her mother returned to the table to collect the untouched cups of coffee, her lips pursed and forehead creased.

Christmas watched her as she returned to the sink and began to run a dish towel over a clean mug as she stared out the little kitchen window.

"What was that all about?" Christmas asked.

"What was what about?" her mother returned blandly.

"Do you have anything to do with this, Mom?" Christmas whispered fiercely, surprised by her own directness.

Her mother grimaced and turned to face her fully, her eyes injured and filling with tears.

"I'm almost sixty years old, Christmas. Even if, for some mysterious reason, I hated him, do you think I am even capable of beating up Lemy LaSalle and dumping him in the lake?" When Christmas didn't respond, her mother ran a hand over her forehead. "I can't believe you'd even ask me. I can't believe you think so little of me..."

"For God's sake," Christmas's father said from the doorway.

Christmas didn't turn to look at her father. Instead, she continued to regard her mother. Her chambray shirt brought out the blue in her shining eyes. Her stringy gray-blond hair, piled up in a messy bun, framed her pretty face. In the dim kitchen light, she looked lovely, despite her frown, despite the deep wrinkles around her mouth. At the same time, she seemed older than she ever had before, maybe even a bit frail. Christmas wanted to put her arms around her mother, to cry into her neck, to apologize, to comfort and be comforted.

Instead, she turned to leave the room. It hadn't escaped her that her mother hadn't answered the question.

16

CHRISTMAS COULDN'T DECIDE WHICH WAS WORSE: being at work with Lexi and being ignored, or being at work and not having Lexi there at all.

Shelley was really mad—and made no effort to discourage Christmas from feeling like it was her fault that Lexi had called in sick—which made Christmas even more upset and uneasy. She hated disappointing people, especially people in charge.

It was almost physically painful not to text Lexi, and several times during the day, Christmas would touch the phone in her back pocket then stop herself from pulling it out, checking it, or sending a text to test the waters: "Hey." Anticipating Shelley's disapproval stilled Christmas's hand, but when Shelley was in the kitchen, or when Christmas took a group of kids to the bathroom down the hall and she was out of sight, she'd take out her phone, stare at it, and wonder if she should turn it off and restart it, just in case something was wrong with it, and Lexi's texts hadn't been coming through.

The plan to go on a bike ride with Rory, though, was a good distraction, a bright spot on the horizon, and she spent a great deal of time thinking about where she'd take him. She settled on the colorfully but misleadingly titled Old Devil's Swamp Road, which led to some breathtaking vistas, mountain views, and then, farther along, to an old stone arch bridge, long neglected but still standing, that she and Lexi loved to visit. Allowed to roam freely on their bikes at twelve and thirteen, they would go there to act out elaborate fantasies: the bridge was their fortress, and they were beautiful, tragic—but nevertheless heroic—princesses, forced to fight and scheme their way out of captivity. Christmas felt a pang remembering, in part because both she and Lexi still liked to play pretend after other girls their age had grown out of it, or at least said they had.

Pedaling to Rory's house, she wished she could talk to Lexi and get some moral support and reassurance. She was so nervous that her fingers tingled and her breath was a little short. It was a good thing she didn't have Rory's phone number because even though she'd been really looking forward to seeing him again, she knew she would have totally canceled. It was only because she lived in fear of ever upsetting or offending anyone, even someone who was basically a stranger, that she didn't simply stand him up. This, she tried to tell herself, was a good thing. She had, in the ensuing twenty-four hours, developed an aching crush. She suspected she was getting ahead of herself. Was she taking this summer person too seriously, spinning out a whole romance when really he was just bored and lonely? Maybe, but she didn't think so. She'd sensed something— maybe his own nervousness, a little twitching of his lip—that made her think he liked her too. At the same time, it was possible that he wasn't looking for a girlfriend or anything like that. If he just wanted to be friends, that was cool. Especially since there was currently a vacancy in her friendship roster.

This last thought was like a needle in her heart.

There was the irony, of course, that if Lexi hadn't been acting so weird, hadn't blown her off the day before, Christmas would not have gone on an afternoon run and met Rory. And even if she had met him, she still probably still wouldn't be going on a bike ride with him if she had Lexi to hang out with. She didn't like this thought and was happy to pull up in front of the blue house where Rory, dressed in jeans (cuffed on one side) and a white T-shirt, his curly hair not yet shoved into the confines of the helmet, stood waiting outside. She almost immediately felt more easy.

She was glad to be wearing something a little less bizarre than last time—her best cutoffs and a well-worn Patagonia tee that Lemy had said he'd liked—and that she'd taken the time to put on some hoop earrings and lip gloss. She didn't want to look like she was trying too hard to look good on their bike ride, but she also wanted to make sure he knew she didn't always wear fluorescent colors.

Rory smiled and picked up a large backpack.

"Hey," he said. "What's up? I didn't know how long we'd be out; I packed some food."

"Like a picnic?" Christmas put one foot on the ground and tilted her head.

"Yeah," he said, clearly a bit embarrassed. "Like a picnic." He wrinkled his nose.

Christmas laughed. "Who doesn't like a picnic?"

Rory put the backpack on and mounted his bike. "Awesome," he said. "Lead the way."

It had been another overcast, humid day, and Christmas started to sweat as they cycled slowly down Lake Road, which cut close to the shoreline. A startled blue heron crashed out of tall weeds, close enough that they could hear her huge, beating wings. They watched the bird skimming the top of the water, flying away in search of a quieter spot on the lake.

They continued on toward another, flatter road that would carry them away from the lake and then past farmland and into a deep wood. They didn't talk much at first, but after a while, Rory pulled up beside her.

"So, I think I heard something about you," he began. "Did you save a guy's life?"

Christmas glanced at Rory. "I don't know if I saved his life," she said. "He's in a coma."

Rory was quiet for a moment. "Still. Wow. You did, like, CPR and stuff."

Christmas didn't respond.

"What happened?" Rory pressed. "I mean, if you feel like talking about it. That must have been pretty scary."

"It's okay," Christmas said. "You're right though. It was scary. I wasn't alone. My friend Lexi was with me. But still. I kinda can't stop thinking about it. There are like three things that my mind keeps cycling through." She stopped there, unwilling to tell Rory that he was himself one of those three things. She took a breath and recounted the basic facts of the evening before concluding, "I really hope Lemy's okay."

"He's a friend of yours? The guy you found?"

Christmas nodded. The woods were noticeably cooler. This was one of her favorite roads. The Voigts, a local family, had owned this land for as long as anybody could remember, and they'd posted No Hunting and Private Property signs on trees every acre or so. She always felt grateful that they'd let it stay wild, that they hadn't chopped down or sold off all the trees for lumber, made a clearing and stuck in a suburban-style house that would sit there like a wound.

"Is your friend—Lexi—is she okay?"

"I honestly don't know," Christmas said. She kept her eyes on the road in front of her. "We were actually having a . . ." She searched for the word. "Argument" seemed too serious. "Conversation" was too euphemistic. "I suppose we were having sort of a tense disagreement. And then we heard the splash and, after that, everything happened so fast." Christmas shook her head. "She's definitely upset. But we haven't, like, had a chance to really talk about it yet."

Rory was quiet for a moment before he said, "Maybe she's traumatized or something?"

"Maybe," Christmas said. "I don't know." Christmas paused, remembering Lexi's anger, the ways she said she had something she needed to tell Christmas.

She imagined Lexi announcing that she and Martha would be going backpacking in Europe for the rest of the summer, or that Lexi had decided she couldn't be friends with Christmas anymore because of the trashy people Christmas associated with. Christmas was ashamed to know that, on some level, she had been grateful for the interruption of the splash. She hadn't wanted to hear what Lexi was going to say.

"I'm not sure why she's mad at me," Christmas continued to Rory. "She seems sort of mad at Sweet Lake in general. Lexi is . . . summer people." She cut a glance at Rory. "That's what we call people who don't live here full time."

He chuckled.

"Her grandparents live on the lake," Christmas continued. "Lexi's mom grew up here but moved to Philly as soon as she turned eighteen. She had Lexi pretty soon after that, and she was mostly a single mom. Ever since Lexi was little, her mom would drop her off to stay for the whole summer, so she could work or whatever. Plus, Lexi's grandparents think she's God's gift to humankind." Christmas smiled, thinking of the Hansens' understated, but undeniable, adoration of their granddaughter. "Anyway, we've always been summer friends. We keep in touch during the year—we used to write letters when we were young. Now we text a lot and I guess we probably talk a couple of times a month. But usually in the summer, we're together every day. We used to laugh that we had to have these intense hangouts because we have to store up our time together to sustain us for the rest of the year. But this year . . . it's like she doesn't even want to be here at all. So, I guess what I'm saying is," Christmas took a deep breath. "Things were not normal even before we discovered Lemy facedown in the lake."

Rory paused before responding. "Are you going to try to talk to her?"

Christmas looked at him out of the corner of her eye. "I guess," she said. "I don't . . . God, I feel so stupid, but I guess I'm afraid."

They biked for a while in silence, up a couple of big hills and then recklessly down again, the wind in their faces, the drop in Christmas's stomach as they raced to the bottom.

She realized, as she cruised along beside Rory that she did feel just a little bit relieved to have shared what had been churning around inside her. She *would* call Lexi. Or stop by the house. As soon as she got home that night.

They'd figure it out.

17

TEN MINUTES LATER, CHRISTMAS AND RORY arrived at the dirt path that would take them to the stone bridge. They rode single file now, Rory following Christmas in the dappled light. The path grew fainter until it petered out completely; Christmas dismounted and leaned her bike against a tree.

"Wow," Rory said, appropriately awed. He got off his bike and looked ahead. "This place is amazing."

"It's nice, right?" Christmas said, smiling, pleased he was impressed.

They approached the moss-covered bridge and Rory remarked, "I mean, pretty perfect spot for a picnic, wouldn't you say?"

"It is," Christmas conceded. "Let's keep going. It's even nicer on the other side."

Together, they climbed to the apex of the bridge, gnats and mosquitoes swirling around their heads and the brook roaring below their feet.

Rory snapped photos on his phone. "Everything is just so green," he said. "It's really, really green. Hey, do you mind if I take a photo of you?" he asked.

Christmas laughed and struck a pose, head to one side, tongue out. Then she took out her own phone and said, "Let's take an ussie." She leaned her head close to his for the picture. He smelled good, like laundry soap and boy's deodorant.

"Nice," she said, looking at the photo. "I look like a dork, but that's to be expected."

"Please," Rory said. He laughed. "You look . . . you know. Good, I guess?"

"Wow," Christmas joked. "I may never get over that compliment."

"You know what I mean. I don't want to . . . freak you out. Like, we're out here in the middle of nowhere . . ."

"Ha," Christmas said. "If you keep insulting me, I'll abandon you and you'll probably never find your way back to civilization."

"It's true. This could turn into a *Deliverance*-type situation."

"What's that?" Christmas asked.

"You know, that old movie." Rory sang, "Der der der der der" and Christmas found the tune vaguely familiar, but she shook her head to show she didn't recognize it. "Some guys get lost in the woods and then like, these white-trash guys . . ." Rory looked around, as though he might find the rest of his sentence in the trees above them. "I guess they . . . sexually assault them? Now that I say it out loud, I suppose that's not, like, a cool reference to make. Sorry."

"Yeah," Christmas agreed. "Inappropriate on a couple of levels?" she said, raising her eyebrows ironically and laughing.

They continued across the bridge, to another stone structure, the crumbling remains of a barn or small house, another staging area for Christmas and Lexi's dramas when they were younger. It looked so small—and unmagical—to Christmas now.

She sat on one of the low stone walls, missing Lexi.

"This place is definitely cooler than I thought it would be," Rory said, shrugging off the backpack and sitting beside her. "I like these ancient ruins. This is like an archaeology field trip. Do you know all the secret spots around here?"

"I know a lot of them," Christmas said, happy for the distraction. "But this is probably the best one. It's all downhill from here. I mean, next time I might just take you by the Quartz Walmart."

"Now that could be a sociology field trip!" Rory laughed. He unzipped his backpack. "So, are you hungry?"

"I am," Christmas said. She hadn't eaten her peanut butter sandwich at lunch and was suddenly starving. "What did you bring?"

He placed two metal water bottles on the ground and peered into the bag. "Chocolate chip cookies," he said. "But don't get too excited. They're vegan. And bagels, what we call Megan-style in my house: cream cheese, sprouts, cucumber, and avocado. My sister, Megan, moved to California and now she acts like she invented the avocado. Anyway. I brought a plain one in case you hated sprouts or something."

Christmas internally rolled her eyes at the vegan cookies, but said, "That sounds great. Are you vegan?"

"No," he answered. "But we are vegetarian. And the cookies have loads and loads of sugar, so it's not like they're healthy or anything."

Christmas laughed. "I could never be a vegetarian."

Rory handed her a bagel.

"Sure you could," he replied. "You just don't want to be a vegetarian. There's a difference."

"True," Christmas said, slapping at a mosquito buzzing around her neck. "But I don't know. I might die of missing cheeseburgers."

"Impossible meat—you know, that plant-based stuff? It's actually pretty good," Rory said.

"Are you trying to convert me?"

"No. If I was trying to convert you, I'd start talking about the abysmal, inhumane, and disgusting conditions at most CAFOs as well as their abysmal, inhumane, and disgusting far-reaching effects, but no. I'm just saying that most of my carnivore friends have told me that they can't tell the difference between plant-based meat and cow-based meat. You should try it sometime."

"I would, I guess, but as far as I know, that stuff hasn't made it here yet," Christmas said. She unwrapped her bagel. "At least I haven't seen it in the market."

"Tell me about it. This place . . . it's sort of like going back in time, isn't it?"

Christmas didn't respond right away. She took a bite of her bagel to give herself a moment to think. His remark was so close to Lexi's complaint that she immediately felt a bit defensive; it was like having somebody poke your bruise.

"The farmers' market has great meat," Christmas said after she'd swallowed, trying to turn the conversation to the town's advantage. "You know, fresh, local, humane. The cows at Cunningham's, for example. They couldn't ask for a better life. They hang out, munching grass all day, enjoying their beautiful view of the lake."

"They are pretty picturesque," Rory conceded. "I guess if I was gonna eat meat, I'd want to eat one of those Cunningham cows."

"This bagel is amazing, by the way," Christmas said, honestly. "Where in California does your sister live?"

"San Francisco. Have you ever been there?"

"No," Christmas said, shaking her head. "I've never been anywhere. I mean, we go to the city sometimes, but I've never even been on a plane."

"Really?" Rory seemed genuinely surprised.

"What?"

"Nothing. It's just . . . you just seem so . . ." He shook his head.

She shook her head back at him and widened her eyes, waiting for him to continue.

"No offense, but you're . . . really normal? Like, you would totally fit in down in Brooklyn, if you know what I mean."

"I don't know what you mean," Christmas said, her response coming out a little more snappish than she'd intended. "It's not like we're another species up here." She suddenly understood his comment about the "sociology field trip," and she felt her mouth turning down at the corners.

"I guess I'm not very good at this," Rory said. He looked at Christmas with concern. "I only meant that I think you are a cool person and I guess I was sort surprised."

"Uh-huh," Christmas said, nodding with fake agreement. "Is this like, 'you're not like these other girls'? I'm supposed to be flattered that I don't conform to the stereotype of the upstate hick?"

"No, that's not what I . . ." Rory began. He grimaced and then tried again, as though he couldn't help himself. "But don't you think—I mean, I'm probably digging myself in deeper here—but don't you think the people here are a *little* backward? Not you, obviously, and I'm sure there are other people like you, too, but a lot of people—"

Christmas scoffed. "Now I really am offended."

"This is coming out wrong. You really don't know what I'm talking about?" he asked plaintively.

Christmas took a deep breath. Of course she knew what he was talking about. Lemy—one of the more sophisticated people Christmas knew—was missing an incisor tooth and, when he wore his overalls and trucker cap, well, she had to concede he was leaning pretty hard into redneck-chic. Even her own dad, who literally bought his clothes at the hardware store and whose winter beard, she joked, often looked like a bird had skipped a birdhouse and nested there instead, could sometimes pass for an extra for a Netflix drama about the meth epidemic.

"I know that we don't dress and talk and act the same way as people in *Brooklyn* do," she said, rolling her eyes. "But that's the point. People can be themselves here." She took a breath, thinking of her parents, of the way they valued their privacy, of her father's crazy birdhouses and the fact that he would only sell them on the "honor system"—a locked wooden box in which buyers could insert cash—because he never wanted to have to interact with strangers. She thought of the guy who had a ten-foot wooden sculpture of a Bugs Bunny-esque creature on his front lawn, of the Lopezes, who had painted their house fluorescent pink, and of Shelley, who kept peacocks. The idea that they could all be explained, dismissed as "hicks," that people like Rory assumed they already knew everything about them without knowing anything at all—it made her heart pound and she felt, again, the sting of injustice, of being misunderstood, misrepresented. "People from downstate come up for one weekend and they think they've got it figured out. And if we're so terrible, why is it that all the Brooklyn people buy everything they can, driving up prices to the point that regular folks can't even afford the rents? And what is it these summer people are trying to escape from anyway? I've never wanted to escape where I live, because where I live isn't terrible and competitive and mean and stressful."

Her final words echoed back in her ears, and she thought again of her argument with Lexi, and the reality that while she did not want to escape Sweet Lake, it was possible that in her desire to defend it, she willfully overlooked some of its shortcomings. And aware, too, that she sounded provincial and defensive, the wave of rage crested and transformed, retreating and leaving behind only regret and sadness. Her eyes filled with hot tears.

"Oh my God," Rory said. He put a hand gently on her shoulder. "I'm sorry. I feel so bad. Please, please don't cry."

"It's okay," Christmas sobbed, feeling acutely absurd. "It's not just you. I feel like an idiot for crying. I'm just sick of everyone—you and my friend Lexi and really, everyone—looking down on us. And what happened with Lemy—" Here she dissolved completely, unable to finish the sentence.

Rory took her bagel from her hand placed both of their dinners, carefully, still in their waxed paper, on the ground. Then he turned back to her put a tentative arm around her shoulder. "Maybe you should let it all out?"

And leaning into him, she did. She let herself cry, hard and loud, as he held her.

WHEN CHRISTMAS WAS CALM ENOUGH TO TALK AGAIN, she apologized for making Rory witness her nervous breakdown, and then they sat for a long while, listening to the birds and the wind through the trees and the croaking frogs. Even though Christmas thought she should probably feel embarrassed for having cried in front of Rory, she didn't, and when they began to talk again, it was easy, and their conversation ranged over all sorts of subjects: the city, and video games they liked, and whether or not fishing was ethical. She felt like she could have gone on talking to him all night, but sighing, she realized that they should start heading back. "It gets dark quickly," she explained, thinking of how the sun dove down behind the mountains without much warning. "Do you have anything reflective on your bike?"

"I do," Rory said. He rose and began to repack the bag and the two headed toward the bridge and their bikes.

They didn't talk much as they cycled home, mostly because they were focused intently on the same goal: getting off the unlit country roads before it became fully dark. As they crested a final hill, they could see the lake in the near distance and Christmas felt a bit relieved, knowing they'd be okay. Christmas planned to deliver Rory to his house and then stop at the Hansens'. Her parents wouldn't be worried; they probably thought she was with Lexi anyway, but she'd call them to check in once she had a signal.

Just as she thought about her phone, it vibrated. They'd been in a dead zone and now they weren't. Hoping it was Lexi, she steered with one hand as she picked the phone up out of the basket on the front of the bike. But it wasn't Lexi; it was a text from Curly. Skimming it, Christmas could see that he was thanking her for what she'd done and asking her to come by the house that evening. She dropped the phone back in the basket, promising herself to think more about that later.

The route they were on would take them past Cunningham's Farm, and Christmas was poised to point out the happy cows to Rory, but as they approached, the bright, rotating red-and-blue lights of a police car burned into Christmas's eyes, making it almost impossible to see. Closer, Christmas saw there were several people and trucks—and the police car—parked at the pasture nearest the lake.

"What's going on?" Rory asked.

Christmas shook her head. Did it have something to do with Lemy? But Lemy had been in the lake in front of the adjacent woods, not in the pasture. Christmas saw Ben and Officer Schaefer walking carefully alongside Mr. Cunningham.

Christmas and Rory biked up to the perimeter fence and stopped. In the waning light, Christmas could see that though some cows stood in clusters around the pasture, many others were down on the ground, lying on their sides, a position that looked strange and unnatural.

"I think there's something wrong," Christmas said, and as the words left her lips, a cow close to the fence collapsed and began convulsing, its legs straightening and jutting in spasms. The poor creature made a groaning noise and white foam began to leak from its open mouth. The cow's eyes were large, brown, and rolling frantically. Christmas looked at Rory, whose own eyes were wide with shock.

"We should get out of here," Rory said, but Mrs. Cunningham, a frumpy woman who stood apart from the various groups clustered in the pasture, spotted them and walked over, wringing her hands. Though Christmas barely knew Mrs. Cunningham, she could sense the woman was looking for someone, anyone, to talk to.

Mrs. Cunningham wiped at her eyes. "They're dying," she called as she approached. "They've been poisoned."

"Poisoned?" Christmas asked. "That can't be . . ."

"Almost all of them, the past two hours." Mrs. Cunningham swept an arm out to indicate the scene before them. "They just started dropping, getting sick. We called Greg—the vet from Grantsboro—and he came over right away, but there's nothing he can do. He said they've been poisoned." Christmas looked out at the field, where she saw a lean man squatting down, ministering to a cow on the ground.

"Oh my God," Christmas said. "I'm so sorry."

"Who would do a thing like this?" Mrs. Cunningham wailed. Christmas noticed, over Mrs. Cunningham's shoulder, two little boys in matching Minecraft pajamas watching from the Cunninghams' front porch. They were the Cunninghams' grandsons, who lived with the Cunninghams because both of their parents were incarcerated for drug-related charges. Pills and meth. It wasn't uncommon. The taller of the two kids waved. This was Jared; he was six or seven and one of Christmas's campers. Christmas waved back.

Suddenly, Mr. Cunningham, who must have just noticed who his wife was talking to, came barreling toward them, shouting at his wife to be quiet.

"Goddammit, Renee," he said. "Goddammit."

Christmas instinctually took a step back, wheeling her bike with her, and Rory did too.

"Get the hell out of here," he yelled at Christmas and Rory. "Sticking your nose where it doesn't belong."

Christmas could see Rory shaking his head out of the corner of her eye. "We were just biking past ..."

"Gonna see if you can resuscitate the cows, little girl?" Mr. Cunningham bellowed nastily. "Get the hell out of here. Pain in the ass—stirring up trouble—you're the one who has the cops all over me!"

Christmas parted her lips to protest, but the old man continued. "This is your fault. And you better tell your friend Curly to watch his back. Messing with my cows. You don't mess with my goddamn cows."

"I didn't ..." Christmas tried. "I don't ..."

"Hey man!" Rory shouted. "Don't talk to her like that."

Christmas laid a hand on Rory's arm. "We better go," she said.

Mr. Cunningham's face was so red that Christmas was momentarily afraid he might have a heart attack and then she really would have to use her CPR again.

As they started to bike away, Mr. Cunningham continued to berate them, and Christmas was grateful they were separated by an electric fence.

They coasted the rest of the way down the hill, past the scene still unfolding across the pastures closest to the lake. Mercifully, the road jogged away from the lake, and they were soon out of sight of the farm.

"What the?" Rory said, catching up with Christmas. "I can't believe he was so rude to you. What's his problem?"

Christmas shook her head. Her breath was shallow, her heart was pounding. "Do you remember him? He's the one—he used the ... slur at the meeting. And I told the cops. I mean, they already knew, but I guess he thinks that I think ... I don't know."

"Who's Curly?"

"Lemy's husband."

They biked a little farther in silence and, too soon it seemed to Christmas, they were in front of Rory's house. It was now fully dark, though scattered streetlights and houselights illuminated the road.

"Hey, want to come in?" Rory asked. The house, with its glowing windows, looked cozy and inviting. "You seem kinda upset. Have a glass of water? Or I can bike you back to your house?"

"I'll be okay," Christmas said, trying to shake off the horrible feeling of being hated by someone. It wasn't easy. "I'm actually going to stop over at Curly's now. He texted me while we were out. And I guess I should tell him about what Mr. Cunningham said."

"Honestly, I think you should tell the police. The fact that that guy was threatening someone whose husband is already in the hospital is pretty messed up," Rory said.

Christmas shook her head, no. Mr. Cunningham already believed she was persecuting him. In her head, she could already hear her mother accusing her of deliberately stirring up trouble.

"I guess this just confirms your ideas about us," Christmas said, pursing her lips. "About the people here being terrible."

"I never said that," Rory said, taking a step closer to her. "Look." He ducked his head. "I said some dumb, narrow-minded things. But I didn't say the people here were terrible."

"But maybe they—we—are," Christmas said. Before he could object, she added, "Anyway, I'm heading over to Curly's. You can come with me if you want."

"Yeah," Rory said. "As long as you don't mind me tagging along everywhere you go. I mean, were you looking for a sidekick . . .?"

Despite everything, Christmas smiled. "I'd love a sidekick."

They proceeded along the road that ran next to the lake, past the Fords' place and the service station and the small, abandoned brown house next to the shop. No one had lived there for as long as

Christmas could remember, and it struck Christmas as sad, with its boarded-up windows and door like blindfolded eyes and a gagged mouth. They biked past the empty field across from the house, which had an absurd chain-link fence along its perimeter. It always made Christmas think of the poem they'd read in English class sophomore year, "Mending Wall."

> *Before I built a wall I'd ask to know*
> *What I was walling in or walling out.*

They arrived at Lemy and Curly's ramshackle Victorian, with its neon peace sign, prayer flags, rainbow flag, and various antique farm equipment artistically arranged in the front yard. Although most of the house was dark, a light showed through the front window.

As they were parking their bikes, Christmas's phone vibrated with a text. It was from Lexi.

still sick & gonna stay home again tmw. sry.

Christmas felt a flash of impatience and anger and then a wave of sadness.

But she didn't have time to dwell on Lexi. She had to focus, she thought wryly, on further entangling herself in some sort of dangerous feud between local adults.

Christmas knocked on the bright blue front door.

They could hear Curly's footsteps as he approached and, when he pulled open the door, he was red-eyed and disheveled. He usually kept his head closely shaved, but he had dark stubble growing in over his ears and around the back—everywhere except the top of his head.

"Christmas," he said, pulling her in for a hug. He didn't let her go as he said, "Thank you so much for what you did. You truly are an angel. I don't know what would have happened . . . I can't even begin . . ." Curly trailed off, releasing her from the embrace but keeping a hand on each of her shoulders. "I wanted to talk to you earlier, but I've been at the hospital nonstop. It's been . . . a lot."

"Of course," Christmas said. "This is my friend Rory," she added. "He lives in the blue house."

"Naomi's son," Curly said, nodding. He gestured for them to come in. "What can I get you? Tea?"

"Sounds great," Christmas said, following him in and down the hall to the kitchen.

Curly filled a kettle and lit the stove. "I could use something stronger," he said. "But you two are minors and I'd feel like a drunk drinking alone. Plus, what if they call and I have to run over to the hospital? Jesus, it's times like these when you realize how inconvenient it is to live in the country. It takes me forty-five minutes to get to Saint Pat's."

"How's Lemy?" Christmas asked. She and Rory sat at the farm table.

"Still in a coma," Curly said. He put a hand over his eyes and slumped against the counter, but only for a moment, before he took a deep breath and stood tall again. He moved around the kitchen, setting out small plates and a roll of butter cookies. "My poor Lemy. Who would do that to him? He's the gentlest creature."

"So, you do think," Christmas began, "someone did that to him?"

Curly stopped what he was doing and looked at Christmas incredulously. "What do you mean? Of course, someone did that to him. You're the one who found him. You saw his face!"

Christmas nodded, hurriedly. "Yeah, it looked like someone beat him up. But the cops . . . I don't know, they suggested that maybe . . ."

"Oh, I know what the cops are suggesting. He kicked himself in the ribs and then fell into the lake and gave himself a concussion," Curly snapped.

Christmas shook her head. "I didn't mean anything. And I told them that I thought his face looked bad. Curly, I told them."

"I know you did, sweetie," Curly said. "It's not you I'm mad at. It's the goddamn cops. Are they afraid that a hate crime will hurt tourism to the area?" He laughed bitterly. "But the real question is: who would do such a thing? I mean, I know there are homophobic people around here. Cunningham for one. Then there's that Gary George—he's a sort of terrifying weirdo. And the whole Velvet Cup crew, your friend Cash"—he pointed at Christmas as if to suggest that Christmas would deny it—"he's a real piece of work. Still. Would any of them hurt Lemy?"

Christmas wanted to object that she wasn't really friends with Cash, but she saw that Curly was not in the mood to be contradicted. "We need to tell you something about Mr. Cunningham," Christmas said.

Curly looked at her with impatience and dread. "Jesus Christ. What now? Wait." He held a hand up and then turned to shut off the stove. "Herbal or caffeinated? I'm having mint. Is mint okay?" Before they could respond, he answered his own question: "Mint is fine." He poured three mugs, set one in front of each place at the table and sat. "Go on."

Christmas swallowed. She and Rory made eye contact and he nodded his head slightly, as though encouraging her. "It looks like someone poisoned the Cunninghams' cows. We were just out on our bikes, and when we passed by we saw that a bunch of the cows were, like, literally dropping to the ground. Mr. Cunningham saw us talking to Mrs. Cunningham and he got all agitated and start saying crazy things. He was angry with me for, I guess, telling the cops what he'd called Lemy at the meeting." Christmas paused. "And he suggested that you had 'messed with' his cows or something."

Curly's eyebrows shot up. "What?"

"He said you better watch out."

"What the fuck?" Curly said. "Sorry, kids. But really. What the fuck? Like I have time to worry about Cunningham's cows."

"Maybe he thinks its retribution?" Rory asked. "Maybe he thinks you think it was his fault . . . about Lemy."

"Well, he is a prime suspect." Curly ticked the evidence off on his fingers. "You both heard him at the meeting, and Lemy was found in front of Cunningham's Woods. And he knows Lemy and I were planning to go to the next zoning board meeting to complain about the runoff from his farm." Curly shook his head. "But for God's sake, of course I would never hurt the cows themselves. What a stupid fool. Still. He seems to have a guilty conscience, doesn't he?" Curly paused and thought. "Lemy was on fire that night when he headed down to the Cup. All riled up and talking about getting to the bottom of things—the root causes of the algae. And I can think of several people around here who might not like anyone digging around. Who might have something to hide. Hang on."

Curly rose and went into another room. Christmas heard him open and close a drawer. She felt Rory watching her, and she looked down at the farm table. One of the knots in the wood looked like a face, sinisterly smiling. She thought about her mother, who had been at the Cup that night. She wanted to tell Rory and Curly, but she couldn't do it; she was too well trained not to go talking about their family business in public. It didn't matter anyway, she told herself. It was irrelevant.

When Curly returned he was carrying a large, padded envelope.

"This came in the mail," he explained, handing the package to Christmas. "It's the equipment to take a water sample to send to the lab at Cornell. Lemy agreed with you and wanted to test the water, regardless of the Lake Association or stupid-ass Bill Ford's opinion."

"I'll take care of it," Christmas said, peeking in to see two plastic vials and instructions, which she knew would take her an inordinate amount of time to decipher.

"So I was at the Velvet Cup," Rory said suddenly. Christmas's attention snapped to him. "Not that night—but last week," he clarified. "My friend Fiona was visiting, and we went over there, just to get out for a while, play pool or whatever." Christmas caught herself staring at him—trying to picture this Fiona—and biting her lip. Rory looked around self-consciously and added, "It was basically some locals sitting around, listening to crappy music."

"That sounds about right," Curly said.

"The bartender, though. I don't know. A big guy?"

"Owen," Christmas said.

"I don't know his name," Rory shrugged. "But he basically let us know that if we were looking for drugs, he had a hook up."

"Owen?" Christmas said again, disbelieving.

"Oh, honey," Curly said. "Everyone knows you can buy drugs at the Cup."

Christmas's cheeks burned. Apparently not everyone knew.

Her mind flickered over recent interactions with Owen and Madison. Did Madison know that Owen sold drugs? And what kind of drugs? She wanted to ask but was suddenly afraid to make herself seem even more naïve.

"I'm just surprised," she spluttered. She looked at Rory. "He's dating one of my friends."

"Maybe you can use that to your advantage," Curly said. "You can innocently ask some questions. See if you can find out anything about that night."

"I'm sure the cops already talked to him," Christmas said.

Curly rolled his eyes.

"But yeah. Of course," she added.

Christmas took the package and rose. Rory followed her as they said their good-nights and let themselves out. She was glad he was behind her and that he couldn't see her working so hard to assemble her face into something not so shocked and sad-looking.

Though she never would have said she was the most tuned-in person, she was apparently totally tuned-out. Was Christmas, really, the only person who didn't know what was going on in Sweet Lake?

19

CHRISTMAS'S MOTHER HAD CALLED when they were talking to Curly. She left a message that made it clear that she believed Christmas was at the Hansens'. Christmas didn't call back.

"So, is this a normal day around here?" Rory asked as they approached their bikes. "Like, if we go for another bike ride tomorrow, will there be a whole new adventure waiting for us?"

"God, I hope not."

Christmas stooped to pick up her bike and then tossed her phone and the package in the bike's basket. When she glanced up, she realized that Rory was looking at her funny and she became aware that she'd been rolling her neck—a tic that she'd had since she was young that she often didn't even know she was doing.

"Sorry," she said, blinking hard. Now that she was conscious of the neck roll, it became almost impossible not to do. She knew she looked like a freak, and she wished desperately she could resist doing it, but again, thinking about it made it even worse.

"I just do this when I get stressed," she said, midroll. "I'm sorry. It's so weird. I'm so weird."

"No," Rory said. "It's fine."

"You don't have to say that," Christmas said, a little more energetically than she'd meant to. She thought, for a moment, that she would actually die of shame. She deliberately shook her head, hard, twice, hoping to just get it out of her system.

"I do weird stuff too."

Christmas almost laughed. "Like what?"

"I don't know," Rory confessed. "I was just trying to relate."

Christmas did laugh, then. He was ridiculously sweet.

"So, when are you going to test the water? And do think Curly's right, that maybe someone wanted to shut Lemy up?"

"I don't know," Christmas said, mounting her bike. Christmas felt a ping of annoyance at the eagerness in Rory's voice. Was this going to be his summer adventure, his plan for a way to pass the time in boring old upstate? He was talking about Lemy as though he knew him. And who was that Fiona, the girl he'd brought to the Velvet Cup, anyway? He'd called her a friend. And maybe she was. But why had she come up to visit him if she was just a friend? Of course, Christmas had no right to be jealous. She and Rory were just becoming friends.

It was none of her business. But still.

Rory must have caught a flash of something on her face because he added quickly, "I wasn't trying to be a jerk. Again. Sorry. I don't mean to try to insert myself..."

"No, I'm sorry," Christmas said, rolling her neck. "I'm just frustrated. Look. Owen, the guy we were just talking about? The, um, apparent drug dealer? Anyway, he's having a Fourth of July party this weekend. I'm supposed to go. I'll try to see if I can get any info." Christmas cleared her throat, even more nervous as she considered what she was about to say next. "And, if you're around, you're welcome to come with me. They'll have fireworks and stuff. I mean, personally I can't stand fireworks. But other people seem to really like them."

"That would've been great," Rory said, picking up his own bike. "But we're heading to Brooklyn for the weekend."

"Oh, cool," Christmas said quickly. She rolled her neck. Would it never cease?

They continued to stand under Lemy and Curly's porch light. Christmas wondered if Rory would be seeing Fiona in Brooklyn.

"But," Rory said, also suddenly awkward. "You know, like, we could make other plans. Before then? You're probably busy, but if you wanted to hang out with your sidekick—"

Christmas smiled. "Honestly," she said. "I'm kind of pathetically unbusy. Except for work."

"Great," Rory said, smiling too. "Can I give you my number?"

They swapped phones. It was strange to have experienced such wildly different emotions all in the same day, even sometimes in the same minute, as well as to be aware of it as it happened. Christmas realized she'd cried that day, laughed, panicked, gotten super anxious, and was ever more intensely crushing on this cute, curly-haired guy and had become, if not wild with jealousy, certainly preoccupied with thinking about *Fiona*. She was exhausted but not totally unhappy as she said goodbye to Rory and pedaled the short distance home.

Leaving her bike against the garage, she trotted around to the back of the house and let herself in the sliding glass doors on the lower level. Her parents might still be up, but she didn't feel like dealing with them. If she slept on the couch downstairs, they might not know she was home at all.

Inside, she rolled her neck, exasperated and acutely embarrassed at having started twitching out in front of Rory. She could see the look in his eye when he first noticed: surprised and maybe even a bit uneasy. She wondered if he thought, *What is wrong with her?*

She knew she shouldn't care. For years she'd been telling herself that other people's discomfort with her eccentricities were their problem, not hers. It was not something to ruminate about. Easier said than done.

She was especially jittery as she sprawled out on the couch to look at the paperwork that came with the lab kit. Though the process seemed pretty straightforward, she couldn't get her mind to really focus on the instructions and she put it aside, promising to really buckle down in the morning.

This evening anxiety and brain fog could be the ADHD, it could be the medicine, it could be simply situational. Really, she should do some meditation. Instead, she looked at dumb stuff on her phone. She tried to remember the name of Rory's high school, tried to look up girls named Fiona from Brooklyn. It turned out that there were a lot of them.

Surrendering to indolence, she watched several TikToks about ADHD and autism, becoming increasingly convinced that she might actually have a bit of both. It would explain a few things, like the compulsive skin picking she sometimes did when her meds weren't quite right, and the way she found fireworks too loud and bright. She then googled "CAFOs," something Rory had mentioned earlier, and watched a video on industrial farming that contained images that she knew she could never unsee. The next video was about to load when a loud thump on the glass doors to the patio had her sitting up with jolt. If there was someone outside in the dark yard, they would have a clear view of her in the well-lit room, while she could not see them. She pretended to look at her phone, her mind racing and her heart pounding. Had she locked the door behind her? Probably not. They never locked their doors. Should she jump up and lock them now?

She told herself to stop being such a baby, such a scaredy-cat. If anything, it was probably a raccoon or a deer or even a bat; or maybe it had been nothing at all, just her imagination. Still. She couldn't sit there and look at her phone with the door unlocked. And the longer she waited, the more she certain she was that she was being watched.

She turned on her phone's flashlight and rose, striding quickly to the door. She slid it open and even before she was able to shine the light on the patio, she could hear something—someone—moving, crashing away, off into the small woods at the side of the house.

By the time she shone the light, though, they were gone.

More scared than she had ever been in her life, she shoved the door closed and threw the lock. She ran up the stairs and locked the front door too.

What was that saying? Just because you're paranoid doesn't mean there isn't someone after you.

20

IN THE DAYLIGHT THE FOLLOWING MORNING, Christmas was sure she'd overreacted. She was on edge and hypersensitive. And self-absorbed. Why on earth would anyone bother spying on her? To see how many hours she could waste watching TikTok?

Nevertheless, she'd been unable to fall asleep until practically dawn. It hadn't helped that she'd started to drift around one o'clock only to be jolted awake by the popping and screeching of fireworks over the lake. She'd sat straight up, furious, knowing it was probably stupid Cash Ford, gearing up for the Fourth. What was wrong with him? It was so selfish to set off explosions in the wee hours of a week-day morning. Why didn't he just go to sleep like a normal person?

At breakfast, Christmas, exhausted and sweaty, returned from her run to see her father sitting at the table in a collared shirt and khakis.

"Why are you dressed up?" she asked between gulps of water.

"I got a job," he answered.

"What?" Christmas asked, genuinely surprised.

"At Home Depot."

"As a senior greeter?" Christmas said.

"Not nice," her father said. He rose and carried his empty bowl to the sink.

"I'm sorry. I wasn't trying to be funny. But why?" Christmas asked. "Is everything okay? What are you—"

"Gets me out of the house," he said, shrugging. "Your mom says Home Depot is my hangout anyway. Might as well get paid." He moved toward the doorway, reminding Christmas of a gentle, awkward crane. "I have to get going. There's oatmeal on the stove."

"Mom up?"

"Nope," he said.

"Well, have a good day at your new job," Christmas called after him.

Before heading out to her own job, Christmas shoveled down some oatmeal and then went quietly downstairs, to the ground-level room she'd been sitting in the night before. She stood looking out the sliding glass door for a moment before stepping outside, her eyes scanning the ground. Maybe she'd see raccoon scat, or even something to indicate a larger animal.

Instead, a few feet from the door, she saw a cigarette butt. She crouched and read the word *Parliament* in blue letters around the cigarette's base.

Had it been Cash? He was one of the few people she knew who smoked cigarettes. Was he spying on her?

Suddenly self-conscious, Christmas stood and turned, as though aware she was being watched at that moment. But save for the birds, chipmunks, and squirrels, Christmas was alone.

21

THAT DAY, THE KIDS AT CAMP SEEMED extra bratty, and the activities —making dream catchers and collecting interesting rocks— tedious. By the afternoon, Shelley, who was also in a bad mood—although that seemed to be her default setting—looked up at Christmas and said, in a severe tone, "If your friend doesn't want the job, you need to let me know. I need to hire someone else if she's not coming back."

"She's just sick," Christmas spluttered, annoyed with herself for feeling like she was responsible and annoyed with Lexi for putting her in this position. "She'll definitely be here tomorrow." Christmas wished she could take that back as soon as she said it; she had no idea what Lexi's intentions were.

It was with lead feet that Christmas, then, forced herself to bike over to the Hansens' after work. She longed to avoid a confrontation, to try and dispense with the hard work by sending a "We okay?" or "Feeling better?" text, clinging to the off chance that Lexi would respond with an "All good. See you tomorrow!" But Christmas knew that the time for texting was past. Plus, she couldn't stand the nervous dread much longer, the bad, bubbly feeling she'd had throughout her since that night on the dock. She needed to know what was up. And whether or not whatever was broken could be fixed.

Christmas dropped her bike on the front lawn and approached the door. Though she often let herself right in at the Hansens' when Lexi was in town, she knocked, tentatively, and then, when no one came to the door, a little louder. Eventually she heard padding feet and Mrs. Hansen pulled open the door.

"Hi there, Christmas," she said. The comfortably built Mrs. Hansen was not usually an excitable person—at least on the surface—but Christmas could see Lexi's grandmother's eyes lighting up behind her cat's-eye frames. "She's up in her room."

"Thanks," Christmas said, heading toward the stairs.

When Christmas got to the landing, she saw Lexi standing at her door, watching glumly.

"Hey," she said, and then turned and went into her room. Christmas followed.

Though Lexi's room was vacant most of the year, her grandparents left it alone, so it served as a time capsule, a museum of obsessions from summers past. Christmas took in the half-joking shrine to Harry Styles and scores of hand-woven friendship bracelets from a few summers earlier. On the Bert-and-Ernie style twin beds, pink bedspreads were evidence of the year the girls had decided they wanted all things in millennial pink; face masks that looked like animal snouts from the first pandemic summer; a collection of crystals and gemstones from the summer they wanted to be geologists. This year, Christmas noted, Lexi hadn't really unpacked. The two duffel bags on the floor by the dresser looked half-exploded, or like garbage that raccoons had gotten into. The narrow bed on the right—the one that Christmas usually slept in—was covered with more clothes, as well as various chargers and devices.

Lexi herself looked a bit unkempt in gray sweatpants and a ragged-looking T-shirt. She sat on her bed while Christmas, unsure of where to put herself, slid down against the wall next to the dresser until she was on the floor, her knees pulled into her chest.

She wondered if Lexi really had been sick, and a feeling of guilt immediately replaced the surge of hope she experienced.

"Do you have . . . like a cold or something?" Christmas asked weakly.

Lexi gave Christmas a withering look. "I'm fine," she said, as though Christmas was the stupidest person in the world. Her phone buzzed beside her on the bed and Christmas waited, watching her, as Lexi responded to a text. When she was finished, she put the phone facedown and rolled her eyes. "What?" she asked, snootily.

Christmas hunched her shoulders. She wished she hadn't come.

"I'm not sure why you're so mad at me," Christmas said into her knees.

"I'm not mad at you," Lexi snapped.

Christmas couldn't bring herself to ask the follow-up question —*then why are you treating me like this?*—because she realized, with an acute pain, that she might not truly want to hear the answer.

They sat in silence.

Lexi's phone vibrated, but she didn't pick it up. Instead, she continued to stare, bored and blankly, at a space in the center of the floor.

"I guess . . . I'm not sure what happened," Christmas tried. "I was so excited for you to come. And I thought we had fun skiing the other day. And then, I know the stuff—that finding Lemy like that—was upsetting, but—"

"It was more than upsetting, Christmas," Lexi interrupted archly. "You just don't get it."

"What don't I get?"

"He was gay-bashed, Christmas."

Christmas nodded. After a beat, she said, "That might be true. The cops said—"

"Don't give me that. You're just as bad as the rest of them. That's why I'm upset." Lexi made a disgusted noise in the back of her throat. "I'm *disappointed*. Disappointed in you."

Christmas swallowed, hard. Her mouth was dry, and her throat felt as though it were constricting. Why hadn't she stopped at home? She could have had a big glass of water or taken a cool shower. She should have collected herself before this difficult situation.

She realized, dimly, that she hadn't let herself go home because she would have lost her nerve, that on some level, she'd known this would happen, and she had to force herself to come, unthinkingly, or she wouldn't have come at all.

Christmas wished she could stick her head out the window, or better yet, make a dash for the door, run out of the house, jump right into the lake and swim home.

Instead, she hugged her legs more tightly and swallowed dryly again. "I know you don't want to be here," she said, her voice wobbly. "Maybe you have cooler friends in Pennsylvania, but I thought—"

"You're right. I don't want to be here," Lexi interrupted. "The only reason I am here this year is because my grandparents threatened to take my mother to court if she didn't bring me. Once I turn eighteen in August, I swear. Fuck this place."

Christmas closed her eyes and then opened them again, Lexi's words clicking into place in her mind. She no longer felt as though she would cry. Instead, she felt a searing, painful clarity. She put her palms to the floor and rose, slowly. "All right," she said. "Fuck this place? All right." She rolled her neck twice, but she didn't feel embarrassed. "Well, fuck you, Lexi. You think you're so much better…" She laughed, bitterly. "As if you're not white trash. Fine, you're also Dominican," Christmas said, waving a hand in the air. "'Cause your dad's a real prince, too, isn't he? I'd be really proud of him if I were you," Christmas sneered. "You're not better than anyone from Sweet Lake. You're not better than your mother or grandparents.

Or me." She shook her head. "Have a great summer, hot shot," Christmas said. She left the room.

"Christmas," Lexi's called after her in a thin, annoyed voice. "Christmas, wait."

But Christmas couldn't wait. Mrs. Hansen, in the kitchen, asked, "Everything okay, honey?" But Christmas didn't stop. She let herself out the front door and got on her bike and rode the short way to her house, where she dumped her bike in the driveway.

She walked down the lawn and out onto the dock, hardly noticing the stupid algae as she dove out, swimming, hard and far, stopping only when she was in the middle of the dark lake. Panting, she floated on her back, her ears filling with water, only her face breaking through the surface, like an iceberg, she thought. Like an iceberg on this terrible, hot planet, she wished she would simply melt away, and she could almost feel it, first her edges and then the rest of her, dissolving and disappearing, yes, giving up the fight.

IFE WITHOUT LEXI: this was the refrain in Christmas's brain as she ran the next day.

She was tired, having woken during the night to the cracking and popping of fireworks over the lake in the predawn hours, startling noises that felt somehow consistent with her mood, the eerily quiet darkness jolted through with intermittent rage. She lay in bed listening, thinking of Lexi's scowl, the contempt on her face, the bite in her words.

It might have been her ADHD, or some sort of knee-jerk coping mechanism, but as she ran, she was grateful to find that the wound felt almost cauterized. Her break with Lexi still hurt, but in a new and different way. It was a matter-of-fact, predictable ache. The worst had happened.

The other shoe had dropped. There was nothing more, it would seem, for her to really worry about.

When she got back from her run, a text was waiting from Shelley. Lexi had quit. Did Christmas have another friend interested in starting right away?

Christmas texted Rory:

Do you want a job? The day camp needs someone, 9:30-3:30 Monday through Thursday, starting today.

He texted almost immediately: *Awesome!*

Despite the weight on her heart, Christmas smiled down at her phone.

She liked him more than anyone else she'd ever liked before. She had gone out with a guy named Marshall for a while, and though Marshall was nice-looking and sweet, she'd really only dated him because she was so flattered that he liked her and sort of didn't want to disappoint him. She'd found kissing him interesting, but not exciting, which pretty much encapsulated the whole dating experience for her so far.

They'd parted ways amicably. There'd been someone else too, a little more recently, but Christmas dismissed him from her mind, the way you dismiss a proposal that is simply out of the question. That kiss, or encounter, or whatever, had been a total fluke.

A mistake.

But this, with Rory. This was something new.

Getting ready for work, Christmas thought about him, reviewing the things he'd said and how he'd said them, wondering how he perceived her, what he'd been doing since they last saw each other, and whether or not he thought about her as much as she was thinking about him.

She imagined kissing him, spending the summer wrapped around each other in the woods by the old bridge, or even on the couch in the den. She imagined the two of them deciding to be serious; she imagined going with him to Brooklyn and visiting him at Cornell.

As she descended the steps to the classrooms in the basement of town hall, Christmas wondered if she should have warned Rory that Shelley could be a bit abrasive. Too late, though: he was already there. Shelley was giving him a rundown of responsibilities while he nodded and smiled. Christmas waved and went to stow her stuff before joining the two of them, just as Shelley wrapped up her introduction.

"Is this one gonna show up?" Shelley asked Christmas, gesturing at Rory.

"I guess you'll have to ask him," Christmas said awkwardly, unsure of herself when it came to banter with authority figures.

"I'll definitely be here," Rory assured them both. "I'm happy to have a job. Plus," he said, shrugging adorably, "kids really like me."

"Hmmm," Shelley said, moving off, clipboard in hand. "Let's hope so, because here comes a batch now."

The kids did like Rory—he seemed to have an endless supply of knock-knock jokes—and he dove into the day's pet-rock project with enthusiasm and apparent expertise.

The morning, though hot—the AC was apparently already on the fritz—went quickly. With the kids parked in front of a video, Rory swept up scraps of yarn while Christmas scraped Elmer's glue off the tabletops, thinking of Lexi, but also remembering her own words, her nastiness about Lexi's parents.

"Hey," Rory said, nudging her with his elbow. "You okay?"

"Oh," Christmas said. "Yeah. Just thinking. Just hot."

"You two," Shelley said, waving a clipboard at them. "Justine's mom is picking her up early. And with the twins absent, I can handle the group if you'd like to take your lunch break together."

"Awesome," Rory said quickly, leaving Christmas to look at her feet and wonder if there were a class or something that they offered in Brooklyn that taught young people how to interact confidently with adults. "Thanks, Shelley," he added, smiling.

"Half an hour," Shelley said, glancing at the wall clock. "Be back by twelve thirty."

They grabbed their sandwiches and ascended the stairs to sit at the picnic tables in the field next to the parking lot. Settled in the shade, Christmas inhaled deeply, liking the summer smell of the hot asphalt.

"What do you think so far?" Christmas asked. "Are you glad you took the job?"

"For sure," Rory said. "It's easy, right? And it makes my mom happy. She was harassing me about finding something to do. She started generating these long lists of house repairs and when I'd say I didn't know how to do what she wanted, she kept insisting I could just watch YouTube videos to figure it out."

"Are you handy?" Christmas asked.

"Not at all," Rory said, biting into his bagel. "I can fix a bike, but that's about it. Hey, did you run already today?" he asked, chewing.

"I did," Christmas said. "I go most mornings." She looked at her own sandwich. She wasn't hungry; it was a side effect of her medicine, she knew. She forced herself to take a bite and then added, "I saw one of Shelley's peacocks. Over past the old railroad stop. It made this incredible noise—scared me half to death."

Rory smiled. "She keeps peacocks? That's cool." When Christmas nodded he said, "I guess you probably encounter a lot of animals on your runs."

"Yeah. Wild turkeys and vultures, possum. I saw a coyote once. But mostly it's just deer and dogs. I was chased by a dog one time."

"What happened?"

"I was going along and then it came running up at me—snarling and snapping. I was terrified. I kicked him, right in the mouth. I didn't feel good about it—I mean I love animals, but it was a him-or-me moment. He sort of backed up and he looked like he was ready for round two, but the owner came running out, screaming and hollering, and grabbed the dog and then the dog bit him—it was a scene. I carry pepper spray usually, but I didn't have it that day." Christmas shuddered, remembering. "The whole thing was pretty horrible, to tell the truth. I really thought for a minute that I was gonna die. Like, I thought, *I'm gonna be mauled by this dog.* But then, I don't know, it was like a reflex to protect myself."

"You're a fighter," Rory said. "That's what you found out that day."

"I never thought about it like that," Christmas said.

Christmas noticed Mr. Ford's shiny gold pickup pulling into the lot.

"So, did you send off that water sample yet?" Rory asked.

Christmas cringed.

Being reminded of a looming task, feeling as though she had something important to do that she'd neglected: these were depressingly familiar old friends. "I forgot all about it," she admitted. "I don't know, I guess I set the kit down somewhere at home and . . . out of sight, out of mind?" She shook her head. "If I don't write things down or take a note in my phone, I usually don't remember to do them."

She was going to say more, but was distracted by Mr. Ford, who was getting out of his truck and carrying a bunch of those cardboard tubes that hold plans and blueprints. Rory said something reassuring and she took another bite of her sandwich.

Mr. Ford, noticing them, waved. She hoped he would just keep walking, but being the friendly type of guy he was, he approached the picnic table.

"Chrissy," Mr. Ford said, nodding. He turned to Rory. "You're Naomi's boy?"

"Yeah," Rory said. "Hi. I'm Rory Gold-Kelly."

"Rory Gold-Kelly," Mr. Ford repeated, and Christmas heard just a note of amused sarcasm in his voice. She had never heard Rory's full name, and it sounded beautiful, musical, to her. "You and your mom enjoying the house this summer?"

Rory nodded slowly. "Yeah."

"And you," Mr. Ford said. "I heard about what you did. You and that friend of yours deserve medals." He beamed at Christmas.

Christmas ducked her head. "We just did what anyone would do."

"Don't be modest," Mr. Ford chided. His smile disappeared as he transitioned to solemnity. "How is Lemy doing?"

"As far as I know, he's still not great," Christmas said.

Mr. Ford shifted on his feet and squinted. "I should stop over there, see if Curly needs anything." He shook his head. "What a terrible thing. And now, Chrissy, don't you worry about the lake or the Lake Association. We'll have another meeting and get it all sorted out soon. Once everyone has calmed down."

"Okay," Christmas said. She shrugged. "But I planned to go ahead . . . you know, Curly gave me some equipment. I can send the sample over to that lab or whatever."

Mr. Ford nodded slowly, as though to demonstrate just how impressed he was with her initiative. "Thatta girl," he said. He pointed one of the cardboard cylinders at her. "I want to be the first to know what you find out."

Before Christmas could respond, Mr. Ford winked and began to back away. "You two stay out of trouble." He turned and climbed the steps into the building.

Rory opened his mouth, but Christmas preempted him. "Everyone used to call me Chrissy."

Rory laughed. "Can I call you Chrissy?"

"I'd prefer not."

"So, that guy. He was the one running the Lake Association meeting."

"Yeah. He owns that service station on the lake," Christmas told him. "My dad always says he thinks he's the mayor or something."

"My mom calls him 'that game show host,'" Rory said, and Christmas remembered how Mr. Ford had treated Rory's mother at the meeting. She felt embarrassed all over again, as though she were to blame for Mr. Ford's rudeness. She wanted to tell Rory that Mr.

Ford hadn't meant anything, that he was just teasing, and then she wondered why she even cared about defending Mr. Ford.

She realized she was rolling her neck. *Not this again*, she thought.

She took a swig from her water bottle. With effort, she was able to stop herself from any more neck-stretching. She'd go to the bathroom and try to get all the rolls out before returning to the campers. "We better head in."

"I think Shelley likes me," Rory said, packing up his reusable bag.

"I wonder what would lead you to that conclusion," Christmas joked.

"She has a twinkle in her eye whenever she snaps at me," Rory returned. "Hey, you busy after work? Want to come over and go swimming at my place? Or we could paddle around the lake or something if you don't want to swim."

"Swimming sounds great," Christmas said. "I'll just bike home and get my suit."

Rory smiled broadly. *He likes me too*, Christmas thought. *And maybe not just because I'm the only girl he knows for fifty miles around.*

23

CHRISTMAS LEFT HER BIKE IN RORY'S DRIVEWAY and walked around the side of the house. Rory and his mother sat companionably in Adirondack chairs at the edge of the water, and she watched them for a moment as Rory laughed at something his mother said. He turned then and saw her, and she waved and headed down the lawn.

"Hey, Christmas," Rory said. "This is my mom, Naomi."

"Hi," Naomi said, smiling warmly. She wore a black belted cover-up and black sandals—very downstate, Christmas thought—which set off the gold and red highlights in her curly hair. "I remember you from the lake meeting. You are a true superwoman. Good for you for agreeing to serve on that board! And for apparently saving someone's life. And now I hear you're the one who rescued my kid from a summer of indolence and lassitude."

"I don't know about that," Rory said. "The summer's just begun. There's plenty of time left for me to waste my time."

Christmas smiled, a little struck by the ironically teasing way in which Rory and his mother spoke to each other, the way they seemed in some ways like people from a TV show about wealthy New Yorkers.

She sat in the empty chair beside Rory. "Rory's a natural with the kids at camp."

"He has a juvenile sense of humor," Naomi remarked, her eyes smiling. "You'll stay for dinner? We have tofu hot dogs."

Christmas opened her mouth and looked at Rory to see if that's what he wanted. "Stay," he said. "If not for the company, for the tofu. I know you can't resist it."

"The hot dogs are actually pretty good," Naomi said.

"Thank you. I'd love to stay," Christmas said.

"Wonderful. Enjoy your swim." Naomi rose, her gold bracelets tinkling as she shook a glass of ice and moved off toward the house.

Christmas and Rory stood, too, and walked out on the dock, upon which there were a variety of tubes and inflatables. In the water, on either side, floated clusters of the blue-green algae. A fish darted past and disappeared into the cloudy deep.

"Maybe we should take the boat out to the middle where there's less algae and jump off there," Christmas proposed, wrinkling her nose. "I don't like to swim in the algae."

"Good idea," Rory said. He jogged to where some oars leaned against a tree while Christmas went to untie the boat. When Christmas picked up the rope that held the boat to the dock, she saw that it, too, was draped in algae strands.

"Do you want to row?" Rory asked, placing the oars in the boat.

"Sure," Christmas said.

"Great, because I'm terrible at it," Rory said.

They clambered in and pushed off, and Christmas moved them out, away from the dock.

"Do you guys have a boat?" Rory asked.

"We have a canoe and a kayak. My friend Lexi, the one I'm always talking about? Her grandparents have a speedboat, and her grandfather takes us—used to take us—waterskiing all the time. Do you waterski?"

"I've never tried it," Rory answered.

Behind her, as though conjured, Christmas heard the roar of a motor. She didn't turn, instead keeping her eyes focused on Rory's blue house as she pushed them away from it. She told herself she was being ridiculous; it could be any number of boaters or Jet Skiers making their way across the lake. There were, in fact, several other boats on the water, although none seemed to belong to anyone she recognized. And then Rory said, "There's somebody skiing right now."

Christmas turned and there, of course, was the Hansens' red-and-white speedboat, Lexi towed behind it. At this distance, it almost looked like they were moving in slow motion, but Christmas knew that, to Lexi, it felt like she was going a hundred miles an hour, the water flying past as she slid and sluiced.

"That's her, actually," Christmas said. She stopped rowing and frowned. "That's Lexi."

"Oh. Sorry," Rory said. "Maybe they won't come over here."

"This is deep enough anyway," Christmas said, pulling up the oars. "Let's just jump in the water."

"Wait," Rory asked. "How do we get back in the boat?"

Christmas smiled a little. "With difficulty?"

She slid off her T-shirt and hurried to get out of her shorts. She didn't want Lexi to see her with Rory. She wasn't sure why, but she felt somehow guilty, as though she had moved on to a new friend too quickly, as though she should be at home sulking and crying instead of having fun with some new guy. At the same time, she considered it a complete betrayal that Lexi was out skiing: Lexi was the one who should be at home sulking, missing Christmas. And even if she wasn't devastated by the end of their friendship, she should at least declare a moratorium on skiing, on this one particular activity that they had always enjoyed together.

Christmas eased herself over the side of the boat, careful not to tip it. In the water, she pretended not to watch as Rory took off his shirt. He had a nice body, but Christmas had been able to tell that even when he had a shirt on. He was slim, with defined arms, and a little bit of hair on toned abs.

And then the speedboat was upon them. Christmas knew Mr. Hansen wouldn't change his route and she knew that Lexi, on her skis, probably didn't realize it was Christmas in the unfamiliar rowboat. They cut pretty close to where Christmas and Rory swam and though Christmas faced away, she would have sworn she could feel Lexi's eyes on the back of her head.

Rory dove down and then came up, pushing his hair out of his face and slicking it back. He looked handsome, glittering in the sun, but he frowned. "You okay?" he asked.

"Yeah," Christmas said. "I'll feel less weird when they're not, like, circling us." She floated on her back. "But the water's nice, isn't it?"

"It's amazing," Rory said. "That sucks about the algae, though. Do you think it's dangerous?"

"I don't know," Christmas said, diving and then coming back up to tread water beside him. "Last summer Lexi said the water bothered her eyes when she stayed in too long. But other people—like the Cunninghams—they let their dogs drink it and stuff. They say it's no big deal."

"I mean, I wouldn't drink this water even if there wasn't algae in it," Rory said.

Christmas made a face. "You know, I wonder."

"What?"

"I wonder if maybe . . . I wonder if Mr. Cunningham lets his cows drink this water? You know, the whole poisoning thing?"

"That would make sense," Rory said. He grabbed a pink noodle from the boat and draped his arms over it. "We should look that up. See if that could be a side effect or if it's ever happened before."

Christmas swam a bit, her body slicing through the water, as she reviewed this idea. It ruined being in the lake, thinking about it being contaminated, but at the same time, the theory seemed to make sense somehow—and it would clearly exonerate Curly—if it turned out that the cows had somehow ingested the algae. But how would she prove something like that?

Returning to Rory, who floated with the noodle under his back, she opened her mouth to ask him if he thought they'd autopsy the cows, when she heard the boat coming back around again. This time, as they neared, Christmas swam to the other side of the boat so she'd be out of sight. Then she ducked under the water and tried to stay submerged. It felt so soothing and cool to be under the satiny water. But then she thought about the water being poisoned and she pushed herself back up, gasping for air.

The boat moved away, the droning noise receding. Twice around the lake was their standard routine. Lexi would be finishing up now.

Glad to know they were gone, Christmas grabbed a tube off the boat and tried to climb on top of it. It was quite undignified—she would have preferred for Rory not to have seen her with her rear end in the air as she tried to scramble aboard the big yellow donut—and she and Rory both laughed at her failed attempts, as, each time, she lost her grip and slid, or flipped, splashing back into the water. When she finally made it and had herself situated, she was panting and smiling. "That was so much work," she said. "I don't think I can ever get off this tube again. I'm going to have to live here."

"I'll bring you meals," Rory said. "And a blanket at night."

"Thanks," Christmas laughed.

"It's the least I can do," Rory said. "My mom's right, you know. You really saved my summer."

Christmas smiled. "Ah, you would have figured something out."

"Maybe." He shrugged. "She made me come up here. I had a rough senior year. I was pretty depressed."

"I'm sorry," Christmas said. "Is that something that . . . happens with you?"

"Not usually. The past few years . . . The divorce was no picnic. And then I kind of lost it after a bad breakup." Rory looked into the distance.

"That sucks," Christmas said.

"It was a while ago now. Back in March. But I had a hard time with it."

"Were you together a long time?"

"Yeah," Rory said. "A year. And I honestly thought . . . It seems stupid now, but we said we were gonna try to go to the same college and stuff like that. I really believed we were going to be together. Like . . . long term."

"Is she going to Cornell too?"

"No," Rory said. "She's going to Amherst. So, maybe it was good that we broke up when we did. But it was hard." Again, he looked into the sky and squinted. "I was totally taken by surprise. She'd been so great. I don't know how I would have gotten through the whole divorce thing without her. She was amazing. And then, suddenly it was over. At least it was for her. From where I am now, I guess I understand it. But when it happened—when she broke up with me, I couldn't function. I acted like an asshole." He made a cringing face. "And when acting like an asshole somehow didn't miraculously make her want to come back to me, I just gave up. I stopped going to school, stopped hanging out with my friends."

Christmas didn't know what to say. She kicked her feet to bring her closer to where he floated on the noodle and put a hand on his shoulder. "I'm sorry," she said.

To her surprise, Rory leaned his head back and rested it on her hand, so that she would keep it there a little longer. His skin was sun-warmed and smooth. He lifted his head, and she took her hand away. "Thanks," he said. "I am better now. I was on antidepressants for a while, and I guess that helped, but I stopped taking them and I've been feeling all right. Graduating was a relief. Getting out of town—it was huge. Coming up here and just leaving the whole, I don't know, the whole scene behind."

"I'm glad," Christmas said.

"I think I need to tell you something," Rory said, breaking eye contact and looking back toward his dock.

Here it comes, Christmas thought. *Fiona.*

"When I was in high school, my friends, well, I don't know how to say this. But we took ADHD meds—you know, Ritalin, Adderall, whatever—we would buy them from kids who had prescriptions. We took it for studying, but also sometimes for fun."

"Oh," Christmas said, surprised. "Yeah. That's a thing. People have tried to buy meds from me. My friend Madison . . ." she began.

Rory waited.

"There were a couple of times, especially senior year, when she'd ask me for pills. She's not the best student—she probably isn't going to do the college thing—and she just really needed to graduate and so I would give them to her." Christmas was hot suddenly, and she considered diving back into the water. "She wanted to pay me for them, but I wouldn't let her."

Rory nodded and Christmas wondered if he was putting it together, that Christmas had given drugs to Madison, who was engaged to Owen, who they'd just learned was a drug dealer. Christmas shifted uneasily in her tube. Was she, technically, a drug dealer as well?

"Whatever," Christmas said. "It's not a big deal. They're just . . . they can be addictive. I didn't want her to . . . you know. Be careless."

"I think it's great that you were responsible about it," Rory said, reassuringly. "And I just wanted to tell you I'd done that. I felt funny about it. Like, you need the medication, and I was taking it for fun."

"No, I appreciate it," Christmas said. "If I didn't need it, maybe I'd take it for fun too," she said.

"Somehow I doubt that," Rory said.

Christmas laughed. She rolled off her tube into the water and, when she came up, saw that Rory had left his noodle and was treading water beside her.

"I'm so freaking glad I met you," he said. He moved closer, and their heads bobbing in the water, he leaned in and kissed her, his lips cool and wet.

"Is this okay?" he asked.

"Yes," Christmas said, smiling. She reached forward to kiss him some more.

WITH MORE SPLASHING AND LAUGHING, they eventually managed to climb back into the rowboat. Christmas's heart soared as she rowed them back toward Rory's dock. He'd meet her eyes and they'd smile, and she'd pull harder on the oars, and they flew across the water.

Closer to the dock, Christmas began, as usual, to note the algae, a reminder of not only all the recent unpleasantness, but also of her conversation with Rory about whether or not the cows had been poisoned as well as her resolution to get a water sample as soon as she got back home.

This idea that she and Rory had been swimming in poisoned water had apparently been waiting patiently in her mind, and, like a bird of prey perched on a tall branch, it now swooped in to clasp her in its talons. Christmas felt a prickly panic. Her breath became shallow, and her mind began to race. Had she swallowed any of the water? Would she, like the cows, soon fall into convulsions? What about Rory? Or even if they were fine in the immediate, had she so saturated her skin that she was now, already, in this moment, hatching a cancer, something sinister and untreatable growing inside her?

SUMMER PEOPLE

"What's wrong?" Rory asked, clearly sensing the shift in her mood.

"Would it be okay—I just . . . I feel like I need a shower. After the lake. Maybe I should head home . . ."

"No, don't go home. You can shower here." They disembarked and grabbed the towels they'd left on the dock. "We're lousy with showers. We have an outdoor one and an indoor one. Whatever you'd be more comfortable with. But—I mean, you don't have to stay, but . . ."

"That's fine," Christmas said quickly.

Though she would have preferred to shower at home, she didn't want to leave. But even more to the point, she felt as though her skin were on fire.

The sooner she was able to rinse off, the better.

Christmas hustled into the outdoor shower, which, with its beautiful blue mosaic tiling and the killer water pressure, was nicer that Christmas's family's indoor shower. She soaped and scrubbed, used shampoo to clean her suit, which she then rung out and put back on, and emerged red and fragrant, her mind, if not completely soothed, at least quieted for the time being.

"I hope you're hungry," Rory said when Christmas emerged, wearing the dry T-shirt and shorts she'd had the foresight to bring. Naomi stood at the grill on which sizzled something that smelled smoky and delicious.

"Starving," Christmas confessed. Her stomach grumbled.

"So, Christmas," Naomi began, turning to face her. "Rory tells me your family moved up here full time when you were in elementary school?"

Christmas nodded. "Yeah. My dad was able to retire, and my mom got a teaching job up here."

"And you like it?"

"Sure," Christmas said.

"Rory said you thought the schools here were better?"

"Yeah, I mean, I'm sure the schools downstate were fine. But I have some processing disorders. And I also have ADHD."

Christmas wondered if Rory had told his mother this already as well.

"I'm an educator, too, so I find this stuff intensely interesting," Naomi said. She crinkled her eyes and laughed. "I know. I'm the only one. Tell me, you feel your needs have been met?"

"I guess," Christmas said, a little surprised by Naomi's directness. "I don't even use most of my accommodations anymore." She shrugged. "I'm on Ritalin, and that's made a huge difference. I also had a lot of anxiety—"

"I've heard the two often go hand in hand," Naomi interjected.

Christmas wondered if Naomi meant ADHD and anxiety or Ritalin and anxiety. She took the seltzer Rory offered her and said, "I manage the anxiety pretty well with exercise and meditation."

"Do you have a cognitive behavioral therapist?"

Christmas smiled, appreciating that Naomi knew what she was talking about. "Not anymore. I used to see someone. But she was far away. And, apparently, expensive. She didn't take our insurance. It's okay though. Like I said, we've got it pretty much under control. I do well in school. I'm happy."

Naomi turned back to the barbecue and began plucking off pieces of corn, placing them on a large yellow plate. "Do you think you'll stay on the Ritalin?"

Christmas shrugged. "Why wouldn't I?"

Naomi waved a hand apologetically. "I don't mean to suggest you should stop your meds. Just, sometimes as people get older, they find they've outgrown their symptoms. Or they start to consider alternatives."

Christmas screwed up her lips, considering. "I really don't mind the medicine. It's helped me so much."

"Of course," Naomi said, putting the plate of corn on the wooden picnic table. "It's just that—"

"Mom," Rory groaned. "Christmas isn't one of your students. Maybe you're the one who should have a summer job. You seem to have excess intellectual energy."

Naomi's eyes brightened as she looked at her son. "Oooh, fresh, but I like that phrasing."

Rory laughed.

Christmas wasn't ready to move on though, and she said, as Naomi returned to the grill to attend to the hot dogs, "I don't mind. I actually kind of like talking about it with people who truly understand." Naomi nodded, and Christmas continued. "I did try to get off it a couple of times and it was rough. I felt really bad. It was partly withdrawal I guess, but I also couldn't concentrate. I couldn't get comfortable. It was almost like having a sunburn, you know? I was so . . . sensitive."

"It looks like you might have a literal sunburn too, sweetheart," Naomi said, using the tongs to gesture to Christmas's shoulder. "I hope you two were wearing sunblock before you went out to float on the lake. Rory, will you grab the aloe from the upstairs bathroom? And really, Christmas, medication is a miracle. If it's working for you, that's wonderful."

"I guess I do worry a little bit about . . . being dependent on something," Christmas said, as Rory walked toward the house. "But when I've gone off my meds, it's like," she searched for the words. "Have you ever gone to a wedding and tried to talk to, like, your elderly aunt and you just can't hear each other 'cause the band is so loud?" Naomi smiled and nodded. "And then the band takes a break and it's such a relief? That's what it was like when I went back on my medication. It was like I didn't have to work so hard just to do the simplest things."

"What a wonderful analogy," Naomi said. "That makes a lot of sense."

Rory returned with the aloe and Christmas slathered some on her shoulders before joining them at the table to eat. "Salud!" Naomi said, raising a glass of wine. "It's good to have you here, Christmas."

"Man, I am so glad you didn't sell this place, Mom," Rory said, taking a bit of his faux dog.

"Were you thinking of selling?" Christmas asked, a little alarmed.

"Well, we got an unsolicited offer." She lifted her eyebrows. "From that game show host. Well, it was from an LLC, but I looked it up and the company is owned by William Ford, who, I believe, also owns the repair shop. Anyway. It was a lowball offer. He must have noticed that we didn't really use the place last summer and figured we might be looking to unload it. And I did consider it, what with Rory's *former* disdain for the place and the fact that, honestly, I'm not that interested in doing a lot of the maintenance work myself." Naomi smiled at Rory. "But I'm happy I didn't take him up on the offer. Although I am concerned about that algae. Was it bad today?"

"It wasn't good," Christmas conceded. She rolled her neck. Her skin felt itchy, despite the aloe, although she also thought that maybe she'd take another shower once she got home. Just to be on the safe side.

Christmas looked out over the lawn and down to the lake. They had a nice piece of property, a spot where they could watch the sun setting behind Cunningham's. From here, the lake and the woods looked peaceful, clean, and calm; it was hard to believe the fields themselves had been the recent site of a cow mass-poisoning or the woods the site of an attempted murder.

"I wonder," Christmas said. Rory and Naomi looked at her expectantly. "I wonder if the algae thing will wind up driving people away. My family has no intention of leaving, obviously, although if the lake is polluted, then a big reason for us living here is . . . well, spoiled."

They sat in silence for a moment, then, each of them looking out at the lake.

"Well, that sucks," Rory said, and Christmas smiled grimly.

They stayed at the table for a long time, talking about college, about the improvements Naomi wanted to make on the house, and about the day camp.

The sun set and they brought the plates inside and then, when Naomi's phone buzzed with a call from Rory's sister, Christmas took it as her cue to leave. She thanked them both and said she'd bike home before it got too dark. Rory rose and walked her to the driveway.

"So, I know I might have mentioned this, but the worst thing in the world is happening this weekend," Rory said and, when Christmas looked up, alarmed only for a moment before she realized he was being funny, he added, "I'm going home to Brooklyn. I had been looking forward to it, but now I'm dreading it."

"Dreading?" Christmas asked, looking up into his face, thinking, *Fiona.*

"I mean, I'd definitely rather hang out up here with you," Rory said.

Christmas smiled. His words resulted in some sort of joyful, swelling sensation in her chest. It felt good, but also a bit scary.

Rory took a step closer to her. "Is it okay if I kiss you again?" he asked.

"Yeah," Christmas said. "That would be . . ." But she didn't finish her sentence because she, too, had leaned in, and their lips met. She put her arms around his neck.

At first, they kissed gently, lips closed, and then Christmas pulled Rory closer, and he wrapped his arms around her waist. Christmas parted her lips and pressed against Rory even harder, a sudden and new understanding of what it meant to want to be close, closer, to another person.

They kissed for a long time, until, aware that they'd be revealed by the headlights of an approaching car, Christmas stepped back, releasing him. "Now I really don't want to go," Rory said.

Christmas smiled too. "Well, I guess we have something to look forward to when you get back."

25

KISSING RORY HAD BEEN EXQUISITELY WONDERFUL. Reviewing each moment of the evening, and especially all the kissing, occupied Christmas's buzzing mind as she showered again and got ready for bed.

But no good thoughts go uninterrupted, it would seem, and her happy reveries were punctuated by interludes of ruminating about Fiona and the "amazing" ex-girlfriend. It occurred to Christmas that the ex might be in Brooklyn that weekend, too, might run into Rory and see the error of her ways.

And, of course, exhausted and lying in bed, Christmas couldn't help but replay the argument with Lexi. She truly regretted cursing at Lexi. It really was out of character for her. Sure, she had fought with her parents—her mom especially—but that tended more toward cold wars, withering looks.

At the same time, it had felt sort of good to lash out at Lexi. And Christmas almost wished she had said more. She wished she'd been meaner, had gotten in a dig about vaping, had nastily asked Lexi why she was so ungrateful to her grandparents. But while wallowing in her self-righteous rage, it occurred to Christmas that perhaps

Lexi had been traumatized by finding Lemy. The guilt rose up again, until Christmas realized that worrying about how Lemy's attack affected Lexi was pretty insensitive; Lemy was the one who'd been assaulted. This line of thought brought Christmas around to Curly, and to Madison and Owen and the continuing mystery around what had, in fact, happened to Lemy and the reality that no one seemed any closer to finding out. And then she remembered Lemy's face, streaked with the green algae, that potentially toxic substance that was poisoning her beautiful lake.

The night was hot—the only air conditioning they had was a window unit in the living room—and Christmas tossed and turned, alternately sweating and kicking off her sheet and then shivering, trying to pull it up using only her feet and then surrendering to consciousness, sitting up and pulling the sheet up properly, only to overheat again.

She did finally sleep, and, when she woke in the morning, all the thoughts and worries were still right there, waiting to be revisited. It was Friday—no camp—and the house was quiet. Christmas took her medication and got out the door.

It was overcast and humid, and running felt like wading through a swamp, Christmas's body heavy in the heavy air. Her clothes were drenched by the time she rounded the last curve of the lake and, although it was slightly disgusting, she didn't bother to go in the house and change; she ran right down to the dock, emptied her pockets, and took off her sneakers and socks.

She was about to jump in, but then she stopped.

She couldn't bring herself to do it.

What? she asked herself. *Am I never going to go swimming again?*

She looked warily at the algae swirling around the dock. She'd been neglecting her raking. It probably didn't make a difference anyway, she thought. She grabbed a floating raft and put it in the water. She'd go out deep, past the algae, and then get in. She would make herself do it. Her freak-out yesterday was ridiculous; she'd let anxiety and intrusive thoughts get the better of her. Maybe she needed a higher dose of meds.

She lay on her stomach on the raft and paddled out, conscious of the algae as it curled around her fingers, thinking of something Curly had said one afternoon when she was over at their place: "The Earth has a fever."

When she got deep enough, she slid off the raft. The lake was too warm for this early in the summer. Did the lake have a fever too? While the warm water was in some ways marvelous, soft against her skin and in her hair, Christmas suddenly sensed a pain all around her, a sickness in the lake, the poison seeping into the clay bottom, lapping on the shores. The idea that the algae was like snot or mucus or pus occurred to her and she tried frantically to climb back on the raft. Panicking, she scrabbled and lost her grip, flipping the raft, sliding back into the water. It was like the scene with Rory all over again, but this time, instead of funny, it felt horrifying to not be able to get out of the water. She took a moment, caught her breath, and then finally mounted the float. Panting, she paddled back to shore, and once on the dock, she picked up her things and ran up to the house to take a shower, to wash the lake off.

She let herself in through the sliding glass doors and went to the couch where she'd left the brown envelope with the lab kit. It wasn't there. Maybe she'd brought it upstairs with her the night she'd been frightened.

But after her shower, she couldn't find it in her admittedly messy room.

"Hi, sweetheart," Christmas's mother said when Christmas, a towel wrapped around her head, came into the kitchen, feeling somewhat calmer, but not eager to get back in the lake anytime soon. "I haven't seen you in days." She laid a cool palm on Christmas's upper arm and rubbed it. She seemed a bit glassy-eyed, spacey even, but also like she was in a good mood. Christmas inhaled deeply. Her mother smelled of sleep and coffee, but not booze. "I'm heading to Honeysuckle in a little while. You don't work today, right? Do you girls want to come with me?"

Christmas wanted to keep her parents in the dark about her argument with Lexi. She didn't think she could bear to talk about it with her mother: too much pity, too much concern. Her parents were low intervention—they would leave her alone if she made it clear that's what she wanted—but she didn't want them worrying about her or feeling sorry for her.

"Lexi is doing something with her grandparents today," Christmas said, thinking it might not be a total lie. She put an English muffin in the toaster. "But I'll go with you," she added.

Honeysuckle, twenty miles to the south, was a surprisingly hip little town. Although the business district was only a few blocks long, it boasted several boutiques, a terrific thrift shop, a bookstore, a supermarket, and a handful of restaurants. Walmart and the Home Depot—where her father was apparently employed—were nearby.

Christmas loved Honeysuckle. She especially loved the thrift shop, Lisa's Amazing Emporium, an island upon the shores on which treasures were almost certain to wash up. Two thoughts flashed quickly through her mind as she grabbed her wallet and her phone: how much she wished Lexi would be joining them, and then, how maybe next Friday she and Rory might go to Honeysuckle. She'd wanted to show him around. She sort of hoped he'd be impressed—most of the boutiques were owned by transplants from Brooklyn, people so rich that they could afford to own stores that never made any money.

Before they walked out the door, Christmas asked, "Mom, I had a brown envelope with some lab equipment in it. Like, test tubes and stuff? Did you see it around?"

Her mother paused and shook her head, no. "What do you need that for?" she asked.

"I was going to test the lake water. There's a lab at Cornell that will analyze it for free." Just mentioning Cornell made Christmas think of Rory and she became aware she was smiling.

Her mother made a face. "Haven't seen it," she said. "But you know, if you can't find something, clean up. Your room is overdue, to put it nicely."

"I know," Christmas groaned, pulling the front door shut behind her. "Or just order another kit."

They didn't talk much in the car, and Christmas gazed out the window, her mind churning, until her mother interrupted her reverie: "So, camp's been good?"

"Um, yeah," Christmas said.

"And how's Lexi?"

"Fine."

Christmas looked at her mother's hands on the steering wheel: her long fingers and liver-spotted skin. Though her mother was apparently "aging well"—other people were often astonished by Christmas's mother's age ("I would have guessed you were much younger!" they cried)—she'd always seemed almost elderly to Christmas, probably because she was always older than her peers' moms.

And, Christmas considered, watching from the corner of her eyes, her mother definitely appeared a little more worn than usual lately; her skin was papery and a bit yellowish.

Christmas couldn't help but wonder if she was drinking again. Her mother had been sleeping a lot during the day, and more significantly, she'd also been going out at night quite a bit. This was something Christmas might not have noticed if she'd been with Lexi or at the Hansens' around the clock; it was certainly not something she was thinking about when she was at school every day. But she realized that recently, though she hadn't fully articulated it to herself, she'd been keeping track of her mother's hours. And yet, as far as Christmas could observe, the clouds of stale alcohol weren't hanging around her mother each morning, and she wasn't acting with the impossible listlessness that was a sure sign of a hangover.

"What?" her mother asked, feeling Christmas's eyes on her.

"Nothing," Christmas said. She looked back out the passenger side window. Rolling hills dotted with cows and red, dilapidated barns scrolled past with such uniform regularity, they began to feel like the repeating backgrounds in old movies, the scenery outside of the pretend cars.

"Mom," Christmas said. "I heard something recently. Something sort of upsetting."

"What's that, Chris?" her mother asked. And then, "Will you hand me my sunglasses? They're in the glove box. It was so overcast before. But it looks like it will be a nice day after all."

Christmas retrieved the glasses and handed them to her mother. She waited.

When it was clear that her mother was not planning to reprise their conversation, Christmas cleared her throat and said, "Do you think it's true that Owen sells drugs?"

Her mother didn't answer immediately. When she did, she said, "Owen? Madison's Owen?"

"Do you know another Owen?"

"You don't need to snap at me," her mother said. "I'm just surprised. No, I hadn't heard that. Where did you hear it?"

Christmas had not embarked on this conversation with a plan. Though the idea that her mother might know more about what had happened to Lemy than she'd been letting on had been nibbling at the corners of her consciousness for several days, she surprised even herself when she asked next, "Why do you hang out at the Cup?"

Christmas's mother shrugged, not taking her eyes from the road.

"Why does anyone go to a bar? As I told our esteemed law enforcement agents: to see people."

"To 'see people'?" Her mother didn't have friends. Well, she used to have a best friend, Aunt Inez, but that relationship had fallen away—been driven away—over the years. Christmas didn't know exactly what had happened with Aunt Inez, but she'd gathered enough clues from listening to her parents that she had a pretty good guess: her mother had been drunk, had said something unforgiveable. And so, no more Aunt Inez.

"What people do you see?" Christmas persisted, through gritted teeth.

"I don't like this," Christmas's mother said, waving a hand in Christmas's direction, "this inquisition. I'm allowed to have a life, Christmas. I'm allowed to have friends you don't know about. Maybe you'll be a parent someday and you'll understand. My life doesn't end when you leave the room."

Christmas let out an incredulous guffaw. "I never said it did. I'm just asking you a question. And I think it might be hard, like, if someone was trying to avoid something, if someone, for example was on a diet . . ." Christmas stumbled over her words.

"What are you getting at, Christmas?"

"I just think it would be hard not to drink if you were hanging out at a bar."

There. She'd said it.

Christmas pretended to stare in front of her, but from the corner of her eye, she watched her mother, who adjusted her sunglasses, pushed a stray hair from her eye, bit her lip, and said nothing.

They continued to drive in silence.

Was her mother going to continue to simply not say anything? Perhaps Christmas's remark hadn't been such a big deal. Maybe her mother was already thinking about something else.

But the silence, Christmas knew, might also be deliberate.

It was a way to show anger. Or, more likely, that she was too injured to speak.

Neither said a word until they arrived in Honeysuckle.

Her mother slowed the car and pulled up in front of the bookstore. When she looked over, Christmas could see that, no, her mother hadn't moved on. She was clearly upset. "I'll text you when I'm finished shopping," her mother said, her lower lip quivering a little bit. "We should go out for lunch. If you want to," she added, peevishly. Before Christmas could respond, she continued, "Do you need anything from Walmart?"

"Shampoo and conditioner," Christmas said, on the verge of tears herself, wishing she could apologize. "Thanks."

Christmas climbed gingerly out of the car and closed the door gently behind her.

For once, Honeysuckle's adorable pastel-colored storefronts were annoying rather than charming, and Christmas wished she had stayed at home, skipped the whole trip.

She sulked her way through the bookstore, which smelled sweetly of glue and ink and paper, and didn't bother browsing. She quickly bought the books she was looking for—a paranormal novel about bullying in a small town and a book called *The Hidden Life of Trees,* which Lemy and Curly had recommended—and then made her way to Lisa's Amazing Emporium down the block.

Christmas and Lexi had loved going to the Emporium together—it was where they'd gotten every costume for every play they'd written (and they'd written several, although most had limited engagements—limited to the Hansens in their living room, that is), the pots for their various candle-making projects, the sad-looking dolls that desperately needed rescuing, the flatware, and the rotary phone (unconnected, but still stylish) for their tree house.

She was feeling slightly better as she made her way to the back racks and then flicked through the endless T-shirts advertising sports teams and fun runs. She stopped at an almost threadbare Hole concert tee featuring a deranged-looking beauty queen. This was so cool as to be almost unbelievable. It looked a bit small, but she took it off the rack. She thought of Rory's Radiohead T-shirt and then, smiling, took out her phone to take a photo to send to Lexi. Her smile faded as she remembered that she couldn't. Still, she turned around, as though to show a friend, but then stopped suddenly, clutching the T-shirt in front of her. Cash Ford stood at the end of the aisle, waiting for her to notice him.

"Hey," Christmas said weakly.

"Hey, Christmas," Cash said. He looked bored, but he took a step closer to her. "Get something good?"

"Yeah," Christmas said. Reluctantly, she held out the T-shirt for him to see. "A vintage band shirt. Or whatever."

Cash looked at the shirt and then at Christmas as though she had just suggested a can of cat food for lunch.

"That's what you're gonna buy?" he asked, screwing up his face.

"I mean, I think it's cool," Christmas said, smiling falsely, despite herself. "I like this band a lot. And it's . . ." she trailed off. Why did she care what stupid Cash Ford thought? He was wearing Oakley sunglasses pushed up on the top of his head.

"Yeah, I don't need to buy other people's used clothes," he said.

"This is a thrift store," Christmas said, with a touch of a tone.

"I was in town for business and saw this in the window," Cash said, holding up a tackle box. "Fucking summer idiots buy all this great gear and never use it. It's not like I have to buy second-hand."

Christmas rolled her eyes. She held back a remark about how shopping at the cigarette outlet and buying illegal fireworks did not count as "business," instead saying, "At least buying things used is better for the environment."

"I don't give a shit about the environment," Cash sneered. "Just decent gear, is all."

"Okay," Christmas said, as usual unsure of how to respond to this strangely angry person. "I guess saving the planet is just a side perk." She bit her lip and waited for him to move out of the way. He didn't, and when she moved sideways to slide past him, he followed behind her, as though they were shopping together.

"Haven't seen you out skiing," he said, smirking.

"Yeah. Haven't been out a lot," Christmas said. "But you know that what you did the other day was totally uncool."

"I just like to piss Hansen off," Cash said.

"Well, mission accomplished," Christmas said. She picked out another T-shirt. This one had a big, ridiculous-looking cat on it and the words "I'm not fat, I'm fluffy."

"Wait, you're not getting that?" Cash asked, making a face.

"It's funny," Christmas said, wondering why they were still even talking.

"You're such a freak," Cash said.

"Wow, you always make me feel so good about myself," Christmas said wryly.

"I was kidding," Cash said, suddenly serious. "Everything looks great on you."

"Oh my God," Christmas said, at once repelled but also, despite herself, flushing. She blinked hard and looked around the store, desperate to escape Cash before he tried to hit on her even more overtly. She knew that he would, too, because on the night of the prom, he'd attached himself to her and behaved quite sweetly, until she'd finally relented a bit and allowed him to kiss her at the bonfire after party.

What was worse, though, was that she'd liked the kiss, but that even as it was happening, she knew she'd regret it. And now, the knowledge that she'd kissed him and it had not been horrible was itself quite horrible.

Was Cash capable of guessing at another's emotions?

He seemed to be, as he looked hard at Christmas before changing tack. "So where's your summer friend, anyway?"

"Who? Lexi?"

He picked up a Mets jersey and then slid it back on the rack. "Yeah, her." He grinned, pulling out a Hooters T-shirt. "You should get this."

Christmas grimaced.

"I thought you two did everything together," Cash continued. He put the shirt back. "You know, lesbos."

"What is wrong with you," Christmas snapped, almost grateful that she had the safety of her rage to cling to. His comment, of course, reminded Christmas of Lexi's criticism, of Lexi's anger, and it seemed suddenly to Christmas that the problems, all of them, were obviously Cash Ford's fault. "You're a homophobe," she said.

Cash held his hands in surrender. "Not me. I love lesbians. You should see my search history."

Christmas shook her head and moved away decisively, not wanting to waste another moment on Cash. And yet again, he pursued her, now into housewares and furniture, protesting, "I was just kidding. God, you're so uptight. But you guys are always together. What? Did you have a fight or something?" Christmas looked at him and she could see he was dying to add another offensive remark but, surprisingly, seemed able to control himself.

"Whatever, Cash," Christmas said. She shook her head as though she'd be able to shake him off. "Just leave us alone when we're skiing. You could really hurt someone."

"I know how to handle myself," Cash said.

"Sure," Christmas said. "You're super cool on your Jet Ski, Cash."

"Why are you such a bitch?" Cash said. A woman looking at the mugs glanced over, concerned.

Christmas made a disgusted noise in the back of her throat. Cash's quick change reminded her of when he was child, how unpredictable his anger, how unafraid he was of teachers, librarians. "What are you talking about? I don't like you endangering my life when I'm waterskiing and so that makes me a bitch?"

Cash laughed through his nose and then changed again, shaking his head as though he were suggesting he would be a good sport and overlook Christmas's shortcomings. "You really do take things too seriously. I'm just joking around with you." He leaned against a tall armoire. "I'll see you tonight, right? Owen's party? You need a ride?"

Cash looked at her expectantly, as though she would be a fool not to leap at the chance to be alone in a car with him.

"I'm fine," Christmas said. "I have my parents' car."

"Mmmhmm," Cash said. "You know you really shouldn't drink and drive."

"I don't drink."

"Well then, maybe you should pick me up," Cash said. He held out his hand. "You don't have my number, do you? Let me put it in your phone."

Christmas cast her eyes around the store, as though waiting for someone to reveal the hidden cameras or to swoop in and save her from whatever this conversation was supposed to be. Grudgingly, she took her phone out of her back pocket, unlocked it, and handed it to Cash.

"I like to go home early," she stammered.

Cash laughed as he typed in the numbers.

"You don't really have to drive me," he said, handing her phone back. "I wouldn't get in a car with you anyway. I know drinking and driving runs in your family."

And that was when Christmas had truly had enough. It wasn't a choice; the slap just happened. It felt good, reaching out and hitting Cash across his dumb, smug face, so hard that his sunglasses flew from his head and hit the ground with a clatter.

Cash's head whipped back, and Christmas saw rage. She cringed, thinking he would strike her back. And then, a moment later, he forced a laugh. "Feisty," he said.

Christmas dumped the T-shirt on a random rack and fled the store.

26

CHRISTMAS'S MOTHER, PERHAPS IN AN ATTEMPT to make up for the earlier unhappiness in the car, too-cheerfully insisted that they go to Julian's, the chic farm-to-table restaurant that was only open seasonally.

Christmas sat, quiet and wary, as they waited for their food.

"You got the books you wanted?" her mother asked.

Christmas nodded. "Yeah." She looked at her phone and, a moment later, her mother did too.

Christmas tried to remember a time before phones. If they didn't have phones, would she and her mother just have sat in silence, staring at each other? She supposed that when she was younger, her mother might have brought crayons and a coloring book. Christmas had many memories of being beside her mother in a public place while her mother read a book and Christmas entertained herself.

Now, Christmas was free to pretend to look at Instagram, but really, she kept replaying the slap in her mind. She was ashamed of having lost control. She'd wanted to cry immediately after it had happened, which was why she'd fled the Emporium and returned to the bookstore to hide in the bathroom until her mother texted.

With the arrival of their food, a certain expectation to talk to each other also descended on the table.

"Did you go to the Emporium?" her mother asked. "Get anything good?"

"Yeah," Christmas answered, taking a sip of her iced tea. "But I didn't buy anything. I ran into Cash Ford though," Christmas said.

Her mother looked up, surprised. "Oh, yeah? That doesn't really seem like his kind of place."

"He was getting fishing stuff," Christmas said.

"Did you talk to him?"

"Yeah. He's so rude and terrible."

"Well," her mother said. She speared a slice of grilled chicken. "He hasn't had the easiest time."

"What's that supposed to mean?" Christmas wanted to tell her mother not to bother defending Cash, that he was totally comfortable making a joke about her drunk-driving accident. She thought of him sneering. For a moment, she was not sorry she'd hit him after all. "Poor rich little Cash Ford. Everyone is always giving that guy a break because his dad is so nice and whatever. He really shouldn't even have graduated," Christmas said. "Everyone knows they just gave him a diploma because his dad donated money. And because the teachers didn't want to deal with him anymore."

Her mother shrugged. "Money isn't everything. It was hard on him, losing his mom."

"That was like a million years ago," Christmas said dismissively. "And lots of people have bad things happen to them. That doesn't mean they should go around acting like entitled jerks."

Christmas's mother shrugged and frowned. "I always thought you liked Cash."

Christmas almost choked. "Liked him?"

"He's not bad looking," her mother pointed out.

"Um, what? Cash had a mullet until like, last year," Christmas said.

"Yes. That was unfortunate," Christmas's mother said. "But the mullet itself was around a nice face."

"No, thank you. Maybe he's not objectively unattractive, but I can't see past his awful personality. And since when are you such a fan of Cash's?"

Her mother shook her head and sighed. "I'm not a fan of Cash's. He is rather surly most of the time. But I suppose . . . well I ran into him recently and he mentioned you. Asked after you. He seems to like you. That shows he has some sense." Her mother smiled.

Christmas grimaced. "When were you hanging out with Cash?"

"I wasn't *hanging out* with him," her mother corrected, the smile disappearing. She waved a French fry. Christmas noted a slight tremble in her mother's hand. "Just ran into him."

"At the Velvet Cup?"

Her mother's lips pressed into a thin line. "Enough with that," she snapped.

Frowning back at her, Christmas took a big bite of her grilled cheese.

Christmas had to concede that perhaps her outrage was so acute in part because there had been that thing with Cash at the prom. Christmas hadn't even wanted to go to the prom at all, but Owen refused to go with Madison, claiming that the prom was for teenagers (something he no longer was) and that he had a quota of times during which he would wear formal clothes and that the quota was going to be fulfilled at their upcoming wedding, unless she wanted him to wear his denim shorts to the ceremony. Madison begged Christmas to go with her and then promptly dumped her at the post-prom bonfire (when Owen appeared).

And that was how Christmas found herself sitting on a tree stump next to Cash, who'd told her that his date, Morgan, had gotten so trashed that he'd taken her home, a detail that, at the time, made Cash rise a little in Christmas's estimation.

He'd toasted a marshmallow and then insisted on feeding it to her. The whole thing was ridiculous, and Christmas regretted it, especially now, especially since Cash was such an asshole and would take something shameful and private like her mother's accident and throw it in her face like that.

Christmas let the sandwich fall to her plate, the cheese suddenly like plastic and the bread soggy with grease. She considered scrolling on her phone again, when her mother sighed and said, "What was it you said Lexi was up to today?"

Christmas met her mother's eye and shrugged. "I don't know what Lexi's doing," she said at last. "She didn't want to work at the camp after all. She's doing other things this summer."

Christmas's mother put down her fork. "What? Did you two have an argument?"

Christmas looked down and swirled a French fry in a puddle of ketchup. "I don't know. I guess."

"Do you want to tell me what happened?"

Christmas shrugged again. "I don't think anything 'happened.' I think she's just sick of Sweet Lake. And I guess she's sick of me too."

Christmas was surprised that she wasn't more upset as she said these words. She was relieved that she wasn't crying in front of her mother, but she also felt that telling her didn't ease the weight or make her feel any better either. If anything, it made the rift with Lexi feel more real and more inevitable. She couldn't pretend they'd find Lexi waiting in the driveway when they got home or that any minute now, her phone would vibrate with a text from her friend. That was over. Lexi had dumped her.

"Oh, Christmas," her mother said, reaching across the table and laying her hand over Christmas's. "That must really hurt, sweetie."

Christmas nodded. "I'm okay."

"You know," her mother said, sighing. "It seems like you're having problems with a lot of the important people in your life."

Christmas slid her hand out from underneath her mother's, a sinking feeling in the pit of her stomach. "What's that supposed to mean?"

"You've been . . . a little abrasive lately. And sometimes, when you're having a problem with everyone around you, it might be that you're the—"

"Give me a break," Christmas said, cutting her mother off, glaring. She suspected that her mother was repeating something she'd learned during one of her stints in AA.

"I'm not trying to upset you, baby," her mother said. "It's just . . . you've been combative lately. You're angry with me, with Lexi, with Cash Ford—"

"I never said I was angry with Lexi."

"Still," her mother pressed on. "You have a chip on your shoulder. And now you want to test the lake water? What for? Can't you just let it go? People are really on edge. Are you just trying to call attention to yourself, make yourself the center of everything?"

"Call attention to myself?" Christmas repeated.

The suggestion was misguided and offensive, and yet she felt her face flushing, as though it were true, as though she were some preening narcissist.

"Why would you want to make yourself the face of some sort of campaign—" her mother continued.

"There's no campaign," Christmas tried to interject. "This isn't about anything except for finding out the truth."

"I mean it, Christmas. Let's move on," her mother said. "I've been thinking about it, and I don't want you contacting Cornell or getting any more involved in this Lake Association business. You need to leave it to the adults to take care of it."

Christmas could barely believe her ears. "You mean, like the way you adults have been 'taking care of it' so far? 'Cause right now the lake seems pretty toxic."

"It's global warming," her mother said, as though that settled it. "And while we're on the subject, I don't want you swimming in the lake anymore this summer. Maybe next year will be different—maybe next year—"

"My friend was attacked!" Christmas said, too loudly. An elderly man at a nearby table looked over and Christmas hunkered down, lowered her voice. "How does that not even seem to register with you?"

"There you go again," her mother hissed, leaning forward as well. "First of all, one thing has nothing to do with another. And second of all, if Lemy was attacked, how come the police haven't arrested anyone?"

Before Christmas had a chance to respond to this absurdity, her mother's phone buzzed.

"Excuse me," she said, flipping the phone over and bringing it close to her face to read. "It's just your dad," she said.

But Christmas knew it wasn't her father because she could see it was a text. Dad didn't text.

Her mother stood and, taking the phone with her, slid out of the booth. "I'm gonna run to the bathroom before we head home." She looked meaningfully at Christmas. "And I meant what I said. Let's try to move on with our lives, okay?"

Christmas gaped for a moment. Was her mother actively working against her? She still burned with shame at the suggestion that her interest in cleaning up the lake was really about making herself the center of attention—a charge that was basically the worst kind of insult to people like her parents.

Why did she have the feeling that she wasn't going to find that testing kit back at the house? Had her mother thrown it out?

Her mother was wrong. She was wrong about what Christmas was doing and why Christmas was doing it. And not only that—her mother was lying to her.

While her mother was gone—for what seemed like a long time—Christmas opened her phone, pulled up the Cornell website, and ordered a new testing kit. She'd just hit Submit when her mother returned to the table.

"I paid up front," her mother said, suddenly seeming pale and tired, the fight gone out of her. "Do you want to drive us home? Good practice for when you're commuting this fall."

"All right," Christmas said, sliding out of the booth and following her mother to the door.

They returned to Sweet Lake mostly in silence, Christmas's mother resting her head against the window and, seemingly, dozing off. Christmas didn't mind not talking; her own brain felt like those scenes of the stock market in old movies, with lots of angry voices yelling and waving papers, trying to get her to pay attention.

Almost home, Christmas noticed some kids in the front yard of a house sitting in an inflatable pool. One of the children—a little girl—wore her hair in two pigtails, reminding Christmas of her childhood self, of one day in particular when Aunt Inez had come upstate and Christmas's mother had allowed Christmas to fill her own inflatable pool with dirt and water, making it, in effect, a mud bath. Christmas had loved the cool softness of the mud, of squeezing it through her fingers, rubbing it on her arms, her legs, her face. Aunt Inez and her mother had laughed and encouraged her; Christmas realized that her mother had always allowed her to do things that might make a mess, and how that was sort of unusual, and actually pretty cool.

Christmas smiled and was about to remind her mother of the day with the mud, to share this fond memory as an olive branch, but then she suddenly remembered something else, her mother holding a clear glass, with ice cubes and a small green leaf, maybe mint. Had her mother been drinking on that day? And then she remembered another thing: waking up early one morning—could it have been that same visit?—and coming downstairs to find her mother on the floor of the kitchen, having passed out. She'd peed her pants.

Christmas had gotten on her knees. "Wake up, Mama," she'd said and, eventually, her mother had roused, collected herself, and stumbled from the room. Christmas remembered being glad that she'd gotten her mother up before her father or Aunt Inez had come down and seen, how she'd felt like a good girl for covering for her mother.

She shouldn't have had to do that. She shouldn't have ever had to see that. And thinking of the past in this way, having to wonder what role alcohol had played in her childhood, in her cherished memories, was like turning over a smooth stone to find squirming, wet insects underneath. Christmas pushed down the sob that was rising in her throat, and concentrated on just making it home.

C HRISTMAS, ALWAYS THE FIRST TO ARRIVE, climbed the steps to Owen's back deck, where she was greeted by three huge, squirming, and friendly mutts. Madison and Owen then emerged from the house and their warm welcome made Christmas feel like an honored guest.

Ultimately, Christmas had opted to bike over, in part because Owen's house was only about two miles from the lake, and in part because it would give her an excuse to leave the party early. But really, the reason she didn't drive was because her mother was already out somewhere with the car, and Christmas hated to impose on Madison for a ride.

While Owen worked on tapping the keg, Madison gave Christmas a tour of the new house, a split-level ranch on four acres that Owen had bought just a month earlier. Owen had, until then, lived in a trailer on his parents' property, bartending and doing seasonal work, and Christmas couldn't help but wonder if it was selling drugs that had made the big purchase possible.

As Madison had warned, the house itself remained largely unfurnished and unadorned, save for an old pleather sofa, television in the living room, and mattress in the bedroom. "He's spent more time shopping for fireworks for this party than he has for dishes and cups," Madison complained again, as she pulled open the screen door to the back deck.

However, Madison confessed, she didn't really want him to get too much stuff. She wanted to do the decorating herself when she moved in after the wedding that fall.

A deck overlooked the backyard, which had been set up with tables covered with white tablecloths and lanterns, electric candles, and twinkle lights. "Wow, Mad, this is amazing," Christmas said. Though it wasn't yet dark, the lights glowed enchantingly, set off by the deep woods that ran the perimeter of the yard and, beyond, the red of the setting sun. It was magical, and Christmas found herself again thinking first of Rory, wishing she could share this beauty with him, and then of Lexi, wishing she, too, could see what Sweet Lake had to offer.

"It's nice, right?" Madison asked, so pleased Christmas was impressed. "I did all the lights and stuff. Owen would have just, like, set a mattress on fire or something. But I think it turned out really pretty. By the way, Christmas, you look hot," Madison said, giving Christmas's outfit—her beloved cutoffs and a newish tank top—a once-over as she led her to the keg. "You are so skinny. Did you get skinnier? You need to stop. I'm jealous."

"Mad," Christmas groaned. This was not the kind of compliment she enjoyed.

"You need to start sharing your Ritalin," Madison teased. "At least before the wedding. Right, babe?" She turned to Owen, who handed Christmas a red cup filled with beer. "Just until I get down ten pounds." Christmas looked around uneasily. The new knowledge that Owen sold drugs was like a low hum in her mind and she wondered, feeling paranoid, if Madison had told Owen that Christmas had given her drugs too.

Owen, at least, seemed not to care about anything except Madison, whom he grabbed around the waist, saying, "Baby, you're perfect. No offense, Christmas, but I like a girl with something to hold on to."

"I think Madison is perfect too," Christmas said, taking a sip of the beer, which was bitter but went down easily. She immediately felt a warm, pleasant sensation in her chest and stomach and resolved to dump the rest as soon as no one was looking.

Madison smiled up at Owen, and the two continued to stand there with their arms wrapped around each other.

Christmas could picture them in twenty years, thirty, a middle-aged couple: Madison a chubby, happy housewife and Owen, tall and beefy, pretending to be long-suffering, but really the happiest man on earth. It was so easy to see that future in the waning light. And yet, Christmas thought, the chances of this outcome were slim if Owen continued on the path he was on. No one ever retires and says, "Well, I've got the good pension from selling drugs for twenty-five years and we're thinking of getting a place down in Florida now."

"So where's Lexi?" Madison asked, interrupting Christmas's thoughts. "She didn't come with you?"

"Oh, she's not hanging out," Christmas said. She knew this was a possible opening—had considered using Lexi's absence as a way to ask Owen about that night at the Cup—but found herself unable to begin. How could she ask Owen about it without seeming as though, as her parents put it, she was either stirring up trouble, or drawing attention to herself and her own role as a "hero"? Or worse, accusing him? Instead of forging ahead, she said, lamely, "She hasn't been feeling well."

Madison made a slight frowny face to suggest sympathy and then charged ahead, "And what's this about this mystery man I heard you were hanging around with?" Christmas opened her mouth to answer but was interrupted as Madison announced, "Let's put a pin in that. My sisters are here!"

Two of Madison's sisters came through the sliding back doors, and there were hugs and chirped greetings. Moments later, a steady stream of people began to stomp up the deck stairs: a handful of Owen's friends and some other kids from their graduating class. Cash was among them.

Owen slapped Cash on the back. "How's your old man?" he asked. He grabbed a sleeve of red cups and began to pass them around.

"You probably see more of him than I do," Cash replied. He turned to Christmas. "Hey, slugger." He feinted backward as though Christmas had made to hit him.

Christmas froze, uncertain. They were already joking about the slap? She shook her head. "I'm sorry about that," she murmured.

Madison had returned to Christmas's side and, never one to let an awkward moment pass unexplored, leaned in, wide-eyed. "What happened?"

"Nothing," Christmas said. "We just ran into each other earlier today."

"I pissed her off, as usual," Cash said. He moved toward the keg to fill his cup. He winked at Christmas and then turned to Madison. "You know it's all an act though. She's crazy about me. Just mad I won't take her for a ride on the back of my Jet Ski."

Christmas rolled her eyes.

"I don't think so, Cash," Madison said. "Chrissy has a new guy."

"Stop," Christmas groaned.

Cash turned to Christmas with real interest. "Is that so? Who? I hope it's not that Harry Potter wannabe again. What a dick."

"Marshall hasn't worn those glasses since middle school," Christmas said, annoyed at herself for taking the bait. Marshall was the self-proclaimed class nerd, an overachiever who constructed a personality around his disdain for his peers. He'd always made an exception for Christmas, though, and for that he'd earned her loyalty. "And he's a really nice person. And we were together for, like, fifteen minutes."

"Seriously, though," Madison crooned, ignoring Cash. She held her red cup with both hands and raised her eyebrows. "Owen saw you biking around with some cute dude."

Christmas shook her head. She would have loved to have talked to Madison about Rory.

Just not with Cash as an audience.

"We work together at the camp. He and his mom have that blue house, you know the one—"

"Summer people," Cash interjected.

"Yeah," Christmas said. "He is summer people."

"You can tell I'm not summer people because I got them autumn teeth," Cash joked. Everyone waited for a punch line they'd heard several times before. "Autumn had 'em fixed years ago." He smiled widely, revealing a missing lower tooth and some overlapping canines. "Does your new boyfriend have summer teeth, Christmas?"

"Some are here, some are there. Ha, ha," Christmas said, pretending boredom, but smiling. The old joke, the twinkle lights, maybe the sip of beer: it all made her feel disposed to forgive Cash, and despite the weirdness with Owen, she felt almost safe, as though she were among friends. "No, he doesn't. You know city people, with their fancy orthodonture and what not," she joked.

"So, is it serious?" Madison asked, angling her body in such a way as to suggest that Cash should move along. "With this guy? What's his name?"

"Rory. We just met," Christmas said, trying to act casual. "But he's really nice."

"Why didn't you bring him?"

"He and his mom had to go back to the city this weekend," Christmas explained. She wished she could tell Madison about Fiona and the ex-girlfriend. She longed for someone with whom she could dissect every conversation she'd had with Rory over the past week.

But Cash loomed, and then, suddenly, music began to blast, too loud, from the outdoor speakers.

"Oh my God. Let me get him to turn that down," Madison yelled. She went into the house in search of Owen.

Christmas walked toward the other side of the deck, out of the direct line of the speakers, and stood at the rail, looking out at the backyard. Cash followed, placing his beer on the rail, before leaning forward and resting his elbows.

From the deck they watched the newer arrivals milling in the yard below. She knew every single one of them, but there wasn't a person she'd go up to and talk to. She thought of Marshall, who, unlike herself, had enough sense to stay home.

The music was abruptly lowered and, as though reading her mind, Cash said, "Just like the old days, huh, Christmas? The two of us together. The two misfits."

"Hmm," Christmas said, surprised. "Were we misfits?"

He smiled, apparently genuinely amused. "Aren't we still? You never wonder why we were always paired up, put in the same groups for projects?"

Christmas cut a look at Cash. "They knew I'd carry you," she said. "Do the work."

Cash nodded and sighed. "That's probably true. And it's 'cause we had some of the same learning problems."

Christmas nodded. "Maybe. I have ADHD," she said.

"You don't say," Cash said, laughing. "Everybody knows that, Christmas. It's like the joke, how do you know someone is a vegan? Don't worry, they'll bring it up every fifteen minutes. How do you know Chrissy has ADHD? Don't worry, she never stops telling you about it."

Christmas turned away, looked back into the yard and the woods beyond, stung. Did she really talk about her ADHD all the time?

She wanted to get away. She was about to say that she needed to go see if Madison needed help with anything when Cash put a hand on her arm.

"Oh, don't get all pissy. I'm just giving you a hard time. You know I have it too?"

"What?" Christmas said. She pulled her arm away and Cash let his hand fall back on the rail. He took a long swig of his beer.

"ADHD, ADD, whatever," Cash said. "Unofficially. My mother always said I had it, but my father refused to have me tested. They'd fight about it." He took another, long drink. "That medicine sure did work for you, though. I wonder if things would have been different for me if I had gotten on that medication. I might have done real well."

Christmas snorted. She didn't mean to. She'd thought, for a moment, that he was joking. It was only the angry darting of his eyes that let her know that he'd been serious. And then she felt awful, realizing that maybe Cash believed that he could have achieved more if he'd had the kind of help that Christmas had received. Or if his mother hadn't died.

"Whatever," he said, his lips curling down. "I'd rather not be a drug addict. You think that runs in your family, too, Christmas?"

"What?" Christmas asked. She felt her eyebrows pulling down, her face crunching up in anger. "What is wrong with you?"

"Nothing's wrong with me," Cash said, again drinking jauntily and turning to look back at the house. "You can say what you want about my family, but we don't do drugs."

"I have a prescription," Christmas hissed. "I don't know why you always have to be such an asshole."

"Whatever you say, Chrissy," Cash said, pulling a pack of cigarettes out of his back pocket. He lit one and walked away, leaving her alone on the deck.

Christmas sighed and lifted her beer to her mouth. On impulse, she chugged it, taking long gulps of the cool beer.

It was a dumb thing to do, of course. But when she lowered her empty cup to the rail, she felt better. She laughed and went to get a refill.

28

THOUGH SHE'D SNEAKED SIPS FROM VARIOUS BOTTLES in Mr. Hansen's liquor cabinet with Lexi a few times when they were younger—the sweet liquid burning her throat and making her cringe—Christmas had never been drunk before. And, at first, it was pretty fun. Cheerful and slightly dizzy, she had a fascinating conversation with one of Madison's sisters, Vanessa, an older girl who had always scared her before, but who now made her laugh with her frank, wry observations about their fellow partygoers. Then, her arm linked through Vanessa's, she was escorted to the grill, where she enjoyed a cheeseburger so delicious that she had to tell Owen numerous times that he was a great chef. She only discovered she'd been repeating herself when Vanessa, giggling, informed her, "We get it, Christmas. It was a perfectly cooked burger."

The cheeseburger, though, made her think of the tofu hot dogs she'd so recently enjoyed, and Rory himself, and this initiated a mood shift. Sad and fretful, she went into the house and texted to ask if he'd gotten in okay. He'd not texted back right away, which sent Christmas into a desperate spiral. She was about to call him when her phone buzzed with a message from him, saying yes, he'd made it, and he already missed her. She was sitting on the pleather couch, a dog drooling beside her, conscious of the dumb smile on her face, when the fireworks started. The dog woke and darted away to hide, and Christmas too was glad to be inside and buffered by the glass doors. Even so, the noise of the supposedly glorious starbursts was still a bit startling, the colors too busy for her to enjoy. Suddenly jumpy and uncomfortable, she wished she could go home. Unfortunately, it was too dark, and she was too drunk to bike. She was not, however, too drunk to know that no one else at the party was sober enough to drive her home either. She wondered if she should text Rory to ask his advice. But the idea of revealing to Rory that she'd been drinking also made her panic and she began to wonder if he already suspected that she was drunk. Would he be judgmental about that, or would he think that was cool? She wasn't sure. Scrolling through their messages, she searched to see if anything she'd written would indicate her inebriated state. The words swam in front of her, and she had to close one eye in order to make the letters behave.

So involved was she in trying to decipher her own messages that she barely noticed when Cash sat beside her.

"I saw you hiding out in here," Cash said, handing her a fresh beer, which she paused before taking. Madison would let her sleep over, she figured, nodding a thanks and taking a sip. "I thought you weren't into partying. Since when do you drink?"

"Since tonight, I guess," Christmas said. She hiccupped and felt absurd. "Why do you care?"

"I don't," Cash said, and then added, "Maybe I do. Either way: cheers?" He clicked his plastic cup against hers, finished his drink, and put his cup on the coffee table. "But you should come back out. Me and Owen got some totally illegal shit we're gonna set off."

"Fireworks aren't really my thing," Christmas said.

"Is that right?" Cash said, considering. "Well, I could just hang here with you if you want."

"You don't have to do that," Christmas said, although she didn't exactly want him to leave, either.

Being with Cash, the two of alone among the other revelers, reminded her of prom night, of how he'd charmed her into "going somewhere private" with him. He'd been uncharacteristically sweet, and he'd taken her by the elbow, and though in the past she'd always found Cash a bit scary, she hadn't that night. They'd kissed up against a tree, his breath hot and beery, and she hadn't disliked it. In fact, she'd been surprised at how nice it felt to be with Cash, how much it meant to her that he seemed to like her so much, at how much she, apparently, liked him too.

She might have gone on kissing him, might even have begun to believe that kissing him could be something they could do again sometime in the future, but then Morgan, his date, had staggered up, swearing—not having been deposited home after all, but left passed out in Cash's truck—and Christmas had gasped, disgusted and distressed, before darting off into the night, leaving him to deal with the mess he'd made.

On the pleather couch, Christmas sighed and met his bright eyes. He moved toward her, taking the cup from her hand and putting it on the coffee table beside his own before leaning in, putting a hand on gently on the nape of her neck and bringing his lips to hers.

He smelled of beer and cigarettes, but his lips were soft and familiar in a way that Christmas found at once comforting and exciting. He ran his thumb along the side of her face, which sent electric shivers down her spine, and she kissed him back before remembering herself, putting her palms to his chest and pushing him away.

"No," she said bluntly. "This is not happening."

"What's wrong?" he said, looking injured, withdrawing his warm hand. "Don't tell me you don't . . . I mean, am I imagining it?"

"I don't know what you're talking about," Christmas said, although, of course, she certainly did. She was attracted to Cash.

But she didn't *like* Cash. And she suspected he felt exactly the same about her.

His face changed and hardened. He leaned back, away from her. "I forgot. You've got a boyfriend now."

Christmas shook her head, too tired to even be exasperated. "I don't know why you have to make sure that our every interaction is so unpleasant."

Cash laughed and stood. "Even when you're drunk you talk like a nerd," he said. "And it wouldn't have to be unpleasant, you know, if you ever gave me a chance." He raised his eyebrows, and waited for a response, or maybe an invitation.

"I'm not drunk," Christmas said, and then, much to her chagrin, hiccuped again. She couldn't meet his eyes anymore, and so she plucked her phone from where it had slid between the couch cushions and pretended to focus on it. He waited a moment, then blew out his lips, turned, and sauntered back toward the sliding doors.

As though synced with the explosions outside, her heart pounded in her chest. She couldn't deny that she was drawn to Cash—and she wasn't happy about it. He was like the fireworks: exciting and maybe a bit dazzling, but mostly upsetting, too much. It occurred to her that he was probably the guy waking everyone up every night with all the noise and yet he didn't even seem to care all that much about watching them. Did he truly like fireworks, or did he just like setting off explosions?

29

WHEN OWEN AND CASH HAD FINALLY run out of things to blow up, Christmas rose on unsteady legs and let herself back out on the deck. She'd been sitting, stewing in the living room, and, in between saying "hey" to the various partygoers who came inside and walked past her on the way to the bathroom, decided it was a good idea to seize the opportunity of her drunken boldness and to speak to Owen. She approached him where he stood with Madison at the keg. As he refilled her cup, she said, "I heard you were working at the Cup the night Lemy was attacked."

Owen looked back blankly. "Attacked?"

"Christmas," Madison said, as though disappointed in her.

A few people standing nearby stopped talking and Owen raised his voice for their benefit. "Give me a break. Lemy was trashed, Christmas. I don't know why everyone is making this into a big deal. He got drunk and probably stopped to take a leak and he fell in the lake. It's good you rescued him or whatever you did, but don't try and build it up into something it isn't."

"I'm not . . . I didn't . . ." Christmas began, remembering her mother's similar admonishment. Owen seemed angry. She already regretted having initiated the conversation. "He looked really bad," she said weakly.

"Yeah, well," Owen said. He lifted the hand holding the red cup and pointed his index finger at Christmas. "Like I said. He was fucked up that night." Owen took a long drink and made a move as though to walk away but turned back. "And you know what, Christmas," he said. "Lemy was asking for it anyway."

"What?" Christmas said, shocked. She took a step backward.

"Owen!" Madison cried.

"I'm just saying," Owen said. "He was shooting his mouth off, making accusations. I wouldn't be surprised if he pissed someone off."

"What was he saying?" Christmas asked. "Who was he—"

"The guy was a pain in the ass," Owen said. "*Is* a pain in the ass. And to tell you the truth, Christmas, you're a pain in the ass too."

"Hey," a voice called out from behind Christmas. "Watch how you talk to her."

"Fuck you, Cash," Owen said. "She's not your girlfriend. She doesn't even like you, bro. Give it up."

Someone laughed, and then someone else threw a beer and then Cash moved swiftly, an arm cocked, and in a moment he and Owen were throwing vicious, powerful punches. Christmas moved away but couldn't take her eyes off them. She'd never before seen a fight in which neither party seemed to hold back even a little bit, trading blows that landed with sickening thumps.

Moments later, they'd crashed to the deck floor where they wrestled, each trying to free an arm up enough to get in another hit. Soon enough, others had swarmed up to the deck and joined in to separate the two, and Christmas, overwhelmed with the screaming and the shouting and the pushing, fled back into the house and then straight to the bathroom, where she was sick.

The rest of the night was a blur: dry heaving over the toilet, and then crying on the pleather couch, Madison assuring her it would be all right, that everyone had just had too much to drink, that she should try to sleep. And Christmas did pass out, at least for a little while, waking at dawn and blinking in the weak light, looking at the red cups littering the almost-empty living room. She waited until eight and, still not feeling as though she could manage riding her bike, crept out to the trashed deck, called her dad, and asked him to come get her.

Her head was pounding when he pulled up and she worried she might be sick again. Gingerly, as though any sudden movements might upset whatever equilibrium she still had, she mounted the bike on the rack and got into the car.

"How was the party?" he asked. "It sounded like about ten thousand dollars' worth of fireworks."

"Fine," she said, leaning her head against the car window.

She could tell that the smell hit him then, and he didn't say anything else. She had never before experienced such profound self-loathing. She hated herself for disappointing her dad, for making him worry, and she hated herself for everything else too: for kissing Cash, for trying to interrogate Owen, for allowing Madison to see her sob and wretch. As they rode along in silence, she reviewed every one of her poor decisions and, when she got to the end of the list, started all over again at the beginning.

As they rounded a bend and approached the lake, she noticed some trash on Rory's front yard.

"Dad, slow down," she said. "Here, pull over."

As they neared, Christmas saw more clearly the red cups and beer bottles scattered around, but also that the front windows of the house were all broken.

"What happened here?" her father asked, leaning forward in his seat to look past Christmas.

"I don't know," Christmas answered, her voice still scratchy and weak. "Looks like somebody broke the windows."

"What the hell?" her father asked. "Do you know the people who live here?"

"Yeah," she said. "This is my friend Rory's house. He and his mom went downstate for the weekend."

Her father pulled the car into the driveway and parked.

Christmas's father called the police and left Christmas to wait for them while he went home to get boards for the windows. Christmas texted Rory and asked him to give her a call if he had a minute. He called back right away.

"Hey, good morning!" he said. "Everything okay?"

"Um, not really," Christmas said, haltingly. She swatted at a fly that was buzzing around her aching head. She told him what she and her dad had discovered and assured him that it didn't seem that anything had been taken from the house (a television was visible from a back window). "The police are on their way. And my dad'll board up the windows, so you guys don't have to come back early or anything like that. But I thought you should know."

"That's so messed up," Rory said. "I'll call my mom and let her know what's happening. And are you okay? You sound pretty terrible."

"I'm fine," she said, glad that the shame enveloping her was not something easily detectable over the phone. "Just stayed up too late."

"Must have been a good party," Rory said, and Christmas shut her eyes, willing herself not to cry. "So, what do you think?" Rory continued. "Was this just some kids being jerks?"

"I don't know," Christmas said. "Whoever it was . . . they must have seen that no one was home, that there wasn't any car or anything."

"They waited until we went away to do this," Rory said. "That's so rotten."

"Yeah," Christmas agreed.

Rory told Christmas the code to open the front door and, when the police arrived they confirmed that the house did not seem to have been broken into. They called Naomi and, when they were done, Christmas also spoke to her and repeated that there was no need to hurry back, that they wouldn't get anyone to come and install new windows that day anyway. Naomi was upset, but also grateful.

While Christmas's father boarded up the windows, she and her mother, who'd returned with Christmas's dad, began to collect some of the trash. Thankfully, Christmas's father had also brought big yellow gloves for them to wear, so the job was marginally less disgusting than it might have been.

Christmas collected the bottles and cups, her head spinning and stomach in revolt every time she bent and stood up again. All she wanted was to crawl into her bed and stay there, but she made herself do this work under a sun that seemed to grow hotter each minute, as though to punish herself for the mistakes of the night before. How could she have been so stupid? And why had she allowed Cash to kiss her? She had no doubt who was responsible for the broken windows.

"Cash did this," Christmas said aloud. Her mother, who was tying up a bag a few feet from her, moved closer, frowning.

After a moment, she asked, "What makes you say that?"

"This looks like some of the stuff from the party I was at last night."

"Lots of people had parties last night," her mother pointed out, but her eyes flicked around the property and toward the road, as though she was afraid someone might hear.

"I just know it was him," Christmas said.

"You seem to *just know* a lot of things lately," her mother said, her voice lowered. "I doubt Cash has any idea of who lives there. I don't even know the people who own this house. They're summer people, aren't they?"

Christmas didn't quite like the way her mother said the words *summer people.*

"What's that got to do with anything?" Christmas said. "Once upon a time, we were summer people. And, actually, I do know them. This is my friend Rory's house."

"I've never heard of this friend before," her mother said.

"You don't everything about me, Mom," Christmas said, her anger rising now, her words lashing.

"That's true enough," her mother snapped. "You smell like they wiped the floor up with you last night." Her lips turned down in a severe frown. Christmas wondered if her mother was going to cry.

She certainly felt like crying herself. But she spat back, "These summer people got a letter over the winter. An offer to buy the house from them. The letter was from—"

"You stop it right now!" Christmas's mother said, stepping closer and putting her face right up to Christmas's. "Enough."

Christmas, stunned and frozen, locked eyes on her mother. Her father came down the ladder, barreling toward them.

"What is going on?" he asked, his eyebrows drawn together in concern. "What are you two fighting about now?"

"It's nothing," Christmas's mother said, huffily, throwing her garbage bag to the ground. "Christmas's got a vendetta against Cash Ford for some reason." Before Christmas could protest, her mother turned back, her eyes blazing. "And as I said to you last time, that boy's had enough trouble in this world without you running around spreading rumors. I don't even know why I agreed to come over here. My nerves are shot."

Christmas's father put a hand on his wife's shoulder. "We'll get you home," he assured her. "We'll get you home and you can lie down for a while."

Her mother ignored him and moved away, muttering to herself as she walked toward the car. "I don't even know these people."

"I'm almost done around back," Christmas's father said. "Let's finish up and—"

A noisy truck came around the bend, drowning out his words. All three of them looked up.

Lexi watched them from the passenger side window of her grandfather's truck. As a reflex, Christmas raised her gloved hand to wave.

Lexi waved back, unsmiling.

Christmas wondered what it meant. Was she just being polite? Could they be making up? Was Lexi's wave just a reflex too?

30

A T HOME, EVERYONE RETREATED TO THEIR BEDROOMS, fighters back in their corners. Christmas took her medication, slept, and woke up feeling better, although still weak, wobbly, and sad.

The day itself, though, was glorious and sunny, and when Christmas walked down to the lake with her coffee, several motorboats were buzzing around, pulling tubes and skiers. No Cash, Christmas noted. And then wondered at herself. Did she want to see him? Was she looking for him?

It occurred to her that just when she was starting to feel something akin to fondness for Cash, he went and did a mean and dumb thing like messing up her boyfriend's house. Although, she corrected herself, Rory wasn't technically her boyfriend. And she didn't know for sure that it had been Cash who dumped the garbage and broke the windows.

Still. It reeked of Cash, she thought bitterly. Dumb and mean.

She sat on the dock, keeping her feet out of the water and placing her coffee beside her. There was a layer of algae so thick she could see bugs walking on it, like it was a floating carpet. She took a deep breath, looked at her phone, and texted Madison.

Thanks for letting me crash last night. Sorry I was such a mess. I'm really embarrassed. And sorry that I sneaked off without saying goodbye. Do you have a minute to talk?

Madison called right away.

"Stop it! We were all messed up! I'm so glad that you actually hung out! Did you have fun? I know things got crazy at the end, but it was a good party, wasn't it?"

Christmas, unprepared for this line of questioning, croaked out, "It was a great party."

"You sound like you're in rough shape," Madison laughed. "Are you really hungover? Ugh. I am. And poor Owen—he has to work tonight. Although I think he's feeling like crap more because of the fight than anything."

"He's okay?"

"He'll be fine," Madison said. "Could you believe that though? I think Cash really has it bad for you. He's always watching you, covering for you. Too bad you have a boyfriend!"

"I don't . . ." Christmas began, and then abandoned the thought. Protest was useless with Madison. "What do you mean Cash is always 'covering' for me?"

She heard Madison blow out her lips. "You know. I guess there was that thing with—" She abruptly stopped speaking. "I mean," she began again. "I don't know," she said, unconvincingly.

Though she still felt unaccountably nervous, Christmas pushed forward. This might be her opportunity.

"Mad, I just want to say that . . . I'm sorry I pissed Owen off. But I brought up the whole Lemy thing because, well, I know that he didn't just fall in the lake. I know that he was beaten up." Christmas faltered. "That . . . Owen and maybe Cash . . . they have something to do with it."

The silence went on for so long that Christmas began to wonder if the call had been disconnected.

Then, finally, Madison said, "Who told you that?"

Rather than answer, Christmas pushed on. "I know Owen sells drugs."

Madison snorted. "Listen. I love you, girl. I really do. But I know you're bluffing. And whatever it is you're trying to do—trying to trick me into saying—it's not cool."

"Someone almost killed my friend," Christmas said. "And I just want to find out what happened to him. Do you know anything? Please, Mad."

"Stop," Madison said, sharply. "This conversation is over. Try to . . . I don't know. Try to move on," she advised. "Take a run? Eat something. Maybe lie down. Whatever it is you need to do. Go do that."

"But was Owen—" Christmas began.

"Chrissy," Madison interrupted. "Please. I'm begging you."

"And I'm begging you," Christmas replied. "Tell me what you know!"

Madison sighed, and Christmas pictured her in the kitchen of Owen's house, collecting herself. "We all have something to lose, Christmas. All of us. You need to trust me. Let it go."

"I can't do that, Mad," Christmas pleaded into the phone. "You know there's no way I can do that."

"You'll be starting college soon," Madison said softly, cajoling. "I know you're not going away, but you will, won't you? Eventually. And that's good, Christmas. I know you love Sweet Lake, but maybe it's not . . . maybe you should think about leaving it—leaving us—behind."

Madison ended the call without saying goodbye.

31

THAT NIGHT, CHRISTMAS AND HER FATHER worked on an elaborate jig-saw puzzle—a painting of a beehive surrounded by bees—at the kitchen table. Though her father split his attention, sometimes slotting a piece in, but mostly watching the Mets game, which was playing on the small TV on the counter, Christmas was diligent and absorbed, putting together the puzzle as though it were her literal job.

After she'd spoken to Madison, she biked to Lemy and Curly's, but no one was home. When she returned to her house, her father was in the garage working on a birdhouse and her mother was just emerging, bleary-eyed and frowning, from the darkened bedroom.

Later, she heated up a pre-made chicken potpie, which they picked at mostly in silence, all her father's attempts to start a con-versation—"Anyone else looking forward to the game tonight?"—faltering and dying out, like matches on wet wood. Christmas felt as though her mother was on some sort of five-second delay, taking just a beat too long to answer or respond. Finally, she excused herself, mumbling something about going to a book club, which was so out of character for her that it might actually have been true.

When her father had proposed the puzzle, Christmas knew that it was meant as some sort of distraction or consolation; she hadn't even wanted to do it, but she, too, wanted to make peace. Once she'd gotten started, though, she found the puzzle an excellent occupation for her mind, which would otherwise be buzzing around like the very bees she now worked so hard to place.

"You know," her father said, clearing his throat. Christmas froze, holding a puzzle piece in midair. "I don't like you drinking," he said.

"I know," Christmas said, breaking eye contact and looking down at the puzzle. "And I'm never going to do it again. I feel . . . I thought it was fun for about a half an hour, but I feel terrible today."

From the corner of her eye, she saw her father nodding.

"You guys drink," Christmas added, still not looking up.

After a moment, her father said. "I don't anymore. And your mother's not drinking now either."

Christmas didn't respond right away, and her father moved his mouth around nervously. Christmas remembered watching the old *Anne of Green Gables* miniseries when she was a kid. She remembered really identifying with Anne, finding comfort in the idea that someone else had a sweet, strange, quiet father like her own. After a while she asked, "Did you think she had a problem? Back when you first met her?"

Her father cleared his throat again. He picked up a puzzle piece and searched for its spot. "Not really." He looked at Christmas. "It's hard to . . . untangle," he said at last. "It feels wrong to say it, but we had a lot of good times when we were drinking. And your mother and I would never have even spoken if not for alcohol. Inez had us sitting next to each other at that dinner party, but we were both too shy to say more than 'please pass the salt.' We only talked later, in the kitchen, after we'd both had a few glasses of wine." Her father looked up and his eyes shone in the kitchen light. "I think, Chrissy, that you and your mom are a lot alike. I think maybe she had some of the same struggles you did, but that we didn't know what to call them back then. She didn't have the same tools you do now. Do you see what I'm getting at?"

Christmas felt, then, that she might cry. She swallowed it down and said, with an edge in her voice, "So she drank 'cause she had ADHD?"

"Not just that," her father said patiently. "The shyness, the anxiety. Things that come easily for other people don't come so easy for your mom. Drinking helped her to feel all right. Helped her in situations that were hard for her. You know people say it's a social lubricant, that it lessens inhibitions." Christmas thought of her own easiness talking to Madison's sister, of kissing Cash, of approaching Owen. "And I think she used it that way for a long time. But it's addictive. And she couldn't . . . keep it under control. That isn't her fault," her father said. "Believe it or not, addiction isn't a moral failing."

Christmas stared at the puzzle, unconvinced.

When her father didn't continue, she said, bitterly, "Other people stop."

"Your mother stopped."

"Only after . . . only after she almost died," Christmas said, bitterly. "She stopped because she had to." And then Christmas surprised herself, adding, "She should have stopped before the accident. She should have stopped for us."

Her father nodded, noncommittal. "Maybe," he said and sighed. "You don't have to be so hard on her, Chrissy. No one could be as hard on her as she is on herself."

"You tell me she's not drinking now," Christmas said. "That's great, I guess. But something else is . . . something's not right."

She looked at her father, who didn't quite look away, but seemed to allow his eyes to lose focus. "She's been struggling," he said, after a long pause.

Again, Christmas waited for him to continue and, again, he chose not to. When the doorbell rang, Christmas and her father looked at each other, alarmed, just like the time the police had come by. But she could tell that they were both relieved, too, grateful for the interruption.

Neither leaped up and Christmas had the grim realization that their hesitancy was not simply introversion, but dread. Their fear was rooted in traumatic memories of upsetting calls from unknown numbers: "There's a lady here who needs a ride home." Once, a stranger literally dropped Christmas's mother, unconscious, at the front door. And there was the time, of course, when the police had come to say that there had been an accident.

Her father, frowning, finally rose.

Christmas stayed in the kitchen, listening.

She heard the heaving open of the front door, she heard her father's greeting, she heard a woman's voice: "I'm Naomi. The woman whose house you fixed? And this is my son, Rory."

Christmas's heart began to pound. Here? Rory was here? Although it wasn't at its absolute worst, the house was definitely a mess: the half-eaten potpie was congealing on the counter, and there were several pairs of Christmas's sandals and flip-flops strewn around the kitchen. There was not time to straighten up, so instead, she darted into the bathroom and glanced quickly in the mirror. She took her hair out of its messy bun, but then seeing that her hair was at a fire hazard-level of greasiness, quickly put it back up again, trying to recreate the casual pretty-but-sloppy thing she now thought she'd had going on before she'd ripped the scrunchie out.

It would have to do. She couldn't leave them alone together any longer. She practically ran into the hallway.

"Hi, Christmas!" Naomi said. She was handing off a white bakery box and a bottle of wine to Christmas's father. Rory held a bunch of colorful summer flowers wrapped in brown paper. "We're here to express our gratitude. We feel so fortunate to have such amazing, wonderful, generous neighbors."

"That's so nice," Christmas said, looking at her bare feet. "Really, it was no big deal."

"It's a big deal to us," Naomi said. "I honestly don't know what we'd do without you!"

"It was no problem," Christmas's father told Naomi. "This isn't necessary." He glanced at the box in his hand. "Junior's cheesecake, huh? I haven't had this in as long as I can remember."

"And it's real Junior's, from the actual store, not from the grocery or anything."

No one spoke for a moment, and Christmas moved awkwardly from one foot to another. Why was her dad so weird? And why was she so weird? Probably because she'd been raised by two socially stunted weirdos.

"Should I put on a pot of coffee?" Christmas offered at last.

"We don't want to impose," Naomi said, although it seemed clear that she had no intention of leaving.

"Please, come in," Christmas's father said. Without waiting for a response, he turned and headed toward the kitchen.

"Yeah," Christmas added. "We'd love for you to stay. As long as you don't mind the Mets. Or the mess. The kitchen table is covered in a jigsaw puzzle."

They followed her down the hall and into the kitchen. Christmas went to the sink to rinse out the coffeepot.

"That looks like a complicated puzzle," Naomi said, looking impressed.

"It's a tough one," Christmas's father said. "But our Chrissy can be very determined. I bet she'll have it done before she goes to sleep tonight." He winked at her.

"Some might say obsessive," Christmas put in. "Would you grab that for me?" Christmas asked Rory, gesturing to a tall vase on top

190

of the fridge. Their fingers brushed as he handed it down, and she looked at him and smiled.

"These are beautiful," she said, arranging the flowers.

Naomi got the plates while Christmas's dad made space on the table, pushing the puzzle pieces to one end. Rory got the knife, forks, and mugs; Christmas put out the milk and sugar.

Even with the jumble of the half-completed puzzle, the table, set with the flowers and cheesecake, white mugs and blue plates, was a pretty vision. The setting sun came in through the back windows, casting the room in gold. The coffee machine popped and gurgled contentedly. Christmas was tired and still a bit on edge, but also pleased they'd come, happy to be at the table with Rory.

"I'm sorry my wife isn't here," Christmas's father was saying to Naomi. "She had . . . where'd she go again, Christmas? Was it a book club?"

"Yeah, I think so." Christmas had to work to keep the skepticism out of her voice.

"That's lovely," Naomi said. "I've always wanted to join a book club, but there are never enough hours in the day."

Naomi cut and passed around the cheesecake, which was somehow impossibly dense and fluffy at the same time. Christmas ate, her eyes intermittently flicking over to the puzzle; her fingers itched a bit to pick up a piece, but she told herself she'd return to it later. It could wait.

"This is so delicious," Christmas said. "But I'm sorry you had to come back early. Did you have a good trip?"

"It was fine. I had to get the mail," Naomi said. "And Rory wanted to see some friends. But honestly, we were just talking about how we both prefer being here." She sipped her coffee. "I think we're appreciating the house more than ever this year, which is a bit ironic since it would seem we're being driven out of town!" Naomi laughed, but Christmas and her father shook their heads and tsked, trying to reassure her that this wasn't the case. Naomi leaned forward, growing serious. "Do you have any idea who might do something like this? Do you really think it was just a kid pulling a prank? Or do you think we are being singled out?"

"I don't know," Christmas's father said. "But we'll be keeping an eye on the place from now on."

"Thank you," Naomi said. "I really do appreciate it. We're also going to put up some exterior cameras. At the very least, they might deter future vandals," she said. "I suppose I'll need a contractor. Is there someone you'd recommend?"

Christmas's dad rose and walked to the window. "I'd be glad to do it," he offered, looking out at the lake. He turned back. "I'm not a professional, but I'm handy. I work over at the Home Depot in Honeysuckle. And I know how to install windows. You buy the materials, I'd be happy to put them in."

"Perfect!" Naomi exclaimed.

Christmas's dad returned to the table and he and Naomi began to discuss plans and logistics. Christmas saw her father's shoulders creep down as he relaxed into a conversation about framing and double-hung glass.

When everyone had finished eating, Christmas and Rory cleared the table. Christmas dumped the coffee grounds into a small bin on the counter.

"Is that for the compost?" Rory asked.

"Yeah," Christmas said. "I forced my parents to start doing it a few months ago, and honestly, it's so easy. Do you guys compost?"

"No," Rory said. "But maybe we should. You just keep this container on the counter?" Rory reached forward to flick open the lid of the square plastic box. The lid, looser than it seemed, flew up with just the gentlest touch and knocked into a row of pill bottles lined up on a shelf to the right of the sink. Like dominoes or bowling pins, the pill bottles crashed down. While Christmas's mother's vitamins and her father's blood pressure meds landed on the counter, Christmas's ADHD pills did not fare as well. Christmas had not secured the childproof cap, instead leaving the lid sort of balanced on top—a very ADHD thing to do, Christmas knew—and the entire open bottle of pills landed in the sink, which was half full of soapy dishes.

"I'm so sorry!" Rory declared. "I'm such a klutz!"

"Oh, it's no big deal," Christmas said, as she fished around in the soapy water. She found the bottle, but the gel caps were already melting. Although it felt strange to do so, Christmas tossed the whole mess in the trash.

"Shoot. Are those your pills? Don't you need those?" Rory asked.

"It's really okay," Christmas said. She did need them, of course, and she experienced a little sinking in her stomach. She didn't want Rory to feel bad, though, and it would be easy to replace them. She forced a smile and shook her head. "I'll call the pharmacy for a refill tomorrow. I've never lost a bottle before—I'm sure it will be fine."

32

ALTHOUGH NAOMI WAS MORE THAN CAPABLE of holding up both ends of any conversation, her discussion with Christmas's dad naturally wound down, at which point she rose and, effusive as ever, thanked Christmas and her father as she headed toward the door.

"Do you want to hang out here a little longer?" Christmas asked Rory, feeling suddenly shy.

"Yeah," he said, right away. "Yeah. We could . . . watch a movie. Or work on the puzzle?" He cut a glance at Christmas's father.

"You can have my spot," Christmas's father assured him. "I'm not sure I was able to contribute much anyway."

Naomi departed and Christmas's dad adjourned to the living room to finish watching his baseball game. Rory and Christmas worked on the puzzle and talked. They made great progress, although Christmas's neck started to get stiff from bending over the table. "Want to take a break?" she asked. "Walk down to the lake?"

Rory and Christmas let themselves out the sliding door and onto the back lawn into the cool night. Christmas inhaled deeply, enjoying the thick, earthy smell of the lake. Rory reached out and took her hand.

"Is this okay?" he asked.

"Yeah," she said. "It is."

At the dock, he pulled her toward him. "Is this okay?"

"Yeah," she said. She raised his face to his. "You clearly took the sex-ed consent-training class very seriously."

"I got an A," he said, smiling. "Can I kiss you?"

"Let me think about that one," Christmas said, bringing her face close to his. She waited a beat. "Yes."

She did think, for a moment, about Cash, about the kiss the night before, but it was easy to push that from her mind, with her hands on Rory's shoulders and his arms around her waist.

When they finally returned to the house, the baseball game had ended and Christmas's dad had gone to bed, although, Christmas noted, her mother wasn't home from her "book club." They put something on the television, though they didn't watch it, and it was well after midnight when Rory finally, regretfully, sleepily, left, giving Christmas one last kiss as she held the door open between them, saying, "Can we hang out again tomorrow?"

"Yes, please," she said, leaning in for another last kiss.

He smiled and kissed her back. "Text me in the morning?"

"Perfect," she murmured into his lips.

The moment was interrupted by a blast of headlights as a car pulled into the driveway. Christmas stiffened, and the magic dissipated. Rory looked at Christmas, confused, and maybe a little alarmed.

"It's just my mom," Christmas said.

"Should I stay and meet her?"

Christmas wrinkled her nose and shook her head. "That's okay. You should go. But be careful. The roads are dark."

He nodded then smiled and sauntered off into the night.

Christmas turned and moved swiftly away from the door. She knew her mother had seen her, but she didn't want to talk to her.

She felt ashamed, somehow, to know her mother was coming home so late. And, she realized as she practically ran up the stairs to her room, if she were being honest, she didn't want to know if her mother had been up late discussing the great American novel or sucking down vodka tonics. Regardless of what her father thought, she knew which choice was more likely.

33

O N AUTOPILOT, CHRISTMAS WENT TO TAKE her pill in the morning, only to remember, her hand held aloft at the windowsill, that the bottle had been dumped. Though she'd gotten up later than usual, it was too early to call the doctor, so she resolved to run extra hard, to shake off the anxiety about the pills, about her mom, about Lexi and Lemy and Cash and Owen. She'd get her pills later. She looked longingly at the unfinished puzzle, laced up her sneakers, grabbed her pepper spray, and went out.

The morning mist lingered near the ground, not yet having been burned off by the sun. As usual, she got lost in the run and was feeling pretty good by the time she arrived back home, to find her father drinking his coffee, looming over the ragged-looking puzzle. "Surprised to see you didn't finish this up last night," her father said. "Suppose you were distracted." Christmas saw a teasing a smile in his eyes.

Not sure how to respond, Christmas made a face and turned to pour herself some coffee. Again, her eye went to the windowsill where her pills usually waited.

"Mom sleeping?"

Her father grunted his assent and Christmas unlocked her phone. She pulled up the number of her doctor's office, which, thankfully, had Sunday hours. When Adrienne, the receptionist, answered, Christmas explained that she'd knocked ADHD meds into the sink and that she needed a refill.

Adrienne tsked and then said, "Can't you take one of your mother's?" When Christmas paused, her voice caught in her throat, Adrienne continued, "I suppose that's against the rules. I'll speak to Dr. Gerber, and we'll call that prescription in for you right away. Just hold on a minute, hon."

"Thanks, Adrienne," Christmas croaked.

She caught her father watching her.

"Will Adrienne call in the prescription?" he asked. He kept his face pointed at the puzzle on the table.

"Um, yeah," Christmas said, unwilling to tell her father what Adrienne had said about taking one of her mother's. Did her mother have a Ritalin prescription? Did her mother have ADHD? Since when?

Adrienne returned to the line. "Christmas? Dr. Gerber says you have to come see him before he'll give you another refill. He said this is the second time this month and he wants to talk to you about being more responsible with your pills—and possibly upping your dosage if you're having such a hard time keeping track of them."

"Second time this month?" Christmas repeated. Her father met her eye.

"Yes, your mother had that replacement called in on Friday, hon." She paused to read something. "I have you down to come in and see him on Tuesday at ten."

"But I don't have any pills at all," Christmas insisted. "I don't know if I can wait . . ."

"I'm sorry, but it's not up to me." She paused, probably reading from a screen. "You're fine with your other prescriptions, right? It's just this one you'll have to wait on?"

Christmas opened her mouth to respond.

Other prescriptions?

Gerber had once given her a scrip for Xanax, but Christmas had never filled it.

"Okay. Um, thanks?" was all she could muster before ending the call.

Christmas's hands shook.

Was it withdrawal already? Or was it low blood sugar because she still hadn't eaten anything? Or was it, perhaps, that she knew, with one-hundred-percent certainty, that she had not lost her pills last week, and that her mother had just gotten a refill at the Walmart on Friday?

"What'd they say?" her father asked, trying, and failing, to act casual.

Christmas stared at him. She was blinking, hard, and she rolled her neck. "Um, I have to go see Dr. Gerber," she said. "Dad, is Mom . . ."

"What?"

"Has she been taking my pills?"

"Your Ritalin?"

"Yeah and . . ." Christmas opened and closed her mouth, unable to complete the thought.

Her father looked at her steadily. "Not that I know of."

"That's not an answer," Christmas said. She was about to say more, to tell her father she was sick of the secrets, when the doorbell rang.

Christmas jumped as though she'd been shot through with an electric shock.

Something bad is happening, she thought.

"What on earth?" her father said. "Is it your friends again?"

Before going to the door, Christmas glanced out the kitchen window and saw a police cruiser parked in the driveway.

"It's the cops," she told her father. "Maybe they have news about Lemy."

Her phone buzzed on the kitchen table.

She grabbed it and headed to the front hall and, before she pulled the door open, she glanced down. It was text from Curly.

I need to talk to you. Lemy woke up.

Christmas rolled her neck. Good news, then. She was overacting. She was freaking out because she didn't have her pills and because, yes, something was going on with her mother, but Lemy had woken up and she felt sure that that was what the police were here to tell her.

She threw the door open.

"Hey," she said to the dour-faced Ben and unreadable Officer Schaefer. "I just got a text from Curly." She pushed open the screen door and the officers, nodding their greeting, stepped inside. She added, "He said Lemy woke up. He's okay?"

"Is your mother at home?" Ben asked.

Christmas's father's voice came from over her shoulder. "She's still in bed. What's this about?"

"Would you mind going to get her, please, Mr. Miller?" Officer Schaefer said.

"All right," Christmas's father said. "I suppose. What's this—"

"We'd like to speak to your wife," Officer Schaefer said firmly.

"What's going on?" Christmas asked as her father stomped up the stairs. Her mother always complained about how loud he was, how he marched around the house as though he was trying to break through the floorboards.

"We need to talk to your mom," Ben said kindly. Officer Schaefer, for her part, stared at a place just above Christmas's head, refusing to make eye contact.

Christmas stood then, waiting, listening to her parent's murmured voices from upstairs. Finally, they came down and into the hallway, her mother disheveled and acting a little spacey, in her pajama pants and New Paltz T-shirt.

"Mrs. Miller," Officer Schaefer said, her eyes flicking back into focus. "Let's get some shoes on. We've got some questions for you—we'd like to take you over to the station with us."

"What?" Christmas said pitching her voice over the officer's. "Why are you taking her to the station?"

Officer Schaefer spoke only to Christmas's mother, whose face was blank and drawn, like the lake in the early morning. She swayed a little and then moved toward the Crocs by the front door and stepped into them.

"Ben, what is going on?" Christmas demanded, whirling to look at him. "You can't just take her. Is she under arrest?"

This last question hung in the air for a moment.

"She's not going anywhere," Christmas's father said. "What's this about anyway?"

Ben pressed his lips into a thin line and, turning to Christmas's mother, said, "Mrs. Miller, let's talk about this at the station."

"I did it," Christmas's mother said, her voice flat, her face still blank. "This is about Lemy? It was me."

"What are you talking about?" Christmas demanded. She saw Ben and Officer Schaefer exchange a glance. "That's ridiculous. You had nothing to do with . . . It was Mr. Cunningham. Or Cash. Or Owen. Or somebody else."

Christmas's mother stood, blinking, as though trying to focus. "It was me," she said again.

"Mrs. Miller, I'm putting you under arrest now," Ben said. "You have the right to remain silent . . ."

"No," Christmas cried, shouting over him.

Officer Schaefer put a hand on Christmas's arm as Ben continued intoning the Miranda Rights. "I know this is hard, but you need to let us do our job."

She shook off the cop's hand, while her father, who'd stepped closer to position himself between his wife and the door, bellowed, "Don't say anything else, Allie!"

Her mother had turned to let Ben place the plastic handcuffs on her wrists. When she turned back around, Christmas saw that she had her eyes closed.

"Mom," Christmas said. "Mommy."

There was shuffling and repositioning—Christmas's father was jostled out of the way and Officer Schaefer held open the screen door.

"Don't say another word," Christmas's father said as they led her mother out and down the front step.

And then they were gone.

34

CHRISTMAS STUMBLED THROUGH THE NEXT FEW MOMENTS. Her father claimed to have no more information. He was distant, as though he were already gone, his mind in the police cruiser, in the jail, with Christmas's mother, as he collected his phone, his wallet, his keys. He wouldn't meet Christmas's eye and would only say that he was going down to try and see about bail. He said he would find a lawyer. He told Christmas that no, he didn't want her coming with him and that yes, he would call as soon as he knew anything at all.

And then he was gone, too, and Christmas stood alone in the quiet house.

The tears came fast and hot, and she sat at the table, sobbing into her arms. After a while, she forced herself to take deep breaths, to calm down, to think. She got up and had a glass of water. She stood, listening to the sounds under the silence, the buzzing of the kitchen lights, the water tank in the basement refilling.

Outside, birds chirped and a truck barreled, too fast, down the two-lane road. Someone started a lawn mower. How could it be that life was continuing on out there? In the quiet kitchen, it seemed to her that the world had come to a halt. She needed her meds. This situation was beyond what she could handle. But there was nothing she could do about that.

Unless, of course, her mother had a stash.

Christmas began a feverish, frantic hunt. First she checked the usual hiding spots, where, years ago Christmas had found the tiny plastic liquor bottles that her mother called nips: between the couch cushions, in her mother's purse, on the highest kitchen shelf.

When none of these places yielded anything of interest, Christmas bounded up the stairs to her parents' room and with renewed determination began searching methodically, looking in each drawer of the bedside table, and then under the mattress. She picked up each shoe in the closet and tossed folded sweaters on the floor. She stuck a finger into the pockets of each dress and jacket. Nothing.

And then she found it.

A tote bag hung behind a winter coat on a hook in the back of the closet. Christmas took it out, opened it, and found two dozen pill bottles, many of them empty. She tossed them on the bed and looked at each one. The labels identified them as having contained Xanax, Ritalin, Valium, clonazepam, and oxycodone. Some of them had Christmas's name on them, and some had her mother's. The oxycodone were all in Allie's name.

She knew that her mother had a prescription for this painkiller after her car crash. It was famously, horrendously addictive. Christmas marveled that any doctor would prescribe oxy to someone who'd just been in a drunk-driving accident. And yet someone had. And her mother must have gotten hooked.

It made sense and, like watching a mystery film for the second time, all the clues seemed so obvious. The shuffling walk and slurred speech and glassy eyes. The sleepy smile, the disconnection that Christmas often mistook for a chill attitude. All along, Christmas had been searching for signs of booze and missing the evidence right in front of her.

Despite the spread on the bed before her, Christmas couldn't find any Ritalin pills. She opened a bottle of Xanax and slid out one small, football-shaped pill. It wasn't what she wanted, but it would probably help her to calm down, stop the buzzing in her brain and the shaking in her hands.

She could probably take two or three pills and spend the rest of the day in bed, drifting in and out of consciousness of the problems, the disasters, the messes that she felt she was suffocating under. Ten, eleven pills and who knows; she might not have to ever wake up again at all.

She shook her head as though to clear it. She put the pill back in the bottle. She put the bottles back in the tote. She would figure out what to do with her mother's stash later.

For now, she sat on her parents' bed. She put her face in her mother's pillow, which still held her warmth and her familiar smell.

The buzzing of her phone sent her sitting upright again, right back into panic mode. Rory was texting. He wanted to know what time they were meeting up.

Christmas's breath came in shallow gasps as she tried to think of what to text back. She didn't think she could bear to talk to him, to hear the sadness and confusion and pity in his voice.

She couldn't tell Rory that her mother had been arrested because it would simply confirm for Rory that Christmas and her family were trash, that they were the type of people who were addicted to pills and had drunk-driving accidents and got arrested for beating other people up. That his *Deliverance* joke had been right on, not an offensive stereotype.

Although her mother had not done it, Christmas assured herself. This was all just a misunderstanding. She could explain it to Rory once everything was cleared up.

With trembling hands, she wrote:

I'm so sorry, but something came up. Can I call you tomorrow?

She watched the three dots on his phone.

of course. u okay?

She hated to lie him. But she hated telling the truth even more.

Everything's fine. I'll catch you tomorrow.

She sent a fraudulent kissy face. Was it too much? Maybe. But she couldn't deal with him now. It would be easier to explain everything to him, she again reasoned, when this whole mess was sorted out. Unless it didn't get sorted. Unless it never got sorted. Because her mother had clearly said she'd done it.

She couldn't have, though. Christmas remembered the conversation they'd had in the kitchen, the way her mother hadn't quite denied her involvement, but how she'd pointed out the unlikelihood. "I'm almost sixty years old," she'd said.

Christmas considered calling Curly. He had probably wanted to warn her when he'd called earlier. And she knew she could ask him what, exactly, Lemy had said when he'd woken up. But she couldn't bring herself to do it. How could she even start the conversation? "Hey! I heard they arrested my mother for almost killing your husband. What's up with that?"

She felt the shame like a swallowed pit, deep in her stomach.

She leaped from the bed, suddenly claustrophobic in her parents' stuffy bedroom. She ran down the stairs and out of the house, clutching her phone.

She thought it would be better to be outside, but the air was heavy and she felt as though she could get no relief from the heat, the humidity. She went back indoors just as a downpour began dramatically, huge drops splashing to the ground.

Christmas paced the rooms, checking her phone, rolling her neck, reviewing what she knew—and what she didn't. At last, her father called. He was coming home, he said. There would be no arraignment until Monday. Her mother would be staying in jail overnight.

He told Christmas that he planned to go in for his shift at Home Depot that afternoon. She opened her mouth to protest, but snapped it shut again as she realized, with a sinking stomach, that they probably needed the money. They couldn't afford for him to take the day off, especially if they were going to hire a lawyer.

Overwhelmed with dread, she continued to walk the rooms, phone in one hand, the other hand raised to her head, where she ran a finger over a dry spot on her scalp. She stopped pacing in front of the patio doors and stared at the rain-streaked glass, picking at her skin and thinking. When she finally pulled her hand away from her head, it was bloody. She wiped her index finger on her thigh but allowed her hand to return to the now painful spot on her scalp.

She needed something to do. But what? What on earth could she possibly to do help her mother?

At least they owned the house. Maybe they could take out money that way, she thought. A reverse mortgage. Would it be enough? How did something like that even work?

If she could figure it out, they could go to the bank first thing in the morning. Get the process started right away.

She pulled up Zillow on her phone to get an estimate, a ballpark idea of what they would be working with. She was optimistic; the house itself wasn't much, but the lakefront probably increased its value.

She blinked hard, several times, as she stared at the information on her screen. Absurdly, she refreshed the page, assuming she was reading wrong, or that they'd attached the wrong address to a picture of her house. A grainy image of their blue two-story, Christmas's bike sprawled like something dead on the front lawn, the lake just a sliver of gray in the background, with the word SOLD in red block letters stamped across it. It was like seeing her own face on a milk carton.

Christmas's vision blurred. She thought she might be sick.

Christmas read that the house had been sold in May. Their house. The house her father had inherited from his own parents.

It didn't say who had bought the house.

She turned away from the glass doors and to the lake and cast her eyes around her, desperate to quell the panic rising in her chest and threatening to take over. She tried to take seven deep breaths—a technique her old therapist had introduced—but each inhale was increasingly shallow, each exhale filled with a sob. She tried to list every book she'd read recently. She tried to notice three red things in the room. She tried again to breathe. Afraid she would pass out, she stumbled to the sofa, where she sat and put her head between her knees.

There was nothing to do, it would seem, but surrender.

35

WATCHING OUT THE KITCHEN WINDOW, Christmas saw her father pull into the driveway. It was hard to believe her mom had been arrested just that morning.

She remembered telling Naomi that being off her medicine made her feel like she had an emotional sunburn. She didn't know if it was the lack of medicine or the entire situation, but she definitely felt as though the presence of another person right now would be sandpaper on raw skin. She couldn't bear to see her father, or anyone at all.

She slipped on her flip-flops and fled downstairs. She needed to leave, to get out of the house, but she had nowhere to go, no one to go to.

There was one place.

And one person.

Slowly, she slid open the glass doors and slipped outside.

She unlocked her phone, and texted Lexi.

Hi. Can you meet me at the tree house? ASAP? Please?

Lexi texted back almost right away.

K

Christmas had to put her hand over her mouth to squelch her sigh of relief. She closed her eyes, took a deep breath, and began to cross the wet lawn, her flip-flops making a sucking sound and spraying water with each step.

The ground was a bit dryer in the small woods next to the house, and she crunched over the soggy leaves, watching for sharp sticks or rocks that might poke her exposed feet. She worried that the rope ladder to the tree house her father had built over a decade ago might have disintegrated or become unusable, but she again sighed with relief when she arrived to find it intact. She was still in her running clothes, complete with a fanny pack with her Mace; she put her phone in the pack so her hands would be free to climb the ladder.

Her head cleared the platform and then Christmas climbed on all fours into the small, dark space. She inhaled deeply, loving the smell of the damp leaves and wet wood. She lifted a small vase full of dried flowers, but all the petals immediately fell away, scattering onto the floorboards. She looked around. They'd also left a blanket—now covered in nuts and branches, probably a mouse's winter home—a rotary phone, some waterlogged paperbacks, an eagle feather. She pictured them in an earlier summer, so certain they'd be back the next day, and then not coming. Not for years. Not until now.

Lexi's head appeared and then she, too, was pulling herself up and sitting on the tree house floor. "You beat me here," she said, blandly. She cast her eyes around before letting them rest on Christmas. She grimaced. "You don't look so good. What's wrong?"

Christmas shook her head, at a loss as to where to begin.

"Since I last saw you," Christmas said, "my life basically imploded." She sniffed. "You're the only one I want to talk about it with. I kind of need my friend back." Christmas realized she was still holding the tiny vase and put it back down. "But first I need to say: I'm sorry."

Lexi nodded, her face serious and still.

Christmas's hand went up to her scalp, her fingers seeking the spot she'd been worrying, and Lexi reached out to push Christmas's hand away and then, once it was lowered, continued holding it.

Lexi gently squeezed Christmas's hand, a small gesture that gave her the courage to continue. "I know I pissed you off and I think I know why." Christmas met her friend's eye. "We don't have to talk about anything you don't want to. But I swear to God, I never intended to hurt you. And I'm also really sorry about all that stuff I said about your mom. And your dad."

Lexi broke eye contact. She let go of Christmas's hand and picked up an acorn, rolled it between her fingers. "I'm sorry too," she said. "I'm sorry I froze you out. And I also said some really mean things. It wasn't all your fault."

Christmas felt an upswell of gratitude so intense it made her slightly dizzy. Everything wasn't fixed, but Lexi was there, had come, was speaking to her. Christmas felt as though she'd been wearing an anchor around her neck that she hadn't even known about until now, as it lifted away. "And yeah," Lexi said. "Martha's my girlfriend." Lexi looked out the tree house window, just a little square cut into the wood boards that made up the walls. She tossed the acorn through the hole. "I'm a lesbian," she said, raising her eyebrows and shaking her head with mock gravity. "I've known since . . . well, looking back, I guess I've known a long time." She shrugged. "I used to think I liked boys too, but then when I met Martha . . ." She nodded, grinning. "That was when I *knew knew*."

Christmas felt her cheeks going red, not with embarrassment, but with shame. Lexi had chosen not to tell her because she thought Christmas would be weird about it. And she hadn't been completely wrong. "I'm sorry you didn't think you could tell me," she said softly.

Lexi swallowed. "I was afraid . . . not that you'd be homophobic. Not that exactly. Like, despite the whole f-word fiasco, I don't think you hate gay people. But you're . . . I was afraid you'd be not cool about it. Or that you'd be dismissive. Like you'd say it was just a stage or I was just doing it for attention."

"I would never say that."

Lexi shrugged. "I mean, you kind of did. That first night. Maybe not specifically, but still. That's how I took it. And it would have been unbearable if I told you and you didn't believe me or accept me." Lexi's face creased with pain. "Telling you was high on my personal to-do list. But then you laughed when we talked about how that guy called Lemy a fag. I couldn't believe it. It was like . . ."

"I didn't really," Christmas protested weakly.

"You did," Lexi insisted. "You laughed and then you made excuses. And then later, you made some remark about Martha being my girlfriend. I felt like you were trolling me or something. Like it seemed almost impossible that you'd be so obtuse. But the alternative? That you were . . . well, I hate to say it, but that you think being gay is a punchline or worse."

"I don't," Christmas said. "I really don't. Honestly, I think I did know," Christmas confessed. "Not totally consciously. But on some level, I was jealous. Not because I . . ." Christmas forced herself to finish the sentence, "not because I want to be your girlfriend or like you like that. It was just hard to hear about some other person— some other friend—you were so crazy about. I know it's dumb."

Lexi paused to consider. "I guess I would be jealous too if there was some girl you talked about all the time." She smiled wryly. "It's easier for me because everyone here sucks, so I don't have a lot of competition." The smile fell from Lexi's face. "I'm sorry. I didn't mean that. It just popped out. Old habits? I don't hate it here, Christmas. I really don't."

"But this summer—did you not want to come?" Christmas asked. "Did your grandparents really threaten to take your mom to court?"

Lexi nodded. "Yeah. But that only happened after that night . . . the night we found Lemy. I was so mad at you, and freaked out too, so the next morning I called my mom and told her I needed her to pick me up. But then there was a big fight between my grandparents and my mom, and they threatened to take her to court. I kinda took it out of context to . . . well, throw it in your face and make you feel bad. But the truth is: I didn't want to be here without you. The best part of being here isn't the lake or waterskiing. It's being with my best friend. The best part of Sweet Lake is you, Christmas. Aww, Chrissy," Lexi said, pulling her friend into her arms. "Don't cry."

"Please forgive me," Christmas said. She squeezed her friend tighter, Lexi's sweet-smelling curls tickling her cheeks.

"Of course," Lexi said. She released her hold and Christmas wiped roughly at her face.

Lexi continued, "I still think we're gonna need to talk some more about it. But—maybe not today? I want to know what's going on."

A light tapping on the roof: the fickle rain was back. But the noise was comforting, making Christmas feel safe, protected with her friend in their tree house. She took a deep breath and exhaled slowly.

"My mother was arrested. For attacking Lemy."

Lexi's mouth dropped open in disbelief.

"I have no idea what is going on with her," Christmas continued. "I found pills in her room. Oxy, Xanax, Valium. Ritalin too. Maybe she's selling them? Or trading them. I think she's probably addicted to the oxy. Or something. And my dad got a job at the Home Depot, which at the time didn't seem strange, but now I realize . . . obviously they are having money problems. I just found out that our house was sold in May." Christmas shook her head, still too shocked to truly understand what she was saying. "There have been so many lies, Lex. I don't even know anything anymore."

Lexi shook her head. "I can't believe this."

"I can't either. And, oh," Christmas said, closing her eyes for a long time before continuing. "The cherry on top is that I am out of my Ritalin with no refills in the near future." She tried to smile. "It's like the joke from that old *Airplane* movie: 'Looks like I chose the wrong week to quit smoking.'"

"Jesus Christ," Lexi said. Christmas found her shock comforting. It was truly absurd, Christmas assured herself. The situation was out-of-control, ridiculous, and terrible. She wasn't imagining it.

"Are you feeling okay?" Lexi asked. "Are you in withdrawal?"

"I feel bad: shaky and unfocused and emotional. But that's probably just situational," Christmas said, more reasonably than she felt. "I think it might even be too early for real withdrawal."

"Oh, Chrissy," Lexi said. "I'm so sorry. We're going to deal with this, though. We're gonna find our way through. Together."

36

LEXI, A PROBLEM-SOLVER, WANTED TO KNOW what they could or should do next, but Christmas said that all she wanted to do was to hide, to retreat to Lexi's bedroom and lie low. Lexi obliged, hustling Christmas into the Hansens' house as though she were a paparazzi-stalked celebrity, depositing her in the bedroom before returning downstairs to gather enough snacks to see them through the evening. Christmas texted her dad that she'd be staying at Lexi's. He didn't text back.

It was only then, sitting shoulder-to-shoulder on Lexi's twin bed eating pretzels out of the bag, that Christmas could allow herself to be distracted, to talk to Lexi about Rory, to fill her in on all the details she been dying to share with her friend. It was a relief to focus on something other than her mother in a jail cell, although Christmas never really forgot about it, the knowledge buzzing in her brain like a looming headache promising to blossom fully later.

Christmas recounted her first meeting with Rory, and their bike ride, and their swim, and Lexi told Christmas about Martha, showing Christmas all of Martha's wildly creative Instagram posts of her original collages, her bizarre and funny performance-art TikToks.

"Are you in love?" Christmas asked.

"Yes," Lexi said, smiling and staring at an image of Martha dressed in a Princess Leia costume. "Are you?"

"Maybe," Christmas said. "Being with him makes me feel . . . you know how some farmers keep a goat with their horses? The right goat can make the horses feel calm."

"So you're saying he's your goat?"

Christmas chuckled. "I guess so."

"It's good to find your goat," Lexi said.

"Yeah. But."

"But what?"

"Rory is so accepting and cool, but I feel like this stuff that's happening with my mom . . . I'm too ashamed to tell him. And what if he can't handle it? Because . . ."

Christmas didn't finish the thought.

Lexi pursed her lips. "Is this a Rory problem or a Christmas problem?" When Christmas didn't answer, Lexi shifted in her seat. "What I mean is: why don't you let him decide what he can handle?"

"You're right." Christmas ate a pretzel. She may not be in withdrawal yet, but she was hungrier than she remembered being in a long time. "Although to be honest, Lexi, I don't know if *I* can handle this."

Lexi grabbed a handful of pretzels. "It's too much for one person to have to deal with alone," she agreed. "So it's a good thing you've got me."

Christmas put her head on her friend's shoulder and Lexi patted her leg. After a moment, Christmas sat up and said, "I'm so pissed at my mom. I don't mean to be a selfish jerk. I know she 'struggles' or whatever. But her and my dad—for real. They lost our house? What is wrong with them? And, again, I feel like jerk saying this out loud, and I would only say it to you, but there is no way I can afford to buy a car and pay my tuition in the fall without their help. So now

I can't go to college. I'm gonna have to get a full-time job. Which is fine, but—"

"No, Christmas. That is not an option. Take that right off the table."

"My parents can't afford our house, Lexi," Christmas replied. "They definitely can't afford to help me with tuition. Even if it's only community college, I can't ask them to pay for it."

Lexi nodded. "You have to at least go to school part-time."

"I don't know," Christmas said. "I kinda feel like giving up."

"And no one would blame you," Lexi said. "But that's not who you are. I don't really think you have it in you to quit."

Christmas tried to smile. "Rory said I'm a fighter."

"Smart goat," Lexi said.

Though Christmas felt exhausted—emotionally and physically —she did want to fight. But she didn't know who or how. All she could envision, perhaps too clearly, were the coming months of court dates and fees, of loans and debt. Any income she and her dad could bring in wouldn't come close to paying the bills. She imagined them renting an apartment, eating reheated dinners silently or separately, him on the couch, her at the table. She imagined new people in their house: summer people who would probably just tear it all down, put up something modern and shimmering in its place. Stupid summer people.

She thought of how disappointed those summer people would be once they saw that without Christmas raking every day (ha ha), the algae in the lake would grow uncontrollable. What was it Mr. Cunningham had said? That the whole damn thing was poisoned?

And what was it that Mr. Ford had responded? Might as well fill the whole thing in.

She could see him doing it, too, and convincing everyone how much better off they all were. He'd probably turn Sweet Lake into a parking lot.

She thought of the last time she had seen him. Had he been carrying blueprints?

"It's the Fords," she said aloud to Lexi. "I don't exactly know what he's up to, Mr. Ford. But I bet he's the one who bought our house. He tried to buy Rory's house. And I bet he has something to do with my mother too."

"What do you want to do?" Lexi asked warily.

Instead of answering, Christmas looked at her phone. She had Cash's number from that day in the Emporium.

He'd listed himself as "Hottest Guy in the world a.k.a. Cash."

She texted.

I need to talk to you.

37

ASH TEXTED BACK ALMOST INSTANTLY.

i knew u would come around, but i dont feel like jetskiing right now lol.

Christmas wrote: *Did you know that your father bought my house?*

Christmas and Lexi waited, watching the three dots and then reading the rambling words.

lol no i bought ur house

maybe ill still let u live there but we are def subbdividing so maybe well just give you an apartment. anyway sry about ur mom.

Christmas, her vision blurring, pulled herself together enough to write back.

What do you know about my mom?

Cash: *shell be fine.*

Christmas's heart was beating fast. She wasn't sure if she was angry or nervous or even sort of excited.

Why was she arrested? She didn't hurt Lemy.

There was a long pause and Christmas was afraid that Cash wouldn't respond. Then, finally:

Ur mom arrested cause lemy woke up and told the police it was her

Christmas blinked and looked at Lexi beside her.

"What the?" Lexi said.

Christmas wrote: *That can't be true.*

Cash: *believe what u want but im not texting anymore u want to talk come over*

Before Christmas could answer, Lexi said, "No. You are not—we are not—going to his house."

"What should I write back?"

"Write back *no,*" Lexi said.

Christmas bit her lip and thought about it. "Cash is crazy. And kind of an asshole. But—I don't know. I trust him. I feel like—I almost feel like he's been waiting for this. Waiting for me to know about my house, to ask him about my mom. To figure this out."

"I don't think you should go over there," Lexi said. "Apparently he owns your house? So he probably thinks that gives him some sort of power over you. But it doesn't. There's no mystery here. Mr. Ford took advantage of your parents and now Cash is trying to . . . I don't even know."

"There's more to it," Christmas said. "Why does Mr. Ford even want my house? Does my mom owe him money or something? And why did my mother confess?"

Lexi pursed her lips and nodded as the connections began to snap into place.

"You think Mr. Ford is dealing pills? Do you think he's the one who attacked Lemy?"

Christmas shrugged. "I don't know. But I bet Cash does."

Christmas's phone buzzed in her hand.

u coming over or what

"Lexi," Christmas said. "I kind of made out with Cash at the prom. And then again, recently. I mean, he kissed me and I guess I kissed him back."

Lexi's mouth dropped open and she did a full-body shudder.

"Yes, I know," Christmas said.

"I think I need a shower," Lexi said. "And maybe you do too."

"He's not that bad," Christmas said. "I mean, he is that bad. But I don't think he'd hurt me. I really don't. Honestly, I think he kind of likes me."

"Christmas," Lexi said warningly.

Christmas texted back. *I'm with Lexi. We'll come over.*

Cash: *Just u*

When she didn't respond right away, he continued.

I'm not gonna like rape u but I have some answers or whatever not for summer people.

"Honestly, I think it's even creepier that it occurred to him to say he was *not* going to rape you," Lexi said.

Christmas sighed. "I'll have my phone. And I have my Mace." She went to Lexi's dresser and took the black cylinder out of her fanny pack and slid it into the pocket of the sweatpants she'd borrowed from Lexi when the evening had turned chilly. "And if you don't hear from me in half an hour—get Rory and come to Cash's."

"You're not really doing this?"

"I have to find out what he knows."

"My bike has a flat tire," Lexi said, clearly a last-ditch effort to delay the outing. "His house is on the other side of the lake and it's getting dark. Can't this wait?"

"Take me over in the speedboat?"

Lexi shut her eyes and groaned. "All right," she said at last. "At least that way I can wait nearby."

"Okay," Christmas said, reassuring both herself and Lexi.

38

THEY SLICED ACROSS THE LAKE, the gray water reflecting the gray sky, the air still thick, smelling like the rain. Lexi stood to steer, and she looked beautiful and strong, her hair blowing back in the wind, her head held high. Christmas felt small and awkward crouched beside her, her own stringy, wispy hair tickling her cheeks.

They pulled up close to the Fords' creaking dock, a heap of metal and wood that had seen better days. It was incongruous with the recently renovated four-story glass-fronted house looming above.

Lexi maneuvered the boat so that it was perpendicular to the dock and Christmas could disembark. She looped a rope around one of the metal poles. "I'll be waiting right here."

Christmas climbed out of the boat and walked up the dock. The frogs on the shore, clamorous a moment before, fell silent with her approach. She planned to jog up the sloping backyard and to the front of the house, but Cash must have been waiting. His head appeared over the railing of the back deck. Even from a distance and in the dying light, she could see he had a painful-looking black eye.

"Hey," he called down.

"Hey."

"I told you to come alone," Cash said, pointing at Lexi. "She can't park there."

"Whatever!" Lexi shouted back. "I'll just idle five feet out, asshole."

"Lexi," Christmas said, stopping and turning back to face her friend. Loud enough for Cash to hear, she said, "It's okay. I've known Cash since we were kids. You go home. I'll call you and let you know when to pick me up."

"No. I'll take you," Cash yelled down to them. "Right, Chrissy? I'll take you home on my Jet Ski."

Christmas waved at Lexi, letting her know she should go. Lexi, annoyed, shook her head, pulled the rope from the pole, started the engine, and began to back the boat away.

Christmas turned and continued up the dock and then to the deck stairs. She thought they'd be going into the house, but Cash, who she saw also had a nasty swollen lip, gestured to the walkway that led to the front. "I have something to show you over in the shop," he explained. "We'll cut across here."

Christmas followed Cash out to the street and down the road about twenty feet to the Fords' service station.

"So why aren't you with the boyfriend tonight? Did you let him take a dip in the lake and now he's all done with you?" he asked, smirking. She noted his knuckles were red and raw as he unlocked and pulled open the side door.

"What is your problem?" Christmas said as she followed him into the dark garage. "Why do you have to be so disgusting all the time?"

"Why do you have to be so uptight all the time?" Cash returned, though he said it without venom.

They were just rehearsing the same old scene, Christmas thought.

Cash flipped on some lights, which blinked and buzzed above them. "Honestly, I'm just looking out for you," Cash said. "You know how summer people are. Don't want to see you get hurt."

"Whatever, Cash. I'm not here to hang out with you. Why is my mother sitting in a jail cell?"

Cash brought Christmas to the back of the garage, where a metal desk and a mini fridge stood. He took out two beers and handed one to Christmas, who immediately put hers down on a nearby shelf of tools. He popped open his own can.

"I'm gonna need your phone," he said.

"Um, no," Christmas said.

"I need make sure you're not recording me."

Christmas paused, frowned, and took the phone from her pocket. She looked at it to unlock it and handed it to Cash. He checked it and then laid it facedown on the desk.

"I used to think it was an act, but you're really like this?" he asked, not unkindly. He pulled a pack of cigarettes from his back pocket and sat down. "You're so smart in school, but you're not very observant about other things, are you?"

Christmas huffed, impatient. "Will you get on with it?"

"Go ahead and sit down," Cash instructed. When Christmas took the seat across from him, he continued. "Lemy's the one who fingered your mother. No pun intended."

Christmas didn't bother to scowl, and Cash added, "He woke up, and the last thing he remembered was getting in the car with your mom."

Christmas shook her head. "My mother wouldn't—she couldn't—have hurt Lemy."

Cash shrugged. "She'd already agreed to take the fall anyway. Thanks to the fuss you've been kicking up, the heat was on about this Lemy thing. And, as you discovered with your crack-investigation skills, Scooby-Doo, your parents are in the hole, big time. So a mutually beneficial arrangement was made: She confesses, mystery solved, and maybe you guys can keep on living in your house. At least for now."

"Okay, evil genius," Christmas said contemptuously. "So, what is it then? My mother gets drugs from your dad? Is that why she agreed to this?"

Cash shrugged. "Your mom's a nice lady. And she doesn't do meth, if that's what you're worried about," he said. It had not occurred to Christmas to worry that her mother was doing meth. She leaned forward, listening hard. "But, yeah. She does have a thing for pills. She had a legit prescription—from her accident—but with that stuff, you always need more and more. So, my dad helps her out and she helps him out." He lit a cigarette. "You know she's, like, in love with him."

"No," Christmas said, narrowing her eyes. "That's not true." She shook her head, as though to clear it as Cash ashed and shrugged again, almost apologetic.

"Fine," Cash conceded. "Maybe it's just the drugs. But you should see how she acts around him. Like he's this amazing guy or something. He eats it up, obviously."

Christmas tried to process what he was telling her. Was her mother having an affair with Bill Ford? She truly could not imagine such a thing. Perhaps, she thought wryly, she didn't have as good an imagination as she'd thought.

"My mother has a substance abuse problem," she said, keeping her voice neutral. "That can make people do messed up things. Things they wouldn't normally do."

Cash guffawed. "You're telling me!"

Christmas inhaled through her nose, willing herself to calm down. Cash, perhaps taking pity on her, said, almost gently, "You don't have to worry so much. Your mom'll be okay. It's not like they're gonna throw the book at her. Maybe she'll detox in jail. And you're lucky to be rid of your house anyway. All the prices are gonna tank soon."

"The prices for houses on the lake?"

Cash nodded and pushed a stack of papers toward Christmas.

Christmas looked at the documents in front of her: surveyor's maps, drone photos of lakefront homes, deeds, architect's plans.

Christmas shook her head. "You can't possibly buy everyone out. And why do you even want all this property?"

Cash nodded and ashed again into the already-full ashtray. "Actually, I don't want anything. It's my dad, even though I was the buyer on your place. And he'll get it all too. Some owners are hold-outs—the Hansens, the Cunninghams, and of course, your friends Lemy and Curly—but he's working on that."

"The Hansens won't ever sell."

Cash stamped out his cigarette. "Two old people living alone? They'd be better off in a condo. My dad can be very persuasive. But that's that not even the point. Who wants to live on a polluted lake? People are already getting freaked out. And once my dad has taken out the trash," Cash snapped, "we'll treat the algae. My dad already has a company on retainer. He'll restore the lake to its original glory. And the summer people are gonna love it; they'll eat it up."

Cash gestured to one of the large rolls of papers. "Take a look," he said. Christmas reached for the paper and unfurled a large sheet. It was a mock-up titled "Sweet Lake Resort and Casino." Various structures encircled the lake: a hotel and yacht club with swimming pools and tennis courts. Cunningham's Woods were sliced into narrow half-acre lakefront lots. A casino was also on the plan—right where Christmas's house currently stood.

"He can't do this," Christmas scoffed.

"Why not?"

"Because people live here. Someone will stop him."

"Yeah? Who? Relax," Cash said. "Go with the flow. Change is good. Honestly, you should get on board. I know my dad would love to have you working with us."

Christmas squeezed her eyes shut, rolled her neck, and exhaled.

She looked, hard, at Cash. "I don't even care about all of this. I mean, I do care, but go ahead and turn my house into a casino. I just want my mother back."

Cash opened his mouth to respond when Christmas's phone buzzed on the desk. He turned it over to look at the screen.

"Your friend," he said. "She wants to know if you're okay. Is she worried I'm gonna kill you?"

Christmas held her hand out for the phone and Cash gave it to her. "Yeah, a little," she said. "You're not always the nicest guy, you know." She texted:

I'm okay. Getting info.

Cash scoffed. "Are you kidding me? I think I've been pretty friggin' nice, Christmas. Looking out for you, checking on you, even watching out for your mom, making sure she got home all right when she was messed up." Christmas felt a jolt of surprise but didn't interrupt. "And I drove you home that time you were out running around in that storm. And I put that pepper spray in your mailbox after I heard what happened with crazy Gary."

Christmas tilted her head. "I didn't know that was you," she said. Recalling it, her hand went automatically to her pocket. She wouldn't need it, she thought.

Cash wouldn't hurt her.

He might be a narrow-minded asshole, but he wasn't going to hurt her.

"I always thought we had a kind of chemistry," he said. He raised one side of his mouth in a half smile. "It sure seems that way when I kiss you. Maybe I should just stick to doing that."

Christmas rolled her eyes. "Whatever, Cash."

"See!" Cash exclaimed, slapping his palms on the desk. "That's exactly what I'm talking about. You always make sure I know you think you're better than me."

"I didn't say that," Christmas protested.

"We actually have a lot in common, whether you like it or not," Cash said. "You and your mom, going around acting like you're summer people." His laugh was mean and forced.

Christmas heard a key in a lock and then a door opening. A moment later, Mr. Ford appeared in the doorway.

"Chrissy!" he cried, beaming. His work boots made a clumping noise as he crossed the garage. "So glad you're here. Cash, you finally did something right."

Christmas instinctively smiled back, feeling as though she was somehow saved by Mr. Ford's presence, a feeling that was only increased by Mr. Ford's enthusiasm, his greeting her as though she were exactly the guest he was hoping to see. She looked at Cash, who was scowling, his eyes darting from his father to Christmas and back again.

"Cash let me know you'd be coming over." He shook his head, performing solemnity. "A time like this. With all your mother's done for us, Chrissy, you are practically family. Hell, not practically—you are family. And we're going to take care of you." Mr. Ford nodded at the papers on the desk. "Cash brought you up to speed on our plans? Well, like I said. You're family now, Christmas."

Christmas looked from Mr. Ford to Cash and back again, unable to understand what was happening. Mr. Ford's overt kindness, his good humor, it was all so confusing.

"Chrissy, I'll be frank," Mr. Ford said. "Your mother has really been instrumental to our success. Such a help. But, God forbid, if she turned on me . . ." He shook his head, as though he were unable to continue. "Thankfully, we all know she's too smart to do anything like that. But still. It's good to have insurance. I've always believed that. You can never have too much insurance." He winked. "Don't get me wrong, Chrissy," Mr. Ford said, cocking his head to one side. "I don't want this to get ugly. You don't want it to get ugly, do you?"

"No," Christmas said, her heart pounding in her throat. Her eyes darted over Mr. Ford's shoulder, and she was distracted by the framed images on the wall: a licensing certificate, a picture of Mr. Ford and his father in front of the shop, and a photo of a smiling blond woman in a sequined dress, a sash across her chest reading "Miss Sweet Lake." That was Mrs. Ford, Cash's mom, before she got sick.

Aware that her brain was going rogue and focusing on the wrong things, she willed her attention back to the man in front of her. Mr. Ford, who had followed her gaze, said appreciatively, "I believe there would be nothing on earth that could motivate a mother more than making sure her family is protected. That unconditional love is sadly something Cash here never got enough of." He nodded his head to indicate the photo behind him. "One thing my boy did get though, is loyalty to family. Commitment. And I know your parents raised you the same way. Work for me and you'll be able to give back to your family. Now, I heard you want to go over to CCC this fall. You know what I'd like? I'd like to pay for your books. Would you let me do that, Chrissy?"

He winked again. Christmas wondered, vaguely, if Mr. Ford had some of his own nervous tics that came out when he was stressed. Was he stressed? She did notice a sort of strain around the eyes, a tightness in his smile.

Christmas nodded slowly, although a voice in her head mocked her: a people pleaser to the end.

Mr. Ford continued. "You might even be able to introduce us to a whole new market." He nodded, as though impressed with his own idea. "Now, like I said, there's nothing for you to worry about, Chrissy." Mr. Ford folded his arms across his chest. Christmas noticed then that he had a gun holstered at his side. He sighed. "Your folks are gonna be real busy, what with this legal mess. So we're just gonna keep you here. I'll let your dad know exactly where you are."

He smiled grimly. "We want your mom aware that we've got her back during this difficult time."

"Are you kidnapping me?" Christmas asked, rising.

Mr. Ford let out a whoop of laughter. "This one cuts right to the chase! Are you allowed to leave?" He shook his head. "Well, no. But will we take good care of you?" Here, he looked at Cash. "You bet we will."

Christmas turned to Cash, too, and he held up her phone, flashing it at her face so that it would unlock.

"Cash," Christmas said. She went to grab the phone back, but Cash jerked it away and typed a message.

"What are you doing?" Christmas asked, going to stand beside him and looking over his shoulder.

He texted:

rorie came to get me were going to his house will call u tmw

"Kinda convenient for me that you came on the boat," Cash said smugly. "She wouldn't see you if you left out the front door."

Christmas protested. "Lexi will come looking for me. She'll tell her grandparents that she dropped me here."

"Ah, the Hansens don't want any trouble," Mr. Ford said.

They were all still for a moment, Christmas aware of the buzzing of the fluorescent lights overhead and distracted again by the picture of Cash's mom. It kept drawing her eyes back and she remembered the day it was taken; she had been there. It was the Founder's Day celebration and Christmas had fond memories of the boat parade. She wished she had time to take that picture down off the wall and really look at it.

Mr. Ford cleared his throat and said, "Might as well put you to work if you're going to be staying here. Let's take a walk." He patted his revolver. "Don't worry. We don't even have to go outside. I've got a nice tunnel built. Son, lead the way."

39

FOR A SPLIT SECOND, CHRISTMAS THOUGHT she saw resistance in Cash's face. He looked at his father with just the hint of a question, and Mr. Ford shook his head slightly, letting Cash know that his input was not desired nor welcome.

They walked her down the steps to the shop's basement—Cash in front of her and Mr. Ford behind. Christmas's breath came in tiny, fluttering gasps, and she worried that she'd pass out, fall down the steps, and then what? What would they do to her?

At the bottom, Cash stopped and turned, registering her eccentric breathing. "Hey," he said, as though to reassure her. But then he glanced over her shoulder at his father and added, almost nastily, "Calm down. Jesus."

She tried to inhale deeply, to clear her head.

In health class, they'd learned that if a person had a gun and tried to take you somewhere, things were not going to turn out well for you. You should fight, the teacher had told them. Never go willingly.

And yet here was Christmas, following Cash through the tidy basement toward a shelf filled with paint cans and half-empty bottles of automotive fluids. The shelf was on hinges and Cash pulled it back to reveal a steel door. He typed in a code and yanked it open.

Christmas saw a tunnel. This was her last chance, she thought. She should make a run for it now. Dash back to the stairs.

She moved fast, feinting to the left, before springing to her right. But she was too slow, and Mr. Ford anticipated her, grabbing her arm too tight. "Whoa, there," he said, as though she were a skittish horse. He looked downright hurt that she'd tried to get away. "You belong to us now, Chrissy," he said, his voice kind, but his eyes flinty. He turned her around, gave her a gentle swat on the butt and, reluctantly, she followed Cash into the dimly lit tunnel.

The tunnel, only about sixty feet long, had concrete floors and walls. It smelled dankly of soil and lake.

Soon, they came to another steel door. Cash opened this one as well and Christmas found herself standing in a room that reminded her of the bio lab at school with its steel tables and beakers but unlike the lab at school, there was also an abundance of plastic tubing, buckets, and bottles.

Christmas looked from Cash to Mr. Ford and back again. "Where are we?"

"This is the basement of the brown house," Mr. Ford said simply. "It's a small operation, really, but lucrative as hell. You wouldn't believe." He smiled. "This, my dear, is where you'll be cooking. Cash is gonna show you how."

He took Christmas's phone from Cash. "Go stand right there," he instructed Christmas. She moved toward a nondescript concrete wall. "That's right, right there. Let me get a quick photo. Now, smile! Want to send this to your daddy. Let him know you're okay. And then he can tell your mom too. Remind her that we're taking care of you."

Christmas didn't smile.

Mr. Ford took the picture, and then concentrated on the phone.

Looking wonderingly around the room, she noted what seemed to be a large plastic cylinder in the lakeside corner; it looked like a small version of a waterslide. "You dump the by-product in the lake?" she asked softly.

"It's one of the hardest things about making meth," Cash answered. "All that toxic shit. It gets people busted all the time. It's been real convenient to have somewhere to dispose of it."

Christmas's throat tightened. She was afraid that she would cry, and she knew that this would not matter to them. Mr. Ford—and Cash too—were hard, cruel, and greedy. Her tears would only confirm her weakness, her manipulability.

Christmas tried to swallow. She looked again around the room, feeling totally conspicuous as her eyes fell on the still-open door to the tunnel.

She said, almost absently, "You'll break my dad's heart. My mom's, too, I guess."

Cash stared stonily. He cleared throat and then glanced at his father.

Mr. Ford nodded at Christmas, like someone agreeing with an adorable, but wrongheaded, child. She realized that this was the same expression he used with Naomi Gold that one night, which now seemed so long ago. What a fake, Christmas thought. What a liar, jerk, and villain. Her hatred for Mr. Ford began to swell inside her, and she felt an impulse to spit in his face, rip at his hair, grab his gun and shoot him.

She turned, frowning, to Cash, who seemed to be watching her closely. "What would your mother have thought of this?" she asked, her voice high and thin. "I remember her, Cash. I remember when she was crowned Ms. Sweet Lake for Founder's Day that one year— do you remember? We were little."

Cash's eyes went big and his face strangely flat.

"What nonsense are you going on about now?" Mr. Ford said, still bemused, but now with an edge in his voice.

Christmas spoke over him. "It was Founder's Day—a big anniversary year? Everyone put garlands and decorations on their boats and your mom was Ms. Sweet Lake. We—my family—we were only summer people then."

Cash nodded slowly. "You're still summer people," he said, his voice a low croak.

"I thought your mother was a movie star. She was the most beautiful woman I had ever seen," Christmas continued. She thought of Mrs. Ford, all blond curls and sequins, being driven slowly around the lake on the Fords' speedboat.

"She certainly was a beauty," Mr. Ford said, as though annoyed to be excluded from the conversation. "Our own Ms. Sweet Lake. But you know, she was summer people too. She wasn't from here. Grew up in Jersey." Mr. Ford laughed with forced good humor.

"I don't know about all that," Christmas said. "But I do know she would have wanted better for you than this, Cash."

In the flickering light, Cash shuffled his feet.

"I'm sorry, Cash," Christmas said. Her arms hung at her sides. "I'm not just saying this because you and your dad have basically destroyed my family. I'm sorry that I wasn't nicer to you. I'm sorry that you lost your mom and that your dad is . . ." She didn't finish the thought. "I don't want to lose my mom, too, Cash." Christmas's throat closed, and she knew she couldn't speak any more without crying.

"I can see why you like her, Cash." Mr. Ford gave a wry, appreciative smile. "She's a real manipulator, isn't she? But let me tell you something, little girl." He took a step closer and winked at her. "It's not just the lake. This whole town is poisoned. Yeah, maybe it was all right once upon a time, but those days are over. There's nothing here worth saving."

Cash snorted an appreciative laugh.

Christmas involuntarily looked at the still-open door. She crawled her fingers to the pocket of her sweatpants.

"I can take it from here, Pop," Cash said, putting a hand on his father's shoulder, as though to pull him back. "I'll get her set up, show her the ropes."

When Mr. Ford turned to Cash, Christmas moved fast, faster than she had ever moved in her whole life before. She pulled out the pepper spray, flipped off the safety, straightened her arm, and pressed down, aiming for Mr. Ford's eyes.

Mr. Ford ducked his face into his elbow and mostly succeeded in avoiding the direct hit, but still, it was enough, and he howled in pain as he clutched his eyes with one hand, his other hand groping for his gun. Cash, wide-eyed, looked at Christmas and said, "Run!" He grappled with his father, pushing him to the ground and trying to wrest the gun away.

"Get the hell off me!" Mr. Ford snarled.

Christmas dashed to the open door. Behind her, she heard a thunk—perhaps metal hitting flesh and bone—but she didn't have time to find out what had happened. Without hesitating, she was in the tunnel, running toward the next door, hoping it was unlocked.

It wasn't, but the deadbolt was on the inside. She dropped the Mace and, with shaking hands, turned the bolt, pulled open the door, and burst back into the basement.

She slipped on the cement floor, falling hard on her hands and knees and then scrambling on all fours up the wooden stairs. She could hear someone's heavy feet running behind her, but she didn't dare look back.

Up the stairs, she raced directly to the side door, where again, she threw the lock before bursting into the inky evening, kicking off her flip-flops as she hurled herself down the driveway and out into the street, her bare feet slapping the asphalt.

Her mind raced, trying to decide where to run next. There was no way she could go home, as Mr. Ford would simply pick her up and haul her back. Would he know to look for her at Rory's or the Hansens'?

She resolved to get to Curly and Lemy's, where she might be able to hide for a little while in a dense thicket of trees behind the house.

All the running, all the breathing exercises to clear her head, all the times she had to force her brain to stay on track: she had been training for this, she thought. She could do it. She had to.

Taking a left, she ran, as hard and fast as she could. When, after a few minutes, it seemed she was not being pursued, she slowed down, thinking that Cash had won the fight or that Mr. Ford had given up.

Then she heard the roar of a truck engine behind her, felt it gaining speed, getting closer.

She cursed herself, realizing that she'd picked the wrong direction to run. If she had run to the right, there would have been more houses, more potential people around. Instead, she'd gone past the seemingly abandoned brown house that she'd just been under, and had to get by the public access dock, desolate at this time of night. Across the street, the large empty plot had been made inaccessible by a chain link fence. There was nowhere to hide.

She was in the truck's headlights now. She might be fast, but she knew that, in a moment, Ford would be upon her. Would run her down.

She sprinted off the road, rocketing down the slope toward the lake, where he couldn't follow in the truck. She ran right into the water and kept running, her feet sliced by sharp rocks. She waded through the clouds of algae, until the water was deep enough to swim.

Gasping, she swam as hard as she could, until she couldn't swim any more. She turned and, treading water, looked back at the shore.

She heard the truck's engine fading. Had she lost him?

She dog paddled, moving slowly and silently toward Rory's house. She wondered if Lexi was still on the lake and thought about calling out to her for help but was afraid to draw attention to herself. It was dark, but she knew the trees, she knew the lake, and she knew which way to go. She couldn't slow her breathing enough to breast-stroke, so she backstroked, making steady progress across the lake.

The night was deceptively placid, the surface of the water like glass. An onlooker would never have been able to guess what had happened. Christmas herself could barely believe what she'd seen, what she'd heard, just moments before: the dead-eyed Mr. Ford, the confirmation of her mother's involvement in a drug ring, her attempted kidnapping. It was so peaceful that when she first registered the vibration in the water, she didn't really think anything of it; she was used to swimming in a lake, hearing distant motors.

And then she realized that Mr. Ford must have taken one of the boats out. He was going to try to find her. He was going to try, again, to run her down.

40

CHRISTMAS BOBBED IN THE WATER and looked around frantically, straining to find the closest shore. Could she make it to land in time?

Suddenly, she was blinded by the single headlight on the Jet Ski. Was it Cash or Mr. Ford? Whoever it was, he had seen her. He was speeding toward her. And he wasn't coming to rescue her.

She dove deep and began to swim under the water, cutting hard to her left. She felt awkward, slow, and unwieldy, visible, obvious, and vulnerable.

If she could just make it to the shallow water, where the Jet Ski couldn't go, she would be safe. But it was far, and her panic made her breath short.

Bursting up for air, she twisted around to locate the Jet Ski. She could hear it, but he'd turned the headlight off, probably so he could later deny running her over on purpose. It was a good plan: he'd run her down, bust the headlight, and then claim he hadn't realized it was broken until it was too late. And what the hell was the girl doing out swimming in the middle of the night anyway? It would look like a terrible accident.

He'd lost her. The shadowy Jet Ski zoomed over the area she'd just been in.

Then, suddenly, the light flashed back on. The vehicle moved erratically as he scanned the water, searching for her bobbing head. She took a huge gulp of air, dove, and headed for shore.

Beneath the water, she could hear the churning, approaching engine. Coming up for air, she felt the algae plastered across her face, getting into her mouth. She spluttered it away, wiped it from her eyes. The algae was repulsive, but it meant she was getting closer to the shallow water.

And then the blinding light and the roar as he zoomed toward her, this time not bothering to turn off the light and risk losing her again.

She tried to dive, but she had no air in her lungs and she immediately resurfaced. She kicked and paddled furiously in a backstroke, which allowed her to see him bearing down on her.

Just moments from impact, he was so close that she could clearly see his rage-filled face. He looked like a different person, not the laughing, good-natured man they'd all known. She thought of Cash, of having to live with a man like that.

Christmas closed her eyes. *I am going to die*, she thought.

She heard a deafening crash and opened her eyes just in time to see the Jet Ski being violently shoved, Mr. Ford's shadowy shape flying through the air at an impossible angle. The Hansens' speedboat careened to one side, turning over completely with the force of the impact.

Unable to truly understand what was happening, Christmas was carried on the enormous waves that unexpectedly lifted and dropped her.

And then, she screamed, "Lexi!" She battled the waves to swim to the overturned boat, also rocking up and down. Christmas noted the motor had stopped; she was flooded with relief that Lexi, smart girl, must have worn the kill cord, the string attached to the ignition that, if pulled, would cut the engine. But where was she?

Christmas dove, emerging into the silent darkness under the capsized vessel. The space was like another, different world, the air strange and too black.

Lexi was there, gasping and treading water. And someone else was there too. Even in the darkness, Christmas knew it was Cash. For a moment, they floated in stunned silence.

Finally, Christmas spoke. "Is everyone okay?" She grabbed for Lexi's arm and found it. She squeezed and then let go and continued treading water.

Lexi replied, "Yeah. Yeah. Are you okay?"

"I think so."

Cash remained silent.

"I was waiting," Lexi panted. "I was watching the dock. I knew you needed help, but I didn't know what to do. And then I saw him tear out on that Jet Ski. And then Cash came down. He told me . . . Christmas, he said his father was going to—"

"My dad," Cash cut in, his voice husky, shaky, and soft. He dove down, disappearing into the lake.

Christmas took Lexi's hand and they too, wordlessly, dove down. Christmas pulled Lexi along until they were clear of the boat, only letting go once they'd emerged again on the other side.

The lake shimmered in the speedboat's headlights, like the water in a gaudy fountain. Christmas's body was warm; the night was quiet; her friend was beside her. She felt almost serene, as though the excitement of the previous hour was only a bad dream that she'd like to have some time to think about, now that she was awake.

Nearby, Cash emerged from the water, splashing and gagging.

Christmas moved to help.

"No! We have to get to land," Lexi said, treading water beside her. "That man tried to kill you. Leave him."

"I can't," Christmas said.

"Please, Christmas," Lexi cried.

But Christmas swam away. Her stroke less frantic, with purpose now, she crossed the distance quickly to where Cash was looking for his father, and she dove into the black water.

While Lexi swam to shore, went to the nearest house and called for help, Christmas and Cash continued to dive. Again and again into the black water, but it was deep, too deep, and they weren't sure exactly where Mr. Ford had gone down. Christmas's body wanted to stop, to quit, but she couldn't, even after she became light-headed, unsure if she herself would be able to make it back up if she dove again.

And then, another boat, one that Christmas didn't recognize, chugged quietly across the water. It was the old clunker that belonged to the summer people who had the property next to the Hansens, apparently commandeered by the police, with Ben Pappas at the helm and Mr. Hansen leaning overboard.

"Can you climb the ladder?" Mr. Hansen asked.

When he saw she was too tired to even answer, Cash, in the water beside her, said, "Give us life jackets. We're not that far. I'll swim her in." Mr. Hansen handed over a ski jacket and a life preserver, and Cash, his voice ragged, said to her, "Hold still," as though she were a child.

He was gentle, pulling her arms through the jacket and snapping it shut. He draped one of her arms over the tube and the other over his shoulder and then he clasped the tube too. And that was how, together, they swam to shore.

41

THE NEXT DAY, MR. FORD'S BODY WAS RECOVERED. Though Christmas didn't see it, it was too easy for her to picture the scene: an interruption in the algae-covered surface of the water revealing a person floating facedown. Then, the weight of him as they hauled the body to shore. The shock and indignation on his face—pale and distorted and strange—when they turned him over.

It would be a long time before Christmas would be able to bring herself to go in the lake again, to swim or ski or even boat.

It wasn't advisable, anyway. The same day they pulled him out, the police and DEA investigators descended in full force, and orange signs appeared around the perimeter of the lake, warning people not to drink the water, eat the fish, or swim.

Outraged and indignant at the lack of real information, Christmas stubbornly went ahead and sent off a water sample to Cornell. A few weeks later, she spoke to a nice lab tech who explained that the excessive algae came from a combination of forces, including climate change, which resulted in the hotter weather the algae loved, as well as intense rainstorms, which carried phosphorous and nitrogen rich runoff from the roads and lawns, and from Cunningham's

Farm, right into the lake. And then, of course, were the toxic chem
icals from Ford's meth lab. Christmas told the tech about the Cunninghams' cows and he said he'd heard of similar poisonings, that
he'd read about another farmer who piped toxic lake water into his
livestock's troughs, killing them all. When Christmas heard this,
her skin crawled; she'd been in the lake that same day the cows
died, had probably gulped water unintentionally. How close might
she have come to getting sick herself?

The Cornell guy recommended an herbicide to kill the algae,
though he remarked it would probably be too late to do anything
that season. He also agreed with Lemy and Curly's argument that
there shouldn't be any industry on the lake. Finally, he said that
homeowners should be encouraged to plant more trees to act as buf-
fers, filtering out the bad stuff from the roads and lawns.

THERE'D BEEN A TIME when Christmas would have immediately acted
on these recommendations, eager to do the "right thing," to please
whomever she perceived to be in charge, and to save her lake. She
would have shared the information with Curly, Lemy, and the Lake
Association and would have spent her long runs obsessing over
fundraising ideas. Instead, she felt as though this new knowledge
only clouded her mind, and she yearned to rake it away, dump it
somewhere, and just move on.

She couldn't clean up the lake or fight climate change, not all
alone. Maybe it would be better just to accept it, cut her losses, move
on. She didn't even know anymore if Sweet Lake was worth saving.

This was the place, after all, where her mother had been party
to a felony assault.

Lemy was making a strong recovery and his statements, along
with Cash's, let a picture of what had happened that terrible night

emerge. For his part, after the crash on the lake, Cash immediately waived his rights and told the police everything. Christmas, though, heard the story only later, from her mother, who was home for a few days in between being out on bail and heading to a rehab two hours away. Allie would get treatment for four weeks as the various legal and criminal proceedings unfolded. This, their lawyer had assured them, would look good to the judge.

But that Wednesday evening after the arrest, Christmas wasn't completely sure her mother wasn't on something as she sat at the kitchen table, her hands wrapped around a mug of coffee and her stringy hair in her face.

"Cash was bragging," Christmas's mother tried to explain.

Christmas and her father sat across the table. Christmas, for one, couldn't bring herself to look directly at her mother, and kept her eyes glued to a spot on the wall just to the right of her mother's head.

"He was talking about his fireworks. And Lemy—he was sitting at the bar, too—he said something like, 'I bet you can get a lot of fireworks with that meth money.'"

Christmas's mother shook her head. "I called Bill," she said. "I guess . . . I thought I was being useful. I told him what Lemy said, and he told me that Cash and Owen should 'take care of it.' I didn't know, really, what he meant, but I do know that . . . I felt like I was important, like I was his right-hand man. Or something. I said, yes, of course, I'll tell them. And I did."

Christmas was aware of her father in her peripheral vision. He shifted in his seat. She couldn't look at him either.

Christmas's mother told them that when the bar closed that night, she, Owen, and Cash had followed Lemy (who was walking) in her car. Cash and Owen crouched in the backseat. When Christmas's mom pulled over and offered him a ride, Lemy got in. Then, Owen sat up and choked him until he passed out. Lemy never even saw the two men behind him.

"Cash didn't help Lemy, but he never touched him either," Allie said. "Owen was angry about that. I believe Bill was too. Cash suggested that we dump Lemy on the side of the road, that it was enough to scare him. Maybe he'd wake up, not remember what had happened, but know enough to move away, to see that Sweet Lake wasn't such a safe place after all. But Owen insisted they drag Lemy down to the water. I suppose they didn't know what else to do with him." She shook her head. "Those stupid boys. They didn't think they had any other choice."

Christmas couldn't help herself. "What about you?" she said, fixing her eyes on her mother's face. "You had another choice."

"Christmas," her father interjected.

"No, she's right," Allie said. "I was a zombie that night, Chris—and lots of other nights too. The pills . . . my emotions were . . . cauterized. I didn't know what I was doing. Or, I guess I did, but it didn't matter to me, it didn't sink in."

"You don't get to hurt people," Christmas said coldly, "just because you're addicted to drugs."

Her mother began to sob then, her face in her hands. She said, "I was trying to protect you and Dad. Bill threatened to take you long before he actually did it."

Christmas stood, her chair making a painful scraping noise as she pushed out from the table.

"Christmas," her mother started. "You have to understand . . ."

"No," Christmas spat. "Actually, I don't."

She took her phone and went out the front door. She couldn't stand to be in the same room with her parents for a moment longer.

CHRISTMAS INFORMED HER FATHER THAT she wanted nothing to do with any of it: her mother's recovery plans, her parents' financial woes, the potential criminal and civil cases. "You guys never let me know what was happening before," she'd said to her dad. "Why start now?"

And yet she was involved, at least as far as her own attempted kidnapping and Mr. Ford's death. And so one afternoon, she was forced to go with her father to town hall to see their lawyer, who kept an office there. As they left the building, Cash, who must have seen their car in the lot and waited, stepped up to Christmas, asking, "Can I talk to you?"

Christmas's father was ready to object, but she'd raised a placating hand. "It's okay," she said. "Yeah. Let's talk."

They'd walked in the merciless sun toward the trees that lined the lot, taking shelter in the shade.

Christmas did want to speak to Cash, but she didn't know where to start.

"Look," he said, at the same time that she said, "Cash."

"You go ahead," Cash said.

"No," Christmas said, shaking her head. "You go first."

Cash reached into his dirty jeans and pulled out a pack of cigarettes and a lighter. His hands trembled slightly as he lit the cigarette. She watched him, noticing the peach fuzz on his chin and cheeks, the dirt under his fingernails. The wildness that had always seemed to radiate from him was now more pronounced, almost overwhelming. She wondered, suddenly, who he had in his life, and then realized, just as suddenly, that he probably didn't have anyone at all.

"Your friend killed my dad," he said with an almost amused detachment, as though he were stating a curious fact. Even behind the sunglasses, Christmas could see him squinting into the distance. "I don't blame her. But he was my dad."

"I'm sorry," Christmas said gently. "Neither of us wanted to hurt him." She thought of Lexi, who was having a hard time too, although everyone around her, including the DA's office, who had chosen not to charge her, and Cash himself, who had been right there beside her, understood that she had rammed the speedboat into the Jet Ski to stop Mr. Ford from running Christmas over. Still, Christmas knew, Lexi was having nightmares, panic attacks.

"He was never a good swimmer," Cash said. "Goddamn fool to go out on the Jet Ski." He sounded, Christmas thought, like his father. "He died fast though," Cash added. "Impact to the head. So at least he didn't drown." He looked at Christmas. "Yeah, he was a bastard. But he didn't deserve to suffer." Cash swallowed. "He could be a decent dad sometimes. Fun, funny. People always said he was charming, and I guess he was, when he needed to be. But that's not what I wanted to say to you. I wanted to say that even after everything he did, you tried to rescue him. You tried to help me find him. I appreciate that."

Christmas nodded to show she understood. "I only made it to the lake at all because of you. And I'm only alive because you got Lexi. I appreciate what you did too."

They stood in silence, Cash smoking his cigarette too hard so that it grew a dangerously long red ember. "They—'the court' or whatever—are talking about using dad's money to 'remediate' the lake. Thought you'd be happy about that."

Christmas shrugged. "I guess," she said. "I don't even know anymore. Maybe your dad was right. Maybe this whole place is poisoned."

Cash's lips turned down so severely, Christmas wondered if he was going to cry. He let out a puff of forced laughter, but then said, with an almost frightening intensity, "Don't stop loving Sweet Lake, Christmas. If anyone can make it better, it's you. I mean it. You're the only one... Shit, if you give up, what are the rest of us going to do?"

Christmas thought she might cry then, too, and she tried to breathe deeply, to hold it in, at least a little longer. Cash must have been doing the same because a moment later, clear-voiced, almost casually, he asked, "How's your mom doing? I heard she went to rehab. How're you even paying for that?"

"My Aunt Inez," Christmas said. "An old family friend. I called her and..." Christmas trailed off, remembering the humiliating conversation, the way she'd had to introduce herself, to take a lifetime of events and feelings and boil it down, reduce it to a few sentences, ones that ended with a plea: "My mother needs you. We need you."

"Four weeks won't be long enough," Christmas said. Despite her decision to un-involve herself, she'd been reading about addiction, recovery, and relapse. The odds, she'd learned, were not good. They were, in fact, terrible. "But we can't afford any more."

Cash grunted. "I don't have shit either."

When Christmas didn't respond, Cash continued. "I'm just saying. With what they've taken and all that's tied up in the case—the cases—there isn't shit left. Otherwise, I might... you know. Try and help you out or whatever." Cash took a last drag of his cigarette before flicking it toward the trees. It didn't make it, though, and lay, smoking itself down on the pavement. He laughed—a short, mean bark. "Goddammit. Why do I even care what happens to you? Where has it ever got me?"

Christmas felt a wave of grief and guilt. "Cash," she began. "You don't have to—"

He cut her off. "Actually, your place—" Perhaps registering that Christmas sucked in her lips in an effort not to cry, Cash added, "It's all right. Did you even know that your house is in my name? Believe me, it wasn't a gift—it was about the taxes. But it worked out for you, didn't it? I'm not gonna evict you. Maybe the lawyers'll work out a payment plan or some shit like that so you can buy it back."

Christmas nodded and tried to swallow the huge lump in her throat. "Thanks," she squeaked.

Cash blew out his lips and looked at her searchingly. "I always tried to do right by you, Christmas. I sort of thought we understood each other. We're different, but we were the same somehow too."

Christmas sniffed. "We both have fucked-up families and brains that don't work like other people's?"

A sad, half smile appeared on Cash's face. "That's exactly right." He shook his head. "You know, you never gave me a shot."

Unable to meet his eye, Christmas looked down at her worn-out flip-flops and the chipped polish on her toenails.

"Yeah," Christmas said. "And that was a mistake. You're a good person, Cash."

He let out a gaspy laugh. "Shit," he said. "No, I'm not."

Christmas frowned, shook her head. "Fuck you, Cash," she said, stepping closer to him. "I know you're a good person."

Though Cash was smiling, he was also crying a little, his lips pursed and screwed up, tears dripping out from beneath his sun-glasses. He seemed to be holding his breath but then he exhaled suddenly and wiped at his face.

"Fuck you too, Christmas," he croaked. "You're a good fucking person too."

Christmas wiped her eyes, and they stood for another moment, sweating and crying.

"All right," Christmas said at last. "Take care of yourself."

"I would tell you the same," he said, as he slouched away. He threw over his shoulder, "But you always do, don't you? You always take care of yourself."

Christmas watched him. Then she turned back to the trees and looked at the cigarette, smelled the smoke, and under the smoke, the hot asphalt, the fresh air of the trees. She walked over and stepped on it, put out the ember. Just in case.

And then she returned to where her father waited.

43

I T HAD BEEN HARD TELLING RORY ABOUT HER MOTHER; it had been even harder to explain to him why she hadn't told him in the first place. And though initially he'd seemed injured, he quickly pivoted to supportive and useful, looking up attorneys, making phone calls, keeping a schedule for her, and also bringing over food, charging her phone, and sometimes, if he stayed overnight, just being there when the bad dreams woke her up. It did not escape Christmas that Rory behaved a lot like Christmas's own father, whose goal in life seemed to be to ease the way for his wife, but as Christmas's days began to resume a degree of normalcy, she depended on Rory less and found herself simply enjoying being with him more.

And despite it all, Christmas almost had the great summer she'd envisioned. It was fun working at the camp weekdays, and then taking long bike rides and hikes, watching movies, and just hanging out with Lexi and Rory.

Then, suddenly, it was ending.

Lexi's mother, Barbara, was coming to get her. This difficult reality was made a little easier by the news that, not only had Barbara agreed to stay overnight, but she was bringing Martha with her.

Sara Hosey

The night before Barbara and Martha's arrival, Christmas and Lexi lay in their twin beds in Lexi's room in the Hansen house, just like the old days. They talked long into the night, about that summer, about romance, about the coming fall, about Christmas's mom.

Christmas told Lexi about the visit she'd made, under duress, to the rehab, how they'd sat outside on the pretty patio. Though the facility wasn't bad, it still smelled and felt like a hospital, and it was filled with sad, desperate, and angry people. But the grounds outside were lush and richly green, with huge, old trees: weeping willows and stately oaks.

"My dad slipped away, went to get a coffee," Christmas told Lexi. "And when he came back, I went and waited in the parking lot. It's almost like we can't stand the intensity, all three of us together. Which is weird because we used to be so easy together."

Lexi was quiet and let Christmas talk.

Christmas told her about the dark rings under her mother's eyes, and her new wrinkles, and how her dirty hair was streaked with grown-out gray. She told Lexi about how her mother had taken her hand and apologized.

"And I guess I forgive her?" Christmas said. "But I'm angry, Lex. About all of it. Not just the 'my mother's dealer kidnapped me as collateral' part. I'm mad that she's been lying this whole time. That every day, from the time she finally got out of bed until the time she sneaked off at night, was a lie."

"Yeah," Lexi said. "You're allowed to be mad."

Discussing her mother's addiction still felt new, strange, and somehow wrong to Christmas, who had for so long believed that her mother's problem was not something to ever be confronted head-on. But she was trying, now, to talk about it. And the darkness made it easier.

"I know it's a disease," Christmas said. "And I know that you can make a mistake—even a terrible one—and still be a good person. I

252

know it rationally. But I don't know it yet, not really, in my heart." Christmas had started to cry then, and when Lexi asked if she was okay, she said, "Yeah. I guess I just miss my mom."

Lexi listened. She didn't offer advice or say she knew what Christmas was going through, because she didn't, not really. And listening was more than enough.

"I worry a bit about my medication," Christmas continued. Perhaps knowing it was their last night alone, she felt like she had to get as much out as possible, to do all the talking she wouldn't be able to do—at least not in a darkened bedroom in the Hansens' house— for another year. "My genetic potential for addiction," she said with false gravity.

"That makes sense," Lexi said.

"My new doctor seems really good though," Christmas said. She'd stayed off her medication for about a week, suffering through the unpleasantness of withdrawal, and had experienced an almost immediate relief when she got back on it. The clouds in her mind parted, and despite all the noise of her messy family life, she found herself able to also move forward, to complete the tasks before her including (with Rory's help) finding herself the new doctor. "She does want me to get into therapy, like, yesterday," she told Lexi. "Which is obviously a good idea. I figure I'll check out the counseling center at CCC when school starts."

"Yeah," Lexi said with warmth in her voice. "That's great. I'm really proud of you, girl. And not just for that. Look at all you've done! I hope you have to write one of those 'How I Spent my Summer Vacation' essays." She intoned in a high-pitched voice: "First, I saved someone's life. Then, I shut down a drug ring. Maybe next year, I'll take on climate change!"

Christmas smiled in the dark. "Do you think we'll both be here —in Sweet Lake—next year, Lex?"

She heard Lexi turn over on her side.

"I don't know for sure," she said. "But yeah, I have a feeling we'll both be here again. And I bet you'll get that lake cleaned up. I bet we'll be skiing again soon, because if there's one thing I know about you, Christmas, it's that once you set your mind to something, you see it through to the end."

Christmas rubbed her feet together, which was something she did when she was comfortable and almost ready to sleep. "I used to think I was sort of special because I overcame my ADHD. Like, anything good I ever did was because I had worked so hard to make my brain behave. But that's only partly true." She was quiet for a moment, searching for the words. "I do work hard at it. But now I know that my ADHD is what makes me who I am in some fundamental way. It lets me focus on the things that matter to me, even if it means other things, things that are important to other people, sort of fall away. Does that make sense? I'll never have a clean room, or be organized, or be able to fill out a form, but that's okay, because if you give me an article on environmental toxins or water remediation, I can sit there and dive into it, even if there's a marching band going by my window. I might not be able to focus when something doesn't really interest me, but I always have enough things going on in my mind to never be bored. I might have a harder time solving a problem than another person would, but I'll keep trying." She sighed. "It's cheesy, but maybe it's true: ADHD isn't a disability as much as a difference. And it can sometimes be a good difference, sort of an extra-ability."

"You mean a superpower," Lexi said.

"Maybe," Christmas agreed.

Lexi laughed. "This is like in *The Wizard of Oz,* when Dorothy realizes that it was the ruby slippers all along. You always had the power. Now you know how to use it."

44

L EXI WAS LEAVING THE DAY AFTER the annual Founder's Day celebration, and Rory invited them to his place for a barbecue that night. They could watch the fireworks over the lake. "Unless you want to do something else," he'd added. "I know you're not crazy about fireworks."

"I'll be okay," Christmas assured him. "I'll have my goat with me."

They filled their last day with mini-golf and lunch in Honeysuckle, Christmas, Rory, Lexi, Martha, and even Barbara, laughing, talking, and playing.

Later, without Rory and Barbara, the girls took Martha to the tree house, where they ate the donuts they'd bought in town, laughed, and talked some more. Martha was just as marvelous as Lexi had promised, and she seemed to love Lexi, maybe even as much as Christmas did.

At dusk, they biked along the perimeter of the lake, past the Cunninghams' mostly empty fields, the few remaining cows contentedly chewing their cud against the setting sun. And then past Christmas's house, where, Christmas thought, her father was probably bent over the calculator, adding up the bills over and over, as though he might just get a different answer if he tried again. He'd been picking up extra shifts at the Home Depot, and Christmas barely saw him, except for when they went to visit her mom or to the lawyer's office together.

As they passed Lemy and Curly's house, Christmas couldn't bring herself to look. Though both Lemy and Curly had been so kind, had reached out to tell her that they didn't hold her mother's actions against her, she knew it could never be the same. She heard they were thinking of selling after all, that Lemy had a job offer in California. She hoped it wasn't true, but knew it probably was, and that maybe it was for the best.

The bright yellow police tape drew her eyes to the brown house and then the service station, now closed, and the Fords' house, shut up tight, like a fist. She pedaled faster and willed herself to focus on the road in front of her. Maybe someday those places would be just places again, but not yet, not today.

When they finally arrived, they dumped their bikes just as Rory came around the house, beaming. He grabbed Christmas, hugged and kissed her, then hugged her again.

"I missed you," he said, releasing her.

"I just saw you a few hours ago," she reminded him.

"Maybe I'm preemptively missing you," he said. He was leaving for Cornell the coming week.

Settling into an Adirondack chair facing the lake, Christmas wished Madison could have been there too. Madison, however, wouldn't speak to her. The few times Christmas had seen her, she'd seemed not only angry, but somehow unwell: disheveled and sunken-eyed. When Christmas had bumped into her in the canned food aisle at the General Store and offered a tentative, "Hey, Mad," Madison swiveled her head sharply and said, "Owen's lawyer says not to talk to you."

"Are you okay?" Christmas had ventured.

"No, I'm not okay. I'm really *not* fucking okay," Madison spat then swept out of the store.

That was another loss. Christmas had lost Madison as a friend; she'd lost Lemy and Curly. Though she hoped that they would find a way back to each other eventually, she also felt as though she'd lost her mother. And in some ways, she'd lost her beloved lake—or at least the lake the way it had been when she was a child: clean, uncorrupted.

But there had been gains too. At summer's end, she considered, she'd discovered her ruby slippers and found her goat. And she had a plan for a major now too: Environmental Science.

Naomi had been pestering her to register for classes, and she'd put it off because it entailed paperwork and because she wasn't completely sure how she would pay for college. But with Rory's help, she'd started the process and soon discovered that one of the upsides of being dirt poor was that you could basically go to community college for free.

And so she signed up for the core requirements and an elective that focused on local ecology. She thought of what Cash had said, when he'd implored her not to give up on Sweet Lake. And she wouldn't. She couldn't.

She looked out at the water, smooth and bright, perfectly reflecting the houses and lawns and trees that ringed it, and thought again of that one Founder's Day so long ago, when Cash's mother sparkled on the lake. Christmas's own mother had been dressed in overalls and a baseball cap; she was also a beauty, laughing with Christmas's dad, shining in her own way. The three of them had decorated their rowboat, strewn it with flowers, and taken their spot in the line of boats that moved in a slow progression around lake. Christmas, beside her mother, smelling the gardenias, listening to the rhythm of her father's rowing, had felt happy and safe, her family alone in their boat, but part of something bigger, part of a parade, at once in the water and of the land.

Rory, who sat in the Adirondack chair beside her, took Christmas's hand, snapping her back to the present. He was talking about colleges, telling Lexi that Cornell had a great program for transfer students while looking meaningfully at Christmas.

"Let's not get ahead of ourselves," Christmas said.

"How far away will you be from each other?" Martha asked, returning from the cooler with two cans of seltzer, one of which she placed on the arm of Christmas's chair.

"It's almost three hours," Christmas said. "And Rory won't have a car."

"But you will," Rory pointed out.

"My Aunt Inez," Christmas told Martha. "My mom's best friend. She's giving me a 2009 Honda Civic with one hundred thousand miles on it—but she says it has another one hundred thousand in it yet."

"And I don't mind the bus," Rory put in. Christmas smiled and Rory squeezed her hand. Lexi, noticing the exchange, beamed at her friend.

Christmas couldn't talk for a moment, she was so overwhelmed with the sense of being surrounded and understood by friends. She was glad that it was just then that they heard the first firework, a pop and a hiss.

"They're starting!" Rory said.

Christmas reached beside her chair and put on the headphones she'd brought. She thought of Cash and his famous illegal fireworks, for the way he annoyed everyone on the lake by setting them off all summer long, often in the wee hours, upsetting the cows, dogs, and wildlife, waking babies and enraging working folks. Everyone knew it was Cash, though the next day, it didn't seem so important to tell the kid to cut it out, ask him to have a little respect for his neighbors. Christmas felt a dull ache, a surprising longing. It wasn't that she missed Cash, exactly. But now that everything had changed, she missed knowing he was around or knowing that they were still locked in their ongoing, unchanging battle.

He was right, of course, at least in the ways that mattered. She'd come to realize that a lot of people were like Cash, setting off bombs in the middle of the night, pretending it's all in good fun, when really they're wishing someone would pay attention to them, ask why they are up so late, find out why they can't sleep.

Christmas looked at Rory, his face turned up, and beyond him, at Lexi and Martha, smiling at the sky. Rory cast a glance at her, to make sure she was okay, and she nodded. Though it was fireworks and not shooting stars, she turned her face up too, made a wish, then another, and then another. For bright futures for her family and her favorite summer people, for herself, and for Sweet Lake.

AUTHOR'S NOTE

I WAS AN ADULT BEFORE I REALIZED that I had ADHD and, when I started to share this diagnosis with friends, many responded with some version of, "That can't be. You're successful and accomplished!" It was nice to hear that they saw me as a success, and I do feel accomplished, but their comments made me realize that people need to know that you can have ADHD and also flourish.

I'm not saying it was (or is) easy. I struggled with focusing throughout elementary and high school, and I was often in trouble for being messy and forgetful. (I'm thinking particularly about the time that I left my eyeglasses in the driveway and my dad ran over them with the car—ugh!) I also struggled with "spaciness," procrastination, and retaining certain kinds of information. And, as a girl who, according to one unkind relative, "couldn't eat an apple without getting it all over herself," these difficulties were often seen by authority figures as evidence of laziness and a contemptible lack of self-discipline. That I was incredibly eager to please others made the fact that I so often disappointed the people around me extra painful.

While I do feel that I "grew out" of many of my ADHD symptoms, some persisted into adulthood. In college, I briefly worked as a restaurant server, and I can't even put into words what a failure I was. (Apologies to Pizzeria Uno patrons circa 1997!) I was an okay administrative assistant, but to this day, I cannot operate a basic office phone, I'm at sea with most non-word-processing-related computer programs, and, for someone who has a PhD in English, I still struggle with alphabetical order. (L-M-N-O, okay, P comes after.)

In other areas of my life, I've overcorrected in order to avoid the criticism I'd come to expect, so I'm obsessive about "doing it now" when it comes to unpleasant tasks (otherwise I might forget and neglect them completely). I'm militant about being on time, anxious about any disruption to my routine, and sometimes unnecessarily inflexible.

But it isn't all bad. As a child, I was curious and an early and avid reader with the ability to focus on written text regardless of where I was or what was happening around me. I've come to see how my ADHD has also allowed me to be a daydreamer and—ultimately —a writer. And that's been the luckiest break I've had: being able to create a life in which I can generally avoid my nonpreferred activities (including anything involving math and numbers), and instead spend an enormous amount of time reading, writing, and talking about reading and writing.

Professionally and personally, I am allowed to get lost in words, and it's my hyperfocus—my ADHD—that has made this book possible. If you're still struggling: I see you. I know how it feels to watch everyone else floating and playing out past the breakers, making it look so easy while you're stuck getting tumbled around in the waves, spit back on the shore every time you try to swim out.

But I believe you can get there too. It might take medicine or therapy; it might simply take time, or surrounding yourself with people who'll help and support you, or figuring out the workarounds you require to get through the day. Whatever it is, I hope you find it. This world needs us—with our unique and creative brains—maybe now more than ever.

Sara Hosey
November 10, 2022

ACKNOWLEDGMENTS

Thank you to my go-to first readers, Erin Riha and Cathy Plourde, who are so encouraging and who ask the good—and sometimes difficult—questions. I hope that you are relieved to see that I took many of your suggestions! I'm grateful, too, to Melanie Bell, who is always up for a read and offers wonderful insights. A million thanks to my Sea Cliff Writer's Collective, Ayme Lilly, and Julie Tortorici. And thank you to Savannah Gilbo, a terrific editor and podcaster.

I am also grateful to my Fall 2022 Fiction Writing class, my Gen-Z spies, who provided crucial insights about their peers. Thank you, too, to Fiona Brett, whom I can always count on for useful info, and to Vanessa McHugh, who is unfailingly supportive. I'm so happy to have you on my team!

Thank you to my folks at CamCat, especially Helga Schier, who offered enthusiasm and encouragement from the jump, as well as Christine Van Zandt, whose sharp eye and excellent editing really took this book to the next level. It's been wonderful going on this journey with you, Christine. Thank you, Penni Askew. Thanks, also, to Bill Lehto and to Sue Arroyo.

Thank you to my steadfast BFF Lisa Modifica, who might just be the kindest and most generous person I know. I wish for everyone to have a Lisa in their lives.

And, finally, to my other best friend, Jess "Not-That-Kind-of-Lawyer" Rao, Esq. Thank you, dear Jess, for putting up with me and my endless new interests. I'm so lucky to have a partner like you. Not you, exactly, but someone very similar.

Just kidding. It is you. Always.

ABOUT THE AUTHOR

S ARA HOSEY IS THE AUTHOR of two other young adult novels—
Iphigenia Murphy and *Imagining Elsewhere*—as well as a novella
titled *Great Expectations*. She is a community college professor and
a tree enthusiast, and when she's not writing or teaching, she likes
spending time with her family and pets in upstate New York.

If you liked
Sara Hosey's *Summer People*,
please consider leaving us a review
to help our authors.

And check out another CamCat YA title,
Kathleen Fine's *Girl on Trial*.

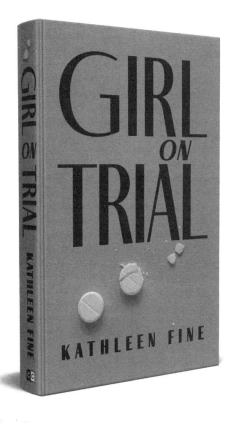

PROLOGUE

January 12, 2022

"The only reason I come here is for my weekly caffeine high," Tiffani with an *i* admitted to Emily as she took a sip of her lukewarm, watered-down coffee. "I'm not no string-out addict or nothin'," she continued and then peered at Emily, realizing that Emily, in fact, was not there just for the coffee. "Sorry, wasn't tryin' to say nothin' bad about addicts." Tiffani sprinkled some sugar into her undersized paper cup and stirred it with the plastic spoon tied to the sugar container with blue yarn. Tiffani glanced around the room and then untied the yarn, placing the spoon into her pocket. She gave Emily a wink. "I gnaw on the edges of this enough and it gives me a sorta sharp blade." Tiffani patted her gray, state-issued sweatpants, keeping the new weapon safe, before taking a seat in the circle with the other women.

"One minute, ladies," the guard announced to the group as the chatter quieted down in the circle. Emily picked up an NA book from the only empty chair left in the circle and sat down in its place.

"Hello, I'm an addict and my name is Darlene. Welcome to the Lincoln Juvenile Correctional Center's group of Narcotics Anonymous. Can we open this meeting with a moment of silence for the addict who still suffers, followed by the Serenity Prayer?"

Emily closed her eyes and took a deep breath as she tried to stop her palms from sweating. She still got anxious even though she'd been attending this meeting every week for the past year. *How has it been an entire year?* she wondered. *So much has happened in only twelve months.*

"Is there anyone here attending their first NA meeting or this meeting for the first time?" Darlene asked. "If so, welcome! You're the most important person here! If you've used today, please listen to what's being said and talk to someone at the break or after the meeting. It costs nothing to belong to this fellowship; you are a member when you say you are. Can someone please read, *Who is an Addict and What is Narcotics Anonymous?*"

"I will," Chantelle volunteered as she reached across the circle, grabbed the paper from Darlene, and began to read.

"Yo, Em," Nikki leaned over and whispered in Emily's ear. "You celebratin' today?" Emily nodded at her timidly. She didn't like speaking in front of people even if it was a group of women she trusted.

"You'll do great," Nikki whispered as she punched Emily lightly in the arm.

"Can someone please read *Why We Are Here and How it Works?*" Darlene asked the group. Emily watched tensely as the paper was passed down to Trina.

"I used last night," Nikki muttered to Emily as she stared down at her coffee cup shamefully. Emily furrowed her brow and placed her hand on top of Nikki's.

She wondered where Nikki could have gotten her hands on drugs since she heard a rumor the guards had been doing weekly bunk checks.

"One day at a time," Emily assured her, trying not to let the guard hear their chatter.

Seeing Emily's tentative face, Nikki whispered, "My roommate sneaked some smack up her pupusa. Had her boyfriend's kid bring it in when he visited her. Whack dude. Whack." She shook her head and rubbed her buzzed hair with her rugged hands. "She's a bad influence on me. I gotta get a new roommate."

Emily frowned, aware that there was nothing she could do to help her friend. She squeezed Nikki's hand tightly and whispered, "Glad you're here."

"No touching," the guard yelled from across the room, eyeing Nikki and Emily. Emily reddened as if being scolded by a teacher in school and instantly pulled her hand away from Nikki's.

Darlene reached below her chair and lifted a shoebox to her lap. "This group recognizes length of clean time by handing out key tags. If you have one coming to you, please come up and get it. The white one is for anyone with zero to twenty-nine days clean and serene." Darlene opened the box to reveal a white key tag and dangled it in the air. Nikki glanced at Emily and then hesitantly got up to collect her tag.

The group clapped and whistled as she crossed the circle and took her tag. She gave a couple of the women fist bumps as the group chanted, "What do we do? Keep coming back!" Emily put her fist out as Nikki gave it a bump.

"The orange one is for thirty days clean and serene." Two women got up, collected their tags, and sat back down. Applause vibrated the room. "What do we do? Keep coming back!"

As Darlene handed out the rest of the monthly tags, Emily began to grip her chair, knowing her turn was coming up. Her palms began to slip down the sides of the metal, damp with her sweat. "The yellow one is for nine months clean and serene."

Nikki peered at Emily and nudged her bicep. "You're next," she whispered. Emily smiled at her, trying to give the facade of bravery.

"The glow in the dark one is for a year clean and serene." Unsteadily, Emily stood up and walked toward Darlene to get her tag. All the women in the room clapped loudly as Emily took the tag and went back to her seat, her face flushing with pride. "What do we do? Keep coming back!"

Darlene placed the box back under her chair and collected the sheet of readings from the women who read. "Today, Emily is celebrating her one-year anniversary with us. You ready, Em?"

The women's applause slowed down and all eyes turned to Emily. She scanned the room at the women and girls before her. Addicts, inmates, and friends. "My name is Emily, and I am an addict. This is my story . . ."

CHAPTER ONE

Trial Day 1: January 7, 2019

The alarm on Emily's phone went off just as Sophie whispered in her ear, *"Wake up Emawee. Wake up."* Emily opened her eyes widely, her body covered in sweat, her sheets soaked yet again. *"Time to wake up."* She heard Sophie's whisper get farther away, humming distantly from somewhere in her dreams. From somewhere in her nightmares.

As she turned off the alarm, she tried to overlook the numerous text messages that had surfaced from numbers she didn't recognize.

"Die killer."

"You'll pay in hell for what you did."

"Murderer."

How can people I don't even know want me dead? With shaky hands, she began to delete the texts as a CNN report popped up on her screen, updating her on the "Trial of the Year," that was beginning that day.

CNN Breaking News
The Biggest Trial of the Year Begins Today, January 7, 2019.
*Emily Keller, also known by the media as Keller the Killer, is accused
of causing the deaths of four family members, two of them being
small children. Being only sixteen years old, Emily is one of the
youngest females to be accused of a crime so heinous.*

Emily buried her face in her pillow, taking a deep breath. She tried to hold back the habitual tears that were creeping out from the corner of her eyes.

I have to be strong today; no crying, she told herself as she rubbed her temples slowly. *I need to put on my protective armor, or I'll never make it through today alive.* She reached under her mattress and grabbed her orange pill bottle, giving it a shake, the rattling sounds of the tablets comforting her.

She poured two pills onto her clammy palm and placed them gently on her tongue. *Protective armor.*

"Emily?" Her brother, Nate, quietly inched open the bedroom door. "You awake? It's time to start getting ready for court."

Without looking up at him, she nodded as she began to roll out of bed, trying not to think about how wrong the prosecution had the facts and how she could be sent to prison because of it. As she attempted to walk toward the door, her electronic monitoring ankle bracelet got caught on her lavender bedsheet. She yanked the sheet off in frustration and dragged her feet to the bathroom to prepare for the first day of her new life.

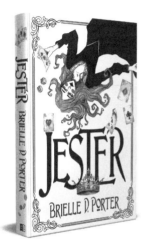